WE'l

An Anthology
of LGBTQ+ Horror

To Meg –

Queer fear for the
win.

GLOOM HOUSE
PUBLISHING

Copyright

Contents

FOREWORD

MARIAN ECHEVARRIA

(Host, *Mothers of Mayhem:*
An Extreme Horror Podcast)

In January of 2022, I set out on a quest. I had just launched my podcast *Mothers of Mayhem* with my friend and co-host, Christina Pfeiffer. We had somehow managed to line up a full season of individual author interviews, and I couldn't believe how lucky we were. Yet, as I reviewed our list, I couldn't help but feel like something was missing.

Oh, sweet Horror. The genre of my heart. Also, a genre stereotypically considered the creative playground of straight white dudes. And there were a lot of them in our first season interview lineup. I mean, *a lot*. All of them were wonderfully talented, artistic minds; but almost every one of them a straight, white dude.

And... that ain't really indie horror, baby.

The independent world of horror echoes with a choir of voices that cross all boundaries of gender, race, culture, class, and health status. It seemed to me these voices weren't getting enough attention, and it was time for that to change. Hence, my "Hidden Voices of Horror" panel series was born. These panels featured POC/Indigenous writers, Women of Horror, Mental Health consumers and advocates, and members of the LGBTQIA+ community.

When May of 2022 rolled around, I finally had the chance to sit and talk with some of the freshest minds in today's queer horror community: Dylan Mottaz, Eve Harms, Rowland Bercy Jr, Angelique Jordanna, and Mick

Collins. We discussed queer representation in horror, respectability politics, and a vast array of other topics. Little did I know but, during this conversation, a creative seed had been planted. After our discussion wrapped up, that seed began to germinate and grow under the loving eye of Mick and Angelique. Eight months after the episode "Extra Sweetness" went to air, Mick messaged me asking if I would write the foreword to this anthology. An anthology that apparently would not have happened had that panel discussion never occurred.

What an honor.

Thank you, Angelina and Mick, for bringing this collection of mischief and madness to life and for shining light on the genius that dwells in the minds of our queer horror creators.

As a bisexual woman myself, and mother to a beautiful 19-year-old pansexual daughter and 10-year-old non-binary human (both of whom are horror fans), I would just like to proudly exclaim:

We're here.

We're totally queer.

Get used to it.

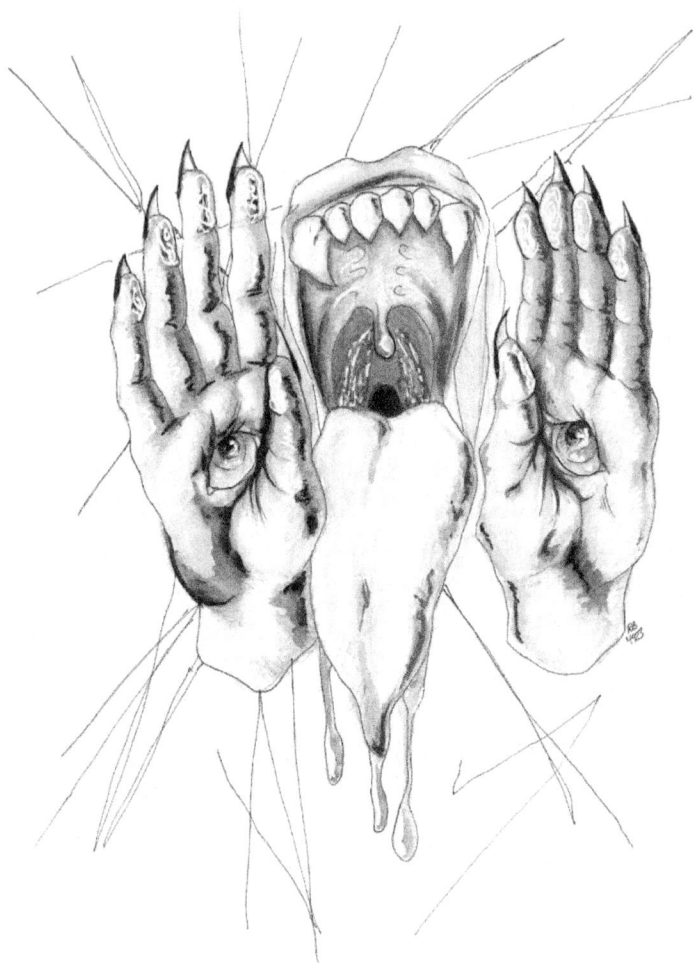

CHASER

JUDITH SONNET

Sometimes, Tulsa almost wished the random men who assaulted her inbox would act like bigots right out the gate. It made her skin prickle when she scanned through the messages she received from men who were obviously looking for praise. She also knew that, inevitably, when she didn't take their bait and tell them that *yes, you really are so good to trans people, a true ally!* they'd start in on the harassment. They'd turn their smiles into ugly examples of transphobia and hatred.

She tried her best to avoid the inbox, but sometimes it needed to be checked. She didn't want to miss any opportunities from potential advertisers, especially since the site was cracking down on "adult" content. Her entire backlog had been demonetized. She didn't see a penny in revenue when ads played ahead of her videos. So, she needed sponsors. As much as she fundamentally detested stopping her videos midway to advertise shaving clubs, VPNs, or mobile games…it paid the fuckin' bills.

Tulsa Raye scrolled through the messages, cringing at what she saw.

Mommy was a big one. Lots of men sent that message, and when she didn't respond within the hour, they'd follow it up with: *Bitch. You're ugly anyways. I was just being nice.*

God, Tulsa hated the internet. But…it paid the fuckin' bills.

Being a public figure—even one as marginalized and niche as Tulsa—meant she had to interact with people. Being an introvert, it had been a hurdle. But she made her boundaries clear. She didn't direct message people, and she didn't respond to trolls.

She used to be accessible at all hours. She talked to people at random whenever they messaged her, simply because Tulsa was beguiled by the fact that anyone would choose to communicate with her. Especially when the video essays had been at their most amateur state! But, of course, she'd learned her lesson after talking to a man named Ben through Facebook Messenger.

Ben had started things off cordially. He wrote her to say:

Hey. Watched your latest video on media literacy. Loved it. You're incredibly smart, and I think it's super cool that you are so public about who you are. I'm not trans, but I support you!

Thanks! Tulsa had written back moments after the message arrived.

Ben started asking her questions. Most of them concerned things she'd discussed in her video, but a few tilted toward more personal matters. Tulsa had been nineteen at the time, and still struggling to crawl out from her shell. She'd answered his questions but hadn't given him more details than necessary.

Tulsa then went to a concert with her friends. It had been a weekend getaway, and she'd left her phone on silent the whole time. Living in the moment was more important than interacting with her video essays, especially since she hadn't made a career of the project just yet.

When she got home, she sat in front of her computer to upload pictures from the concert onto her Facebook and found her inbox stuffed with messages from Ben.

Hey.

Hey.

Hey, what's up?

Don't want to talk with me?

It's cool if you don't want to talk to me. I can handle it. Just tell me.

Hey.

What's up?

You okay?

Listen, I'm sorry I messaged you so much last night. I was drinking and just got worried that I'd messed up or made you uncomfortable. I think it's super cool that you're putting content out there for the world to see. Just wanted you to know that.

Did I say something transphobic? If so, I didn't mean it. I'm sorry. I drink a lot, and sometimes I mess up. I just hope we're still cool. Message me sometime, okay? I'll be here.

Hey.

Yo.

Hello?

Okay, I was trying to be cool about it, but you're really beginning to piss me off.

You know, I think all trans people must have some kind of piss fetish. That's why you're so obsessed with getting into women's bathrooms. What do you think, fag?

Hey.

I'm sorry. I was drinking last night and didn't mean that awful stuff I said. My niece is trans, so you know I'm not transphobic or anything. I'm really sorry.

Hey. Are you mad?

Terrified by the Dr. Jekyll and Mr. Hyde-style messages, Tulsa had blocked Ben after taking screenshots of the chatlog. She'd worried all week that he'd somehow find her based on some incongruous statement she'd made during their pleasant conversations. Then she worried that he'd somehow "cancel" her as if she had been in the wrong for removing herself from his aggressive messages. Those fears waned after a month went by, but it had defined every online interaction since. Whenever Tulsa did receive a polite message, she was weary that the conversation would turn the second she did something that upset a potentially irrational person behind a keyboard.

So, Tulsa didn't respond to direct messages any more than she had to, and she only checked her inbox for sponsorship offers. And the *last* thing she did was follow her hashtagged name on Twitter and Instagram. The few times she had, she saw posts mocking her identity and personhood, or saying she was part of the "woke mob" because she'd done a video on the transphobia displayed by a popular children's author. It was all fruitless chatter to Tulsa, and she had no use for it.

Tulsa saw the online landscape as a waste of time. She put her energy instead toward her hard work on fashioning professional video essays. When she uploaded them, her fans praised her, and her sponsors had no complaints. To Tulsa, this meant that she was doing just fine.

"You really should be more active on Twitter if you want to grow a following." A more popular YouTuber had told Tulsa at a convention last winter. "I mean, you've got a loyal following, and your stuff is really good. You should be trending every time you upload."

And maybe he was right.

When Tulsa turned off her monitor, her face reflected back at her, and she sighed deeply. She'd felt dysphoric a lot lately, and she had been researching facial reconstruction surgeries in her spare time. Unfortunately, she was only making enough to pay rent and buy groceries. She had no cash for cosmetics.

She was told she was beautiful by her friends, but an entire childhood of feeling ugly had given her scars that were slow to heal. That said, she had done a lot to herself to make her flesh feel like a home. Her hair was long and vibrant, and her cheeks were chiseled. She'd developed breasts which could barely be contained, and she had legs for days. In many ways, she was exactly the woman she had always hoped she'd grow up to be…but there was always something that made her hate herself despite her advancements. The way her chin looked at the wrong angle could shatter her heart, and she detested her blue eyes because they reminded her of her father.

She didn't talk about these things, as she'd been called "problematic" for doing so. As if dysphoric trans women couldn't critique their self-image. So, she kept it all bottled up. Just another part of her that was silenced by the masses.

She turned her computer back on and went to her Twitter feed. She hadn't posted since last week, and that had been a picture of her best friend's new kitten. The scraggly cat was mid-meow, and his fur was silky. Tulsa felt her heart murmur at the image.

"Yeah. I'll just let that speak for itself for a bit longer," Tulsa said before shutting her computer back off.

Standing, she walked over to her bed and fell into it. Surrounded by her stuffed animals and rumpled blankets, she instantly felt warmer and better.

Yes. That hits the spot. Tulsa grabbed her stuffed duckie and gave it a long hug.

She felt her phone chirp in her pocket.

11

"Ugh," she muttered as she reached down and yanked the device out. She expected a message from her mother—the only member of her immediate family who hadn't banished her after she began her transition. The older woman was currently vacationing in Colorado and sent a near–constant stream of pictures from her voyage. Tulsa was happy to look at the pictures. It made her feel as if she was out and about with her mother, even though they hadn't seen each other in person since Tulsa's father threw her out of the house at eighteen.

Tulsa felt her mouth go dry. Her eyes felt prickly and wet. She knew she was going to cry tonight. She cried a lot, especially when she thought of her dad and the hurtful things he'd said upon discovering that his "only son was a sissy."

Tulsa turned on her phone and opened the text message.

It was from an unknown number. An icon marked the message as potential spam, but she could see it anyways. All it said was her dead name.

Tulsa felt her heart curdle, and her blood ran cold.

Another message followed the dead name: *I know who you are.*

Tulsa dropped the phone, sat up in her bed, and held her ducky close to her breasts. She ground her teeth together and furrowed her brow. She was angry, hurt, and terrified all at once. If this was a joke or a troll, they'd succeeded in getting a reaction from her.

That's not who you are. They don't know shit about you. They know your given name. So what? You're Tulsa Raye. You always have been, a reassuring voice chittered in her ear. She was having trouble focusing on the affirmation. Her eyes were glued to the glowing screen.

Another text came through:

I'm here.

There was a knock at the door.

Tulsa gasped so hard, she felt as if she'd swallowed an icicle. She spun around on her bed and glanced toward her bedroom door, where the knock had originated.

Her phone buzzed once more. The message read: *I love you.*

"Go away!" Tulsa shouted. She clamped a hand over her mouth, feeling like an idiot. She'd just alerted the intruder to her whereabouts!

The knocking continued. The invader was in no rush. Instead, he tapped at her door in slow strokes.

Tulsa snatched up her phone, dialed 9-1-1, and waited. In her head, she rehearsed what she would tell the dispatcher. Someone was harassing her, and they'd invaded her home. No, she didn't know if they were armed. No, she didn't know *who* they were. Did she have any enemies? Sure. She was a trans woman who created online content. Somedays, it felt as if the whole world was out to get her! Har-Har!

The knocking continued. It was joined with a gentle series of scratches as if the person on the other side was a dog begging to be released from the house.

The phone trilled in her ear. Tulsa was surprised that no one had answered. Didn't they usually pick up automatically? She doubted that they were experiencing a higher call volume than usual.

"C'mon. C'mon. Pick up. Pick up. Pick up," Tulsa muttered.

The line crackled and dissipated. Suddenly, she was listening to a dead tone.

No. That's impossible. Cell phones don't drop 9-1-1 calls. What the fuck?

Tulsa pulled her phone away and gazed at the screen.

Her harasser had sent another message: *We just want to talk to you.*

Her door rattled. The fiend on the other side was jostling the knob. She could hear reptilian hisses emanating from the hallway. Then a long black tentacle wriggled in from beneath the doorframe. It writhed across her bedroom floor, sweeping its nose back and forth. She watched as the blackness cleaved open at its end, revealing a mouth filled with yellowed fangs and dribbling hot venom.

It's a snake! They're sending poisonous snakes into my room!

But it was like no snake Tulsa had ever seen before. It had no eyes and no tongue. Just a vortex of flexing fangs. It reminded her more of a lamprey eel. Like something slimy and aquatic.

Another tentacle pushed its way into the room. It left black streaks in its wake as if it had been lubed with ink before being unleashed.

Her computer monitor flicked on, bathing the room in white-hot light. Tulsa held her breath and looked toward the computer, dragging her eyes away from the writhing tentacles seeping beneath her door.

An image popped onto the screen. Tulsa was surprised to see her own visage staring back at her. Slowly, the image faded and was replaced with shaky video footage. It was shot in the hallway leading to her door.

She could see the person standing on the other side. The figure was clawing at the wooden door, its movements synchronized with the raspy scratching sounds she could hear over her own panicked breathing.

This is live footage. That means…there's another person out there. They're filming my home invasion!

She tried to take in the details of the figure. Maybe it

was someone she knew. But the footage was too shaky and blurry. It looked as if it was being filmed through nylon.

Tulsa swallowed a boulder. She tucked her chin between her knees, sitting in a fetal ball. She tightened her arms together and shuddered as if she'd swam through a cold pocket.

The footage was replaced with red text against a white background.

WE JUST WANNA TALK.

Tulsa shook her head as if the foes on the other side of the door could see her. As if they'd respect her wish to be left alone.

The tentacles flapped loudly against the floor. They sounded like wet fish. Tulsa could smell them too, and they reminded her of the fetid odor that accumulated around a reptile's terrarium.

A mantra rolled over Tulsa's brain. Her thoughts were frazzled, and her nerves were jangled, so she was somewhat surprised that she could conjure a clear plea. *Leave me alone. Leave me alone. Leave me alone—*

Tulsa let her mouth drop open. She wanted to shout out to the intruders and tell them to get out of her house, but her throat was as dry as a desert. All she could release was a muted groan.

On the screen, more text appeared.

WHY WON'T YOU TALK TO US?

The door splintered down the middle. More slippery tentacles writhed through the fractured wood, wriggling like hooked nightcrawlers.

Leaking through the fissure, the face of the intruder made itself known. Tulsa's scream finally broke through her clinched throat. The sound tore through her mouth and filled the room like a swarm of hornets. The creature

15

matched her roar with its own. Only its tone was a jeering snarl.

The thing had a pale face. Its eyes were glazed with a smooth film, and its nose appeared flattened into a piggish slit. Its mouth was toothless. A green tongue swam out from between its lips and tasted the air. The tentacles grew out from the creature's chest like mutated hair. It wore an open rain jacket and nothing else.

The creature held the sides of the fractured door, and tore the pieces back, widening the wound in Tulsa's defenses. She saw that it had only four fingers on each hand, and each digit ended in a curved talon. More tentacles emerged through a vaginal slit on its palms.

Shrieking, the monster—Tulsa could think of no word more appropriate—sloughed through the broken door and plodded into her room. The beast pulled in a wet breath, turning its head to the side as if it had caught a curious scent.

The creature held its hands ahead of it. The tentacles growing out of its palms swiped through the air, flicking like a snake's tongue.

Tulsa unwound her arms and stepped off of her bed. She moved steadily, holding her breath, and pinching the tip of her tongue between her teeth. Her heart pounded like a jackhammer in her chest.

I'm dreaming. I have to be. This can't be real, Tulsa thought. *I fell asleep at my desk and now I'm having a nightmare—*

The monster spun toward her, holding its arms out like a defensive player on a basketball court. It cocked its head to the other side. The beast's movements were jarring, as if the monster wasn't comprised of flesh and blood but was instead a stop-motion model. It added to the unreality of the situation.

A blackened tentacle lashed out from the creature's palm and looped around Tulsa's throat. She gasped once before the noose tightened. Grasping at the surface of the tentacle, she dug her fingers into the juicy flesh. Ink-black fluid wheezed out from where her nails skewered the thing.

The tendril whipped back and forth, threatening to crack Tulsa's neck. She followed its maneuver, stumbling on her bare feet as it drew her closer to the demonic entity.

The creature made a noise that reminded Tulsa of a childish snicker. As if it was cruelly pulling a dog by its leash.

Tears blurred Tulsa's vision. She ground her teeth together while she worked her fingers underneath the tentacle. She could feel her knuckles pressing her esophagus and knew she'd wind up with imprints on her smooth throat.

The tentacle tightened, trapping her fingers.

The creature leaned in. Soupy goo spilled from its toothless mouth, dribbling against the bedroom floor. Its slime sizzled when it hit the ground. Tulsa could feel the heat emanating from the beast's maw.

If it drools on me, it'll melt the skin right off my bones. Oh, God! This can't be happening!

Straining her eyes, Tulsa looked back toward the broken doorway. She could see the secondary invader standing in the crevice, recording what was happening with a digital camera. He was wearing a hood, jeans, and a baseball cap. She couldn't see his face but could tell it was an adult man.

"Puh—" Tulsa tried to plead, but the tentacle cut her words off with another squeeze.

Tulsa watched as the creature's throat began to

17

expand. It filled up like a bullfrog's sack. She heard something thick and wet *slosh* inside the bulge.

She ripped her hands away from the tentacle. Drawing her knuckles down her throat caused instant bruises to swell up along the length of her gullet.

The creature leaned its head back, gargling as if washing its mouth out with Listerine.

Fuck you! Tulsa thought.

The creature snapped its head down, expelling a payload of acidic slime.

Tulsa threw a punch, which directed the stream of goo away from her and across the bedroom. It spattered against the camera, and the intruder. He yowled like a teakettle and peeled away from the crevice, dropping his melting camera as he went.

I can't believe that worked!

Tulsa kicked out, landing her foot on the creature's pelvis. The monster coughed wetly, sputtering more slime. The sizzling goo dotted Tulsa's arm, singeing it quickly. She scrambled back, choking herself on the tentacle.

The two did an awkward dance, attempting to pull apart, but they remained connected by the blackened tentacle lashed around Tulsa's neck.

Tulsa kicked again. Her foot landed on the demon's belly. She felt it give, like a crispy chip crunched between hungry teeth. She heard something s*plash* against the ground.

Looking down, she saw a stream of inky fluid pouring out from between the monster's legs. She'd broken something inside of it, and now all of its juices were evacuating from its belly.

The monster pawed at its stomach, groaning as its liquids sluiced out and stained Tulsa's floor.

Finally, the tentacle slipped loose and flipped back into its spot in the brute's palm. Tulsa sucked in a hard breath, which lit her lungs on fire. She fell back, planting her rump on the bed. She pulled her legs up again and watched as the creature flailed in place, spraying black waves from the gash between its legs.

The monster collapsed, hitting its knees on the ground with a *clack*. It tipped forward, smashing its face against the floor with an eruption of black blood. Its head had broken apart like rotten fruit. She watched as fragmented pieces of meat floated in the black sea like white islands.

The monster lay flat. She watched its liquid contents drain until the body was a deflated sheath of skin and flopping tendrils.

It didn't have any bones. All it had were those…tentacles. No organs, either. Just black goo… and fucking tentacles!

It was sent to kill me. It was going to melt me, and they were going to film it for—for who?

Tulsa coughed harshly. Blood spattered from her mouth and filled her palm. She wiped her hand on her blankets, leaving a rusty smear behind.

She looked back toward the door and could hear the cameraman whimpering from behind it. Evidently, he hadn't been blasted with enough of the acid to kill him.

Tulsa crawled out of bed, ignoring the mushy pool beneath her as best she could. She circled around the monster's corpse and made her way toward the hallway.

The cameraman was lying on his back, rolling on the floor, clutching his face. His skin was pock-marked from the expulsion of sizzling acid.

Tulsa stamped over to him, knelt, and pried his hands away from his face.

"L-let me…see you," she croaked. Her voice sounded

as if she had just swallowed steel wool.

The face wasn't familiar to her, but it was heavily scarred by the acid. The flesh on his left cheek had bubbled over and now melted in a beige stream. His right eye had turned into a milky puddle.

"Please…hos-spittle…" the man groaned before collapsing into sobs.

"Why?" Tulsa asked, still struggling to grasp the reality of her situation. She wanted a motive, an explanation, or at least a clue to the riddle. Why had this stranger brought a demon to her house? What was the point?

"W-we just wanted to… t-talk to you," the man moaned. His sobs hit him like punches. His chest shook, and snot babbled from his nose in twin streams. "But…y-you ignored us!"

"What the fuck do you mean?" Tulsa rasped, holding him by his wrists.

"Please! You need to take m-me to the hospital! Please!" the man cried. "I'm—I—It hurts s-so much!"

"You were going to kill me!" Tulsa throttled him, jerking him by his wrists. "You were going to kill me, you fuck! Tell me why! Tell me!"

Tulsa dropped his hands and planted her thumbs over his eyes. The digits sank in easily. Milk-white juice spilled out from his melted right socket, but her thumb punctured the left eye with a shocking *pop*. Orbital fluids leaked out of the socket and crept up the length of her thumb. Tulsa dug in, churning both of the man's eyes.

"Tell me!" She lifted him up, hooking her thumbs against his orbital plates. She slammed him against the ground, shocking him with a blurt of hard pain. His mouth gulped, and his hands scuttled around like agitated crabs.

"Stop! Please! Stop!" the man whined. "Stop!"

Tulsa lifted his head and smashed it back onto the hardwood. She heard something break inside his skull. A fissure snaked across the back of his head, and blood sprayed out as if from a hose. She watched as crimson sheets crept across the floor ahead of and below the man's dome.

"We just wanted to talk!" the man sobbed. "We just wanted to talk! Please! *Stop!*"

"Fuck…you!" Tulsa roared, lifting and smashing his head into the ground once again. Her hands pushed into his skull, forcing his brains to *flop* out from the gorge she'd cracked into his dome. The pasty organ oozed out like mud from a sewer. Then, the brain began to unwind like a satisfied orgy of snakes.

Tulsa leaned back and tilted her head to stare at the ceiling. She no longer wanted to watch the gory mayhem she'd brought onto her assailant. She was surprised to see that the man's blood splatter had reached the ceiling, painting it a grisly scarlet.

Tulsa tumbled back as if she might make a snow angel in the gore. She shut her eyes, but even her vision was tinted a vibrant red.

I killed a demon… and a fucking creep. I've never killed anything before. Will that fuck me up for life? I'm too exhausted to consider that now. Shut up, Tulsa, she thought in a bleary haze. She wanted to crawl back into her bed and hug her stuffed animals. She could only hope that none had been melted by the acidic spray from the demon. She needed all the comfort she could get and losing one of her cuddly friends would simply add to the trauma.

Tulsa got on her hands and knees and crawled into her room, not caring about the door splinters that pierced her hands or the goopy stains that besmirched her clothes.

She shimmied up onto her bed and drew the covers over her, like a tent. She gathered up as many stuffies as she could, holding them close and sobbing into their furry bodies. After crying, she peered out from the blanket and took in the destruction of her room. Her walls and floor were all dripping with black fluid. But the computer monitor remained untouched.

She saw an image on the screen. It was obviously shot from the same camera the man had used to record the demon as it broke through her door. The blurry, smudged imagery gave her a view into what appeared to be a ritual.

A group of men sat in a circle. They were naked, and their pricks stood up like totems between their hairy thighs. They circled a roaring bonfire, which flickered red and orange in frantic winks.

Tulsa seethed through her teeth. She rubbed her eyes, smearing blood across her rumpled face.

"We offer you this sacrifice, Challl-Irith. The Devil of Unrequited Love! We offer you this sacrifice, so that you may punish the woman who slighted us!"

"Hail, Challl!" the men roared in unison.

The camera flicked back and forth, gathering up as many visions as it could contain. Tulsa saw that each man had a symbol drawn upon his brow. The symbols varied, but the most common was a minimalistic spade tipped with jagged stars. At the center of the spade was an overturned cross.

"We reached out to her and were collectively ignored." The camera turned toward the speaker. She recognized him instantly. It was the man she'd just murdered in her hallway.

She recognized him now. She'd just seen his face while scrolling through the message requests in her inbox. He'd been one of a multitude of men who reached out to her, expecting her attention, affection, and compliments despite not knowing her beyond her online persona.

Tulsa called them "chasers."

There were many men who pursued her with romantic intent, and just like the man who had lashed out at her when she hadn't answered his messages the moment he sent them... these men would have turned on her the second she gave them even a minuscule amount of attention.

The fact that they had summoned a demon to melt her was proof enough that her fears weren't irrational.

"Take this sacrifice, Challl-Irith! Take it and deliver upon us a vessel of *vengeance*!"

The man held out his hands, and Tulsa saw that he'd been holding a delicate organ. She couldn't be certain, but it looked like a heart. It was larger than she expected, but she was sure that whatever it was, it had come from a human body.

The man dropped the heart into the fire. Immediately, the flames bellowed and turned scarlet. The men raised their hands and chanted in a passionate tone. Their dictations were hard to parse, as something was wailing from the center of the flames.

She already knew it would be the demon she had slain. Still, she watched as the creature rose from the flames. It arched its back and cried out like a newborn. Tentacles thrashed madly around it, growing from its chest, its palms, and from the gash in its pelvis—

The image was cut, replaced with a white background and red text.

WE JUST WANTED TO TALK TO YOU.

Tulsa shook her head. "No, you didn't. It wasn't just talking. You fuckers... wanted to hurt me."

"I agree."

Tulsa shrieked and hid under her blanket.

"No need for that. I'm not here to hurt you, Ms. Tulsa Raye." The voice coming from the end of her bed was deep and wet. It sounded like something that would have crawled up from a scummy pond.

Tulsa peeked over the edge of her blanket. Her heart did a backflip when she caught sight of the miniature creature sitting on her bedpost. It was like a toad, with a long mouth, squat frame, and webbed hands. Its feet were tipped with long toes that ended in curved hooks. It bore a lizard's tail, which wrapped around the shaft of the bedpost and ended in a shaky rattle.

The creature lifted a hand and gave her a gentle wave. "Hello, sweet one."

"Wh-who are you?" Tulsa asked.

"I'm Challl-Irith," the creature stated, matter-of-factly.

Tulsa swooned, threatening to fall into unconsciousness. Her body could only take so many shocks before giving up.

"I'm sorry about the demon. I wouldn't have given it to them if they hadn't given me such a scrumptious heart. You see, it's my favorite meal." The creature grinned. Its teeth were stuffed with tattered scraps of tissue. "But I'm sure you appreciate that I sent you a weaker beast. Something I knew you could easily defeat."

"Wh-what are you?" Tulsa muttered.

"Oh, please." Challl-Irith's tail shook, rattling like a maraca. "You know what I am. I may not be listed in the current iteration of the Holy Bible, but you should recognize a demon when you see one."

"A…a demon? An actual demon?"

"Yes, but don't be concerned." He patted his belly.

"I've already eaten today."

Tulsa giggled. Maybe that meant that her brain had finally broken. She shook her head and hugged a stuffed teddy up to her breasts.

"Y-you're a demon. Great. I'm talking to a demon. I can't believe that I don't believe it," Tulsa whispered.

Challl-Irith hopped from the bedpost and landed on the bed. He almost blended in with her multiple stuffies. Waddling toward her, the demon said, "Humans so rarely believe what they see. But I'm as real as the creature you killed. Or creatures, if you count that horrible man."

"Why'd you…why'd you send them a weaker monster if—if they were the ones who summoned you?"

Challl-Irith burped before nestling onto her lap like a slimy cat. She felt his warmth and was comforted by it.

"Because they summoned me for the wrong reasons. One must be careful when one summons a demon. We can be a tricky breed. You know, they all started a club dedicated to trying to get your attention? When that didn't work, they decided to kill you instead. I'm the Devil of Unrequited Love, not the Devil of Jilted Incels," the demon snickered. "The internet has brought on a whole new host of sins, hasn't it? Some are outright pathetic if you ask me." He nuzzled against her, purring. His tail looped around her arm, but Tulsa didn't feel threatened by the contact. Challl-Irith's presence was soothing to her. She laid a hand on his bumpy head and began to pet him gingerly.

"Are the rest of them…still out there?" Tulsa asked. She couldn't believe that she'd inspired a literal cult. She felt like crying again, but her tear ducts were dry.

"They are," Challl-Irith stated, yawning widely. "Which is why I wanted to meet you."

"What do you mean?" Tulsa asked.

"Would you like…revenge?" The creature asked. "Or would you prefer us both to turn the other cheek?"

"R-revenge?" Tulsa groaned.

"I can be a kind ally, Ms. Tulsa Raye. I could protect you against the obsessives who have targeted you. I could keep you safe. But I require payment for my services."

"Payment?"

"Yes," the demon said. "Yes. And I believe that you are well aware of what I accept for my wages."

Tulsa mulled it over. She was literally going to make a deal with a devil, and she was going to do it just to protect herself against people who had targeted her simply for existing.

It shouldn't be like this. I should just be allowed to make silly internet videos and sleep safely in my own bed. But they ruined that. They ruined it before tonight… but they took this step! Not me! This isn't my fucking fault!

Tulsa thought of all the creeps and weirdos who reached out to her, then attacked her when she stayed behind her boundaries. She wanted to feel safe, and she hadn't felt that way for years—

"Yes. I understand," Tulsa said.

She left the devil on her bed. Taking a pair of scissors from her computer desk's bottom drawer, she strutted out of the room and back into the hallway. She straddled the man's corpse, then plunged the scissors into his sternum. The blood inside of him had ceased to flow, so it oozed out in a gushing sheet around the wound.

Tulsa bit her tongue and worked the scissors open and closed inside of him. Then she ripped the scissors loose and slammed them back in. In a matter of moments, she had dug a gory gutter into the man's chest. Then she tossed the scissors aside.

"Fuck you, you fucking chaser piece of shit!" Tulsa

roared as she cracked his chest wide open. His organs squealed and hissed as they were exposed.

She rootled around in the mess of swampy tissues and tattered organs, finally exhuming the heart with a twisted pull. It came loose with a *snap*, clinging onto the man's chest by strands of muscle.

Tulsa stood, wiping her brow. Blood dribbled out of the heart, which rested in her hand like a clump of compost.

Slowly, and on unsteady feet, Tulsa walked back into her bedroom. She held the heart before her, offering it to her new deity.

Sneering, the demon took the heart…and swallowed it whole.

She Tasted
of Good Fortune

Hailey Piper

This city wasn't the kind of place anyone came looking for their good fortune anymore. Certainly not downtown, especially not by the piers, and never at the dockside Eastlight Club. Beneath its marble-columned front, an array of elegant dancers' statues reached their arms eastward to welcome the dawn.

But by nightfall, they likewise welcomed all elements of the city's arcane underworld. They ventured here between twilights, sowing the seeds of many an underhanded deal, each leading down expected paths of blood and ruin. If there were fortunes to be found here, they favored the few and the cruel.

Kate Ligali had to be out of her damn mind for agreeing to come here, weaponless and apparently brainless, with only a bulky coat and the kiss of a promise on her lips. Her billowy dark hair must have filled her skull. She'd been drunk on a good time, and now she'd come too far to go back. Better she ascend the Eastlight Club's steps and find what fortune she could.

And hope it left her in one piece.

Two plain-faced men in dark suits waited atop the marble steps. Their bulky frames cast grim shapes against the shimmering golden entrance like stains on the night.

"Private engagement tonight," one of the men said. He sounded bored, the type who might rather have joined the club's dull roar, host to a couple hundred guests, than stand out here and check the door.

"Your invitation?" the other asked, his voice sea-deep and patient.

Kate reached into her coat and pinched out a paper between olive-skinned forefinger and thumb. She had only been handed it an hour ago and could have gone without touching it again. Nothing in its texture felt natural.

The deep-voiced usher glanced down at the paper and then back to Kate's face. "*Your* invitation."

"It's the one I got," Kate said, a shrug in her voice.

"For Miss Bouquet," Deep Voice said. "I've seen her, a bony thing with scary eyes. Not you."

"Maybe she's hiding in my coat." Kate patted down her curvaceous front and smirked at both ushers. "She gave it to me."

Deep Voice aimed a finger down the steps. "You need to leave."

"Her invitation will let me through," Kate said, insistent now, and the paper bunched against her skin as if ready to growl.

"Lady?" Deep Voice leaned close. "Scram, or I'll bring out people you do not want to meet."

The edges of the invitation crackled against Kate's fingertips. It seemed to wear a threat of its own and the will to make good on it. The paper crinkled across Kate's skin, its texture warm, and then its front spat a thick crimson stream up the steps and into Deep Voice's face.

He reeled back and clawed at his eyes, his cheeks. The red spray vanished into his flesh faster than he could wipe it off. His spine then twisted, and his failing legs dropped him backward against the steps. Every limb jerked in an awkward horizontal dance. He'd given up clawing at his face, too stricken with pain to fight as thin ropes pressed from the underside of his skin. They formed brief hills and valleys as a nest of blood-made serpents slithered in his flesh, and Kate lost track of where they started or where they went. Their every movement bled agony through the screaming man. His voice was no longer deep as the sea.

The once-bored usher clapped a hand over his mouth. Kate almost did the same, but she had to look like she'd known this would happen, like she'd been given clear orders to make trouble for anyone who tried to stop her.

Deliberate steps carried her past the writhing man. The other usher didn't watch her, let alone get in her way. In a small still-aware part of his mind, he understood now. Kate's invitation meant business.

So did Bouquet, having given Kate the damn thing and thrown her into this mess.

Was Bouquet entirely to blame? At the heart of life, Kate got herself into this particular mess the same way she landed in most messes—in a state of undress.

Bouquet's unusually pale skin had marked her as a shut-in or creature of the night or both when Kate first saw her in a midtown bar. Street talk said Bouquet had given herself that moniker on account of the flower-named dragons inside her, and Kate believed it. She made no custom of tangling in the bedsheets of notorious smugglers and gamblers, but she'd never slept with a walking talking nest of dragons before, and besides, she liked the way Bouquet carried herself in that flaring blue dress.

More street talk called her a recluse, hard to find by friends and enemies alike, but she took to Kate. That was usually enough to start a night. A couple drinks and batted eyelashes, a tender touch on the dip in Kate's spine, beneath the curve of her belly, upon her left cheek, her good side? That was more than enough to keep the night going.

Never were the two of them in Bouquet's bed alone. Street talk had its truths. When the lights went down in the steel-doored fortress Bouquet called an apartment, its windows shuttered, the light gone in such absolutes that even vermin might be afraid of the dark, Kate glimpsed Bouquet's secret insides.

Fissures opened in Bouquet's skin, where pearlescent eyes glowed in the curve of her breasts and the shallow of her throat. One eye even glared through the patch of hair between her legs. Kate might have run her tongue across it without realizing during her and Bouquet's enthusiastic tangle, but once Kate knew the dragons were real and partners to this, she let them light her up with sweet stinging kisses and fiery tongues. By sunset, she was ready to do anything Bouquet asked.

And Bouquet knew it. Deep in the throes of gasping and burning, out popped the fateful question and the next step in Kate's disaster.

"Will you get something for me?" Bouquet asked. Her voice was a split-tongued purr in the ear.

"Sure, hon," Kate said, her lips touching fire. She might have been saying it in ecstasy, or in answer. Even she wasn't sure once the words had spilled out, but she chased them just the same. "Anything you like."

Bouquet's smile spread fire against Kate's sun-kissed neck, always a sensitive spot, and the delicious inferno trickled molten down her nerves.

"A future," Bouquet whispered. "Bring me a future. Get it for me, won't you, doll? Make me a promise."

Long story made short, she wanted a fortune teller to

hold her hand and tell her what was to come. The request made sense to Kate. A woman with dragons in her skin might be worried about the long-term effects of said condition. Kate hadn't bothered to ask how Bouquet came to be this way; not Kate's business.

But she knew without asking that sensitives with such god-blooded talents as clairvoyance were becoming a rare type in this city. They might have decided to head inland for greener pastures, or at least less stormy ones. Maybe, at last, typicals without talents were catching on that such sensitives were often imperfect, even flat-out wrong sometimes, and their talents weren't worth the coin.

Either way, anyone who wanted a fortune told in this city needed it done before there was nobody left to tell it.

"I hear Niki Xeniade will show at the Eastlight Club tonight," Bouquet said. "One such fortune teller. I need my sweet Kate to seek her out."

"Eastlight Club?" Kate asked, still reeling from dragon kisses. Eastlight Club was the chief joint operation of the Dorman Brothers. "Why not go together? The brothers got a grudge against you? No invite?"

"Oh, I have an invitation." Bouquet's hand wrestled across the detritus of an unlit nightstand. "The brothers are no trouble to me, but they've invited Big-Heart Cressida, and that's a bird I wouldn't like tempting with my little worms. Take my invitation."

A slim paper brushed Kate's cheek in the dark, and she finally wrenched herself from Bouquet's warmth. The paper was small and coarse, its texture almost scaly.

Kate guessed the Dorman Brothers hadn't sent these out in such condition to everyone. Bouquet must have worked a strange touch into it, the kind Kate wouldn't understand until her arrival at the downtown club.

But even in bed, she accepted she'd hooked up with someone with god blood inside her, or a god's curse, or some fearsome unknown facet to the universe. Strangeness beyond under-skin dragons would follow, even if she would be too engrossed in Bouquet's splendor to notice.

"I've made sure my invitation will let you in, no matter what." Bouquet shook the paper until Kate snatched it. "Tell Niki Xeniade that you have a special friend willing to pay in a big way to have her fortune told."

"I'm not exactly the persuasive type," Kate said, though she'd slid herself between Bouquet's sheets without much trouble.

"I don't need you to be the best," Bouquet said. "I need the one Cressida won't see coming. Somebody she's yet to form a grudge against."

Yet being imperative, but Bouquet's logic made a certain kind of sense.

"Anything you like," Kate said again. She kissed down Bouquet's arm, her lips tingling with dragon heat. "I'll do it."

"What a good lady. Now—" Bouquet guided Kate's head down between her thighs with one hand, and then she dragged a sharp nail across one inner thigh with the other. Dragon eyes glowed over a fresh red slit. "Blood will make that promise mean something, yes?"

Twisting suggestions and shadows blanketed Kate's thoughts. She hardly remembered sliding her tongue across Bouquet's sweat and blood or standing away from the bed to get dressed, only found herself doing so. Her hands were in the habit of dressing and undressing her; they could do so without her thinking about it. Same for when she reached into her coat and plucked out a mint leaf smoke from the pack in her coat pocket. If only she'd found a light in there, too.

"An errand takes longer without a good smoke, and I'm all out of matches," Kate said, reaching her hand toward the bed. "Mind giving a light?"

She expected Bouquet to paw at her nightstand again and snap up an unseen matchbook. Instead, one of the faces within her skin unstitched itself from her paleness in the dark and kissed fire to the tip of Kate's smoke, leaving it to smolder.

"There you are," Bouquet said. Her atmosphere spread in a flower of heat, moistening the air and stinging Kate's skin. "Hurry on, good lady, like you promised. Don't leave me lonely for too long."

Promises made in bed were one thing.

Promises made in bed and in blood were another, especially the god-touched variety. The kind you couldn't escape. Blood was the stuff gods wove into dreams and nightmares, and though radio talk and newspapers said gods were scarce these days, such miracles lingered in all their wonder and terror.

Bouquet had more secrets to her than dragons in her skin. Whether miracle or curse had put them there in the past, she wanted Kate to bring her word on the future and had set a promise to see it through. Would Bouquet's curse spread if Kate broke that promise? Or would she wind up like that usher outside the Eastlight Club?

Better not to know. Best to find Niki Xeniade and be done with the Eastlight Club, soon as possible. Back in Bouquet's arms, against her tongues, Kate might forget what she'd done to the usher. What she'd helped to do, knowing or not.

A vaulted ceiling reached between the Eastlight Club's

high-columned walls, where golden chandeliers dangled in two neat rows. The main room's edges were filled with soft seating and round tables, behind which the Dorman Brothers' guests dined and drank. A live band played brass, strings, and piano on a raised platform far opposite the front door. Waitstaff in white suits slipped in and out of slimmer doors to either side of the room or dogged along a majestic dance floor spread over the club's center.

Its population ran thick with the already-drunk, the soon-to-be, and the few who might genuinely have come to have a good time. They wore tight dresses and oversized scarves, dazzling suits and hats, and some flashed jewelry made of bone.

Kate had seen this before. A dance to forget all troubles, and everyone belonged once they'd made their way inside.

Except her entry had been more troublesome than most would expect. After such a front door scene, somebody might come looking for the attractive round lady with big dark hair and a bigger coat. The invitation had only promised Kate a way into the Eastlight Club tonight. If she were thrown out, or punished via less savory methods, it might not help her again.

She unbuttoned and shed her coat from a sleek black dress, neck-high in the front, low-cut down the back. Same dress she'd worn when she approached Bouquet earlier tonight, and Kate hoped the way she filled it so nicely would encourage anyone here, no matter their usual cruelties, to point her in the direction of Niki Xeniade.

Not that the Eastlight Club brimmed with the most helpful sort. Kate hadn't noticed anyone matching what she knew of Big-Heart Cressida—the tall lady in red—but you didn't need a reputation on the street to bring harm within these walls.

In one corner, cloaks of white draped the Dorman Brothers, a bald pair of twins with graven faces and the ash of funeral pyres in their eyes. At another table, one man sat dining while his tablemate spoke with enthusiastic hands, and Kate wondered if the man with food in his mouth noticed that his friend had dressed their knuckles in what looked like human teeth.

The night drew all manner of the city's arcane underworld, each in search of wretched dealings cut in bone and blood.

And if Kate meant to get what she came for, she would have to ask them for help.

An hour passed of giving the guests a verbal prodding. Kate would have had an easier time had the Dorman Brothers insisted everyone pin their invitations to their suits and dresses and coats, but who was to say that Niki Xeniade had shown up under her own name? She might be another woman clutching a borrowed invitation.

Everyone Kate spoke to seemed as clueless as herself. Either they meant to give her the runaround, or they sincerely didn't know that particular fortune teller, and she couldn't press them harder. She had none of the needed muscle, and everyone had their own problems, even here.

Worse, if Niki turned out to be such a talented fortune teller as worth seeking out, she might be capable of dodging unwanted attention. Could she have seen Kate coming? Street talk said that sensitives needed more tactile sensations to trace anyone, and their talents didn't work on themselves or each other, but street talk had its cracks and potholes, same as genuine streets.

In hindsight, Kate should have asked for payment on Bouquet's little errand. Separation of work and sex life had become crucial now that she'd called it quits on her old pleasure career, and her savings were dwindling. If Bouquet had the coin to pay Niki Xeniade in a big way, she could offer a few table scraps to Kate, too.

Or better yet, she could have let this night be an innocent one. No business, only the pleasure of each other's company. The feeling had started to climb Kate's spine that Bouquet had only taken her to bed for this exact purpose of finding a fortune teller.

A sliver tipsy, a little horny, and a lot hopeless, Kate wondered if she should give up on Bouquet's bed entirely, maybe find another or her own for the night.

She couldn't be sure where the broken blood promise would lead. Only the gods could truly curse typicals like Kate, right? And since all-around chatter suggested they wanted no more business from humanity these days, they couldn't exactly damn anyone.

But Bouquet held enough divine malice of some sort in her flesh to paint vicious blood across her invitation. Kate couldn't say whether her recent paramour was god-cursed, a living miracle, descended from greatness, or just a startling genius when it came to blood and misery, but she knew for certain she didn't want to turn out like the deep-voiced usher left screaming on the Eastlight Club's outside steps.

She was about to risk the club's unsavory corners when tender hands grasped her wrists and yanked her into the depths of the dance floor.

The woman wore baggy black pants patterned by small glimmering stars and a loose top of the same make, its sleeves draping loose beneath her arms in a pair of silken wings. Her bony face flashed a big toothy grin, and the tattoo of a dark eye stared from the bronzed skin beneath her black bangs. Her grip and motion waved their arms back and forth, sending Kate's coat to slide over her forearm. The woman couldn't have noticed; she never glanced down, only kept on grinning.

"Listen, I'm flattered, but I got a little business to work at here," Kate said. She slid one hand free and tossed her coat from forearm to shoulder. "Maybe we'll catch up some other time."

"Oh, there's no other time," the woman said, and her onyx-painted lips peeled back into an even wider grin. Her teeth were large and pretty, the kind Kate wouldn't have minded snapping love nips at her skin. "It has to be tonight, and now, judging by your poking and prodding around the club. I heard you've been looking for me."

Kate staggered to a gentle step and let her mouth hang open. "Niki Xeniade?"

Niki tucked her grin behind her lips and bobbed from side to side, only slowing to catch one of the waitstaff by the arm and snag two glass flutes of golden drink off a tray. She shimmied side to side as she returned and offered Kate one of the flutes. Her fingers had barely closed around it before Niki downed half of hers in one gulp.

Kate took a gentle sip. "Having a rough night? Or is pounding them back your idea of a good time?"

"All sensitives, be us counselors or detectives or fortune tellers, drink more than we should," Niki said. "At least, the ones who care about themselves toss back a few on the daily. It dulls the sensitivity. You'd understand if you could feel what I feel."

Niki gulped what remained in her flute before shimmying it onto another passing waiter's tray. No grins or humor lit her face as she came back to Kate. A dizzied fog instead haunted her silvery gaze. One lock of dark hair curled into the inky eye above her brow as if beckoning Kate's thoughts into Niki's head.

"That's better." Niki took Kate's free hand and began to dance back and forth from her in gentle swaying waves. "It's a tough time for fortune tellers, Miss—"

"Kate."

Only now that she'd finally said her name aloud did she wonder if an alias might have better suited this occasion. Something like Bouquet? Or Big-Heart Cressida? That seemed the flavor of the city these days, as if human names were cursed instead of their blood and fate.

Kate sipped from her flute and tasted a light white wine, the kind you'd have to drink by the barrel to get yourself any kind of hammered. She had no nose for its origin or type, even as the local varieties shrank in number after the Burning and season floods. Alcohol was alcohol.

"Miss Kate," Niki said, almost hissing the first word through her teeth. "Did you know my kind are going missing? There's a dearth of fortune tellers in our good city of Diomarch."

"I heard that was by choice," Kate said.

"Might be?" Niki's shoulders climbed and fell, but whether that was a shrug or part of the dance, Kate couldn't guess. "Better we choose to go amiss than let it be chosen, you know? But then, how could you know? Don't suppose you're in this line of work yourself if you're looking for me. What's your angle? What exactly is it you do, Miss Kate?"

"I'm between incomes." Kate sipped from her drink again. She needed another waiter to take the damn thing away before she finished it. "Used to be in the pleasure

39

business back when that was a safer prospect, but there's no order to this city anymore. No telling who to trust."

"Safer—that's funny," Niki said, tasting the words and curling them into a new grin. "Big-Heart Cressida used to be part of that work. She liked it, too, until her run-in with a god put a stop to it. She wanted none of his touch, for better or worse, and now she's cursed. You think you were safer back when they still paid a moment's attention to us, but one wrong night of their divine affection—oof, that'd put a mean twist in your tail."

"You sound like you speak from experience," Kate said. "Less the pleasure, more the gods."

"Where do you think I got my sensitivity from?" Niki asked. "Family trait. You got the talk of someone with no experience, that's what I think."

"The odds were on my side." Kate sipped her drink again, decided she didn't care for it, and slipped it to a nearby waiter. "Now, not so much."

She let Niki lead them in a quick-paced dance. Giving control to a fortune teller who might glean where Kate's feet would land to avoid stepped-on toes seemed easiest, especially when the waitstaff weren't the only people making rounds throughout the room.

In a faraway corner, one of the Dorman Brothers shooed away someone in a dark suit, their knuckles shining in the chandelier light. Near the oaken bar, behind a line of round tables, a broad man in a derby seemed to be eyeing everyone fetching drinks and finger foods.

No way they were searching for Kate, right? Especially not over what her invitation did to the deep-voiced usher at the door. That was a whole hour ago. Someone else in this vermin hole must have leaned into greater acts of deceit and violence by now. Such was the way of places like the Eastlight Club.

"They say evil is a creature of the wilderness and the sea," Niki said, tugging Kate's attention. "But like all such creatures, with its home paved over by city streets, its water sullied by ships, it becomes a creature of the pier and the alleyway. I'm always on the lookout for that special kind of predator before I get eaten up. Is it you, Miss Kate?"

"Evil as a creature?" Kate asked. "I was thinking you might work for her."

"Cressida?" Niki laughed, teeth aglimmer. "She's one big softy."

"That's one way to put it," Kate said. "I hear that's how she leaves people she's unfond of—soft, like she's crumbled all their bones."

"She keeps an abundance of feelings inside, probably for too long," Niki said. "Sometimes, letting them loose gets a bit harsh, especially for the poor sap she's 'unfond of,' as you put it."

Niki's expression sank into a hollow between her facial bones, her eyes turning dark. Maybe she drank to dull her sensitivity, sure, but maybe she likewise needed to cloud her thoughts a little when stepping too close to Big-Heart Cressida. Niki had seen far worse than Kate could know. She might even be on the hunt for a way out of Cressida's orbit.

"Sounds like you got troubles," Kate said. "But I know money greases all wheels. I didn't come looking for you on my own business. I've a special friend outside the pier district, and she's willing to pay in a big way to have her fortune told."

"Money can't grease all wheels." Niki shook the sullenness out of her face and danced a little closer to Kate. She stood a few inches shorter, forcing her to look up now, and her eyes caught the light from the chandeliers. "But sure, I could use a little extra coin."

"Bigger than Cressida's big heart." Kate hoped she hadn't overplayed Bouquet's offer. There had been no mention of exact numbers; Kate had been too focused on what she herself would be getting in the end.

That bed again. Those dragon kisses in Bouquet's skin.

"Cressida's family owned one of those vineyards gone to ashes in the Diomarch Burning," Niki said. "Bunch of people thought the sacrifice would get the gods' attention. Didn't work, no surprise. Cressida started in the Dorman Brothers' employ then, stamping out smugglers carting around knockoffs in Dorman-labeled bottles. She pays me fine, but not enough to get me out of Diomarch and headed—I don't know, western Aeg? I heard it might be better out in the city-states that way."

"Don't you know for sure?" Kate asked, nodding to the eye tattoo on Niki's forehead. "It's your future."

Niki brushed at her bangs and forced out a laugh. "Sure, if only I could tell my own fortune and learn just where to go."

She lowered her fingers from her forehead and laid her hand against Kate's neck. Outside the dance floor, the band eased into a slower tune. The brass crawled in moody waves, and the strings followed, letting the piano take up the somber melody.

Niki sank against Kate's middle, the strength slipping away from her. There were facets to her trouble she hadn't been keen to share. Too much talk about Big-Heart Cressida's past and what Bouquet wanted, yet nothing clear on the predators of Niki's thoughts, on exactly who and what she'd been running from. Hers had been a lengthy escape, and she needed this gentle moment from anyone willing to give it.

Kate took up the lead as she leaned toward Niki's ear. "How's it work? This fortune-telling business? Are you getting anything off me, or am I clean of thought? It won't offend me if I am. I've heard it before from plenty of partners, of every kind you can think."

Except the gods. She'd never slept with a god, and from the sound of things, she was better for it.

Niki's chest thrummed against Kate's with easy laughter. "It's less a science of thought and more an art of feeling."

"Sounds messy," Kate said.

"It is," Niki said. "Feelings are like the aroma of wine, each vast and complex and intermingling. And like with wine, you need a nose for it. The scents of emotions must be understood, and I have a knack for such aromas, hence my business of feeling people out."

Niki craned her head past Kate's and inhaled across her neck. A tremor shot down Kate's nerves, and she stiffened her arms around Niki's waist. At the edge of sight, she caught dark suits again, still on the prowl. Better to keep dancing.

"You're the patient type." Niki slid her face from Kate's neck. "And coiled up on sex worse than a snake in heat. You got an ache inside, pretty deep, and it'd be nice if someone took it out of your hands and into theirs, even for a little while."

"We both seem pretty perceptive of each other," Kate said. "Can you sniff out my future, too?"

"Not at all," Niki said. "A future must be tasted." She lifted one of Kate's hands and sank her big teeth into the meat of the palm.

Kate flinched to take her hand back, but it was caught in the toothy trap. No getting out of this unless Niki let her go.

43

The dance eased to a stop as Niki ran tongue over skin, spreading saliva and blood into Kate's hand. Its gentle touch sent another tremor up Kate's nerves, and between this caress and the piercing grip of teeth, she wondered if the pain should feel this sensual.

"I'm sorry." Niki lifted her head, drew a violet handkerchief from inside her top, and dabbed at Kate's damp palm. "I see a shut door and a lonely heart. It might be yours."

"That bad, huh?" Kate asked. "Tell me, doc, how long have I got?"

"Could be a year? Ten years?" Niki licked red dots from her dark lips. "Could be tonight. Maybe the gods will start to like us again and grant you a miracle to beat back my little prophecy."

A quiet settled between them. It might have meant to part them, but Kate wasn't ready to let go yet. The longer she tucked Niki close, the longer she could pretend nothing awful would come for either of them tonight. No helping it; she'd taken a liking to Niki. She glanced again past Niki's head toward the edges of the dance floor, the tables, the bar and band, but the dark-suited hunters had disappeared. Maybe they had given up their search, or they had been looking for someone else and found them.

Kate couldn't say, but having them out of sight only riled her nerves. Harder to keep track of what she couldn't see.

"Your talent must be rubbing off on me," Kate said. "I'm getting hints of 'get while the getting's good' and 'move along if you want to see daylight.' Sound familiar?"

"Oh, I do like you." Niki pried her head from beneath Kate's chin. The chandelier light found her eyes again. "Fetch me one last drink for the road."

"You'll have a headache come morning," Kate said.

"The headache of a hangover is nothing to the headache of clairvoyance," Niki said. "Puffs up my brain like I got a skull full of taffy. Please, one more drink and I'll go with you."

Arguing would only drag this out. The sooner they left, the better. Kate slid her arms from Niki's waist, reluctant to let her go, and then turned away.

A bad feeling chased her off the dance floor and toward the bar. She might not have been joking when she said Niki's talent had rubbed off. That, or someone had painted the writing on the wall in such garish colors that even Kate couldn't miss them. Either way, they needed to be quit of this damn place.

One drink for the road. Enough to dull Niki's senses and make life bearable.

She had a grim humor to her. Kate liked this fortune teller enough to pass up the rest of her evening with Bouquet and her dragon kisses once she had her future. If it weren't for the blood promise and that writhing usher who'd defied Bouquet's blood-painted edict, Kate couldn't be sure she would head back to that steel-shuttered apartment at all. There was intrigue to Niki.

More than that, she might carry a means of getting out of the city. She sounded like the sort to have a plan, and she only needed the funds to stamp those ideas onto reality. Kate had been scraping by so long, she'd forgotten what an intentional future felt like.

Or was she fooling herself? Niki might have tasted right when she mentioned a lonely heart and sniffed out an inner ache. Maybe when Kate had sensed that exhaustion in Niki, she had really turned her perceptions inward and found a tired, lost woman at her own core, ready for any hopeful direction or comforting embrace willing to have her.

The night would tell. At some point, she'd have to make a choice.

She had almost reached the bar when a different kind of embrace encircled one arm and then the other. Two men in dark suits, their fists gripping tight.

Kate swallowed hard—too late. "Sorry, gents, I'm out of that line of work," she said. "And my rate was too high for the likes of you anyhow."

"You're not for us," one of the goons said, a derby perched on his head.

His fellow goon leaned close, eyes flecked with gold. "You're wanted by a big heart."

The backroom smelled too clean for Kate's health. A place with its own bar tucked in the corner, a circle of plush seats, and a round green table scratched with coins from card games should have carried scents of wine and tonics, human sweat and linens, and the metallic sting of money. This pristine nothingness, laced lightly with chemicals, warned Kate of frequent spilled blood and hasty cleanups.

She expected more blood to spill, the backroom acting as the sacrificial altar for some absent god. Its copper stink would overpower any coins of same-scented make.

At least until the next cleanup.

The goons thumped Kate into one of the seats and towered at her sides. No restraints, no commands. Both must have expected her best behavior. She had no interest in staring across the table at the other woman in the room, but hope fluttered in her heart that if she acted agreeable and offered a polite ear, she might get out of here alive.

But that meant hoping the woman across the table had

a heart to match her moniker. What typicals took for eccentrics, fortune tellers, and the mad—each of these a safer breed of god-touched than Big-Heart Cressida.

A crimson hood draped her head and covered most of her face, leaving only her mouth and chin showing beneath the hood's frayed hem. Thick patchwork robes dressed her body in varying shades of red. Her naked sun-kissed arms jutted from rolled-up sleeves, their elbows bent behind the far rim of the table. Both her palms lay flat on the tabletop, her right hand bearing a grape vine tattoo.

The left stared with an inky eye tattooed on the back of her hand. A red-brown scab formed its pupil, and the flesh around it wore a purpled bruise.

"I don't know you," Big-Heart Cressida said, her voice scratching up her throat and against the hem of her hood. "In this city, that can mean the good luck of one outside my gaze or the poor luck of an unnoticed insect."

Kate's teeth clacked open and shut behind her lips. She needed to find her tongue, talk her way out of this. *Say something, dammit.*

"I can grab the point, or I can drag this moment to an unhappy outcome. Your call." Cressida's right hand rubbed coarse fingertips into the table's shallow grooves. "I want Bouquet."

Kate's lips at last parted. "Roses or magnolias?"

"Snakes," Cressida hissed. "Worms. Maybe she gave you another word, maybe you're a clueless fool, but I damn well know her. For half her wrongs done, even the most impoverished might spend their last morsels hiring a detective to hunt the likes of Bouquet, and I have greater resources than crumbs." Her fingers inched toward the center of the table. "Luck has helped her dodge me, and my detective, and my fortune teller, my quarry unwilling

47

to touch another soul—such expense! But then in you walk, an answer to all these troubles."

"What makes you think I know her?" Kate asked.

"You flashed her invitation at the front door." Cressida's hood twitched, maybe a nod to Kate's coat, still draped over one shoulder. "Someone brainless enough to torture a Dorman Brothers employee is bound to get attention."

"He was getting handsy."

At a glance, neither goon at Kate's side looked like the deep-voiced usher. The one with flecks of gold coloring in his eyes was too young, and the other's derby looked too small to sit on Deep Voice's head.

When Kate looked back to the table, Cressida's hands had reached the center. The stretch should have taken the full length of her arms, but her elbows remained bent behind the table's far edge. Kate blinked hard, but she couldn't force the arms or table to make sense.

The scab-pupiled eye glared closer from the back of Cressida's left hand.

"You have a contrarian demeanor," Cressida said, voice curling to spit. "I would gamble you had no idea what Bouquet painted on that invitation and not a thought to what it would do. You should have burned the paper, stranger. It reeks of her blood curse. My boys couldn't find you on their own, but on the dance floor, one sniff led me right to it. We only had to wait for you to leave the throng."

"What's with everyone smelling out blood around here?" Kate asked. "I didn't figure the Eastlight Club for a powder house."

"That attitude won't help you." Cressida drummed her fingers, and each made a hollow tap against the table's wood. "You'll want to start being more afraid now."

48

When Kate blinked again, Cressida's hands had nearly reached her. Both elbows remained bent behind the table's far edge, leaving Cressida's arms in stiff snakes across the tabletop. Another few inches, and they would snag at Kate's belly.

"The gods are gone, and they've taken their miracles with them," Cressida said. "But they left their curses behind. You carry the invitation of one so accursed. I can show you another."

She lifted her right hand from the table and arched her fingers over the left. Two jagged fingernails clawed across the inky eye's center, tearing away the scabby pupil and filling the eye with a slender red puddle. The right hand then reached for Kate's face and caressed her cheek.

Cressida grinned from across the table. "You're fond of the woman whose skin writhes with things that crawl, yes? She's not the only one."

A ripple shook the blood puddle across Cressida's left hand. Kate forced herself to watch. The last time she'd turned away, the world had betrayed her in stretching arms. If she averted her gaze again, what nightmare would finish Cressida's crossing?

Except the curse didn't care if Kate watched. Another ripple stabbed from the eye's center, and then a boneless finger of blood climbed from the back of Cressida's hand. It swayed from side to side as if the band's music played only for this crimson tendril.

Both of Cressida's goons flinched away. They must have seen this trick a dozen or more times, and yet they still weren't used to the sight.

Kate was no tougher. Her eyes watered, and at last she thrust her face to one side.

"What, stranger? You dislike the look of what the god

of madness has done to me?" Cressida's breath chased her hands across the table. "Try feeling it. Share with me."

Kate caught the worm's leap out the corner of one eye, too late to duck under the table and pretend none of this was real. She flung her hands out to catch it, to stop this, but the worm of blood jabbed into her tender neck and burrowed into her skin.

Under her skin. The blood worm's body stiffened, forcing her neck straight as if Cressida had shoved an iron rod between Kate's jaw and clavicle. A ragged shriek tore up her throat.

"Here's the thing about having a big heart," Cressida said, arms recoiling back to her side of the table. "I feel everything. The gift and curse of true empathy. The worms crawl inside me at all times, a pain without finality or mercy. Which means I possess a better idea than anyone as to how much this hurts you right now."

The stiffness drooped from Kate's neck, letting her head fall. Her lips parted, ready to pray she'd felt the end of it, no matter how far away the gods might have gone, only for a corkscrew of stabbing glass to wind beneath her sternum. The worm now coiled around her left lung. Or maybe her heart.

Cressida stood from her seat. "And I likewise possess a damn good idea how much more pain you can take."

Kate's chest eased, only for the grinding agony to strike her middle. She clenched the muscles beneath her belly, desperate to crush the worm, but she only forced her insides against its writhing barbed-wire body. A half-sob, half-scream rattled out of her.

"You've the benefit of express treatment," Cressida said, circling the table and nearing Kate's seat. "I had to leave Diomarch and cross a number of sister city-states to begin my journey of true pain. Aeg is a good place for it. Someone told that mad god Tychron to expect Bouquet in his temple. He was curious about her god-curse, or miracle, but she passed her invitation to meet him along—fascinating how she does that, yes?—and it fell to me, some doe-eyed novice in all things true. Why should I argue? Those were younger, different days, and how could a pleasure girl like me turn down a chance to meet a god?"

Kate wanted to argue she'd dodged any such requests, the only kind of partner she'd never slept with, but pain strangled her voice. The burrowing blood worm shot past her muscles, around her intestines, and clutched at her lower spine. Her back arched against the chair, and she let out another jittering screech.

Cressida pressed Kate against the cushions. "When the mad god saw his desired curse wouldn't be joining him, he was—well, as you'd expect a god of madness. He didn't know the details of Bouquet's curse, but he smiled and laughed and put an approximation into me. A little spite and bad humor, like to like." Cressida lowered her mouth to Kate's ear. "Mine is worse. I promise."

Kate flinched from copper-scented breath and closed her eyes. The worm now climbed her spine, eager to squeeze every two vertebrae together and play a shrieking song through her lips.

"But revenge is coming, slow and sure as life's misery." The fingers and thumb of Cressida's unbloodied hand squeezed Kate's chin and then yanked her face toward Cressida's crimson hood. "Tell me where to find Bouquet."

Kate's teeth clenched together. The worm had reached her neck again and now fingered at the back of her skull. Words melted down her throat, alien sounds she couldn't understand or create. These curses meant blood against blood, and her body couldn't tell which to obey, the promise to Bouquet or the pain of the worm.

"You and my curse take some time, get intimate," Cressida said, releasing Kate's face. "But when I come back, I want a real answer, or you'll soon know my big heart in far worse of ways."

Kate had felt unpleasantry from clients in the past, the disrespectful and violent sort on the street, but torture was a new teacher. It meant to educate her in its unique properties.

One was its tendency to linger on the present, stretching every moment. Time could no longer be told by pocket watch or wall clock but instead measured by the heartbeats Kate endured across each winding stab through her insides. Maybe the blood worm feared the future. Why else delay it? The future might bring salvation to Kate, a time when she wouldn't writhe on the backroom floor beside her fallen coat, banging heels and hands and spine against the boards in hope the pain would end.

Tears coated her cheeks, and foam rippled through her lips. She had begun to cry again before she realized she wasn't alone.

Cressida had left her goons here to watch the show. They might not have liked to see the blood worm first rise out of her eye tattoo, but they had a taste for its effects on the mortal body.

Kate sucked spit back into her mouth, blinked away the tears, and tried to steady her breathing. She needed to feel out where the blood worm might head next.

Its fluid body combed across her inner abdomen,

jabbing her kidney, her womb.

She breathed deep, desperate to steady her middle, and then twitched one arm as if it might be more frightened to take in the blood worm than any other part of her body. The hand was a sensitive place. Cressida must have had an easy experience ignoring the jabs of a painful hand tattoo if little curses crawled through her body at all times.

The worm twitched up Kate's abdomen, maybe curious about her arm's new movement.

"Come on, you fucker," she whispered.

Both goons glanced at each other and then back to Kate. "Talking to us?" asked the man with gold-flecked eyes.

The goon in the derby chuckled. "She can't even know we're here."

Kate thrashed her arm again. The worm surged up her chest, rippling the skin against her now sweat-soaked dress. Its narrow hill crossed her ribs, her left breast, the edge of her collar bone, and then shot down her arm and past the elbow. Stabbing pain filled her hand.

There.

Kate wrenched her hand toward her mouth, sank her teeth in, and tore open the skin. Blood pooled between her lips, and she sucked at the wound until the taste filled her mouth. Her throat seized against the flavor, ready to vomit.

Derby Goon flinched to reach out. "Is she choking?" he asked.

Gold-Flecked Goon opened his mouth to answer.

Kate wouldn't get another chance—she thrust her head and shoulders off the floor to sitting and spat the blood worm into Gold-Flecked Goon's face.

She didn't see where it burrowed in. Maybe his gums? His cheek? She only noticed his hands fly up to stop it, same as she'd tried, before he fell screaming to the floor beside her.

Derby Goon flinched again to reach out, retreated, and then started again. What to do? He had no idea.

But Kate did. He glued his attention to his fellow goon's misery, and maybe they cared about each other? Loved each other? Kate had no idea. She hoped it was a weak love, and maybe then whichever survived wouldn't miss the other after she raised the chair she'd been sitting in and slammed it across Derby Goon's skull.

He sprawled onto the floor across Gold-Flecked Goon's legs. The derby tumbled down his back and fell top-down beneath his jittering feet.

Kate raised the chair to hurt him again, splinter his skull if she had to, but his neck didn't look right. She let out a harsh breath and dropped the chair beside him. No sense worrying for the goons' welfare, especially not their necks. Their boss's worm had put a hurt into Kate's neck, and she'd attacked the same place in a contagious curse.

Time to scram. Out of this room and the whole Eastlight Club before Cressida and her big heart came back. One scratch and another blood worm might burrow into Kate's flesh. She never wanted to feel anything like that again. This city couldn't be home for much longer.

She grabbed her coat off the floor, slung her arms into its sleeves, and flung open the backroom. A mint-colored hallway of doors upon doors opened to the left and right. The paint color reminded her she hadn't tasted a smoke since she left Bouquet's and didn't have a light even were the opportunity to strike.

And when would that be? The doors wore no labels, neither hall looked like an exit, and each forked at its end. Where was Kate supposed to go?

Hinges squeaked as one door slid open across from the

backroom. Kate twitched back a step to hide—there had to be somewhere else she could go—but then she saw the face peering from the dark doorway.

Niki Xeniade. Dark bangs parted from her bony face, and an eternal eye stared from her forehead, straight through Kate. Niki gritted her teeth and curled two fingers, a clear message of, *Follow me, damn you*.

Kate had no better ideas. She stepped out the door and let her wounded hand fall into Niki's grasp.

These were poor shoes for running, Kate realized as Niki led her around the—what, third turn? Fourth? Thin soles sent the hard floor aching up Kate's ankles, but she couldn't ask Niki to pause and didn't want her to let go.

These were service halls, narrow side passageways where the waitstaff could scurry out of sight from the Eastlight Club's guests. To waltz back to the dance floor meant getting caught. To slow down meant getting caught. Kate could almost hear Big-Heart Cressida sniffing behind them.

"You came for me," Kate said.

Niki stared ahead without speaking, but her grip tightened around Kate's hand.

Kate squeezed back. "You'll have pissed off your boss."

"Don't you think I know that?" Niki asked, glancing back.

They turned another corner, slowing enough as they hugged the wall for Kate to notice an echo in their footsteps. Her own, Niki's, but someone else's too. Waitstaff had to be slipping in and out, but they wouldn't come running up these halls, not when their profession demanded cautious and deliberate movements.

"Know how my heart got so big?" Cressida called. Faint, but doubtlessly her.

Kate and Niki eyed each other and then hurried. Niki seemed good at running. Maybe Kate's assessment of her on the dance floor had been right. How many desperate nocturnal escapes had Niki seen in her life? How many times had she dipped her toes in treacherous seas for someone else and then regretted it? Kate would make sure she didn't regret it this time.

She believed this all the way until they struck another fork, where clacking shoes beat a rhythm down the halls. Cressida might have been the worst of their pursuers, but she wasn't alone. Which way would more of her goons spill from, the left or the right? Which way to go?

"First, I take an enemy," Cressida said, her voice nearing with each word. "And then I tear out their heart and merge it with mine. There are so many fused in my chest, stranger. The biggest heart you can imagine. Come find out for yourself and decide if Bouquet is worth your trouble."

Kate glanced right, left, and then flinched right. Better to make a choice than let it be made for them.

But Niki pulled her back and drew up her hand. Her front teeth clenched around Kate's wound, and she worried Niki might find traces of the blood worm in that opened flesh.

"I get it, a future's got to be tasted, sure," Kate said. "But how do you know it'll help us tonight?"

Niki pried her teeth free, and her tongue slid between her lips. "Left."

Kate took her hand back. "How can you be sure?"

"I see you in the kitchen," Niki said. "Which is left from here. And it must be now because you're never coming back to the Eastlight Club after tonight, are you?"

She squeezed Kate's hand a little tighter and rushed to the left. "We're out of time."

The hall dead-ended at a slim door. Niki shoved it open, where the garlic-scented atmosphere of a busy kitchen consumed them. Its floor stirred with cooks and waitstaff in white, and every surface gleamed with steel, while off went Niki and Kate in their dark evening finery. They would be easy to spot.

"There's a back exit where they throw the garbage," Niki said, leading Kate between sinks and stovetops across a slick tiled floor.

"Why protect her?" Cressida's voice chased. She hadn't stormed into the kitchen yet, her voice faint beneath the clattering cookware. "You can't get away. Her curse leaves a stink, and it's all over you."

Or did she say, *It's all over* for *you*? Kate couldn't be sure at this distance, and she had zero interest in closing the gap to ask for Cressida's repetition. Had the lady with the big heart used a big brain to figure out Niki had a part in this?

Doubtful. Her thoughts focused only on wondering why Kate would protect Bouquet. Cressida had no clue about the blood promise, and even if she did, no way she'd give a damn about Kate's wellness in the matter.

Only Niki cared.

She thrust open another door and rocketed onto a small metal landing, where the railing overlooked a dark alleyway. The scents of food and seasoning melted into the salt-and-fish odor of the nearby piers. No stars dotted the night; black clouds had filled the sky and sent the air crackling with the still-dry atmosphere of a coming storm.

Niki looked surprised to have found the outdoors after all. How long had she been cooped up in the Eastlight Club at Big-Heart Cressida's whim?

Pots and pans clanged beyond the shutting door. People began to shout and scream, maybe in leaping out of Cressida's way, maybe because she'd decided to hurt them if they took too long doing so.

"No time for gawking," Kate said. "Stick with me."

She took the lead down the stairway and into the grime and guts of the alley, tugging Niki toward the street at the far end. They emerged between a boarded-up warehouse and a dark-windowed restaurant, closed for the night. Beneath the nearest streetlight, a man hunched by the hood of his car, turning a crank to force the engine alive, but otherwise Kate couldn't spot another soul. No crowds to hide in.

Only distance would do. Kate led from one curb to another, up a second alley, around a left turn, and then a right, past another street and warehouse, hugging so many corners in their mad dash, she might have gotten herself lost if she didn't know the city better. She wouldn't have minded forgetting where she was, so long as ignorance kept her far from the pier and the Eastlight Club.

Good enough that she doubted Cressida could hunt them down the city's winding outer corridors. Who could she even ask for directions?

She had lost her fortune teller.

An hour of walking passed before Kate realized where she and Niki were headed. She had mirrored this walk earlier tonight, bundled tight in her big coat as she made for the Eastlight Club, skin still hot with Bouquet's touch. Her plan had meant feeling that touch again.

But now Niki leaned against Kate's arm, exhausted and tipsy. If she went back to Cressida, blaming it on the drink might work.

If carried a lot of weight for its smallness, as if secret dragons nested beneath the word's skin. Or maybe blood worms. Niki must have seen such torture inflicted on Cressida's enemies aplenty, might have experienced it herself. Exactly why did her forehead wear the same eye tattoo as Cressida's left hand? A mysterious past trailed Niki's heels. Her only chance at a future might mean kicking said past off her feet like a pair of lumpy shoes and running as fast as she could.

"When you bit me on the dance floor," Kate said. "Did you see that backroom quagmire in my future?"

"I couldn't tell you," Niki said.

Kate hugged Niki closer. "Why? Would that have changed it? You can tell me."

"Nothing changes it." Niki rested her head against Kate's shoulder. "But you'd blame me if I warned you, like I'd made it happen. And it would have happened anyway. Telling fortunes is an inherited talent, but having genuine skill is something of a god-curse itself."

"Feels like I owe you one," Kate said.

"You can introduce me to your big-paying special friend," Niki said. She kept her eyes glued ahead. "I'll use that to get out of town. My days with Cressida were numbered anyway. I can't read my own future, but I felt her patience sloughing off."

"I suppose a big heart has a habit of giving feelings away." Kate shuddered. "And intentions."

They quieted again until they reached Bouquet's narrow street. Weathered apartment buildings glowered from both curbs, the alleyways between choked with brick dust and crumpled newspaper pages. A slender stairway climbed past the first-floor windows of Bouquet's building to an unsteady landing, where her steel door and closed slatted blinds hid her from the world.

"Leave with me," Niki said.

Kate gave a hard look, and then she led onto the stairway toward Bouquet's apartment. She had pondered this idea before Cressida's goons came grabbing, but she hadn't broached it with Niki. Had she seen them in a future together? Seemed unlikely given the unreliability of fortunes told; more likely that she'd sensed the desire in Kate's loneliness. Thunder growled overhead, muffling their ascending footsteps, and the clouds flickered blue.

"Ever hear of a lightning rod?" Niki asked.

"Sure," Kate said. "Nabs up all the lightning so it won't strike anyplace else nearby." She paused two steps beneath the landing and let the implications slide together.

"You're a trouble rod, Miss Kate." Niki slipped past Kate and climbed onto the landing. "I could really use somebody like you on my travels out of town and beyond. Especially if our poor city of Diomarch isn't what it used to be. I'm not sure anywhere in Aeg is the same without the gods, but I have to try."

They reached the door together, and Kate tapped lightly with one fist. Something stirred inside—Bouquet hurrying to open up. Kate eyed the bottom of the door, where someone had taped a matchstick to the steel. An odd signal by Bouquet, or a reward toward a good smoke?

Affection lingered here. Only Kate had suffered an ordeal tonight and grown closer to someone else. Nothing had changed for Bouquet.

Maybe it would once she had a future in her hands.

"And besides all that," Niki went on. "I've kind of taken a liking to you."

"The feeling's mutual," Kate said. She tapped the door

again and turned toward the stormy sky. "But let me keep a promise first, and then we'll see what happens."

Steel scraped brick as the door flew open. Kate lowered her smiling face in inches to greet Bouquet.

But there was no Bouquet. Kate instead caught Niki's wide silvery eyes and gaping lips as she fell into the open black doorway. Wormy strips of pale flesh coiled around her neck and arms, bunching up the wings of her sleeves.

The damp winding flesh froze Kate in place. Those hadn't been dragons kissing her skin in the dark, but something stranger and closer to Cressida's ailment than Kate could have known. Each scaly tube squeezed and pulled. Niki's face bulged where the milky tendrils caught her throat, and then the darkness stole her every feature.

The steel door clanged shut. A heavy lock creaked behind it, sealing in Niki's muffled screams.

Kate rushed to the door and pounded both fists. "Niki?" she called. "Bouquet, what gives?"

Thunder crashed overhead, and lightning's flicker glowed across the line of tape at the door's bottom. Kate crouched to pluck up the matchstick. What kind of game was Bouquet playing?

The sky settled its growl, and another scream rang through the door. Kate grabbed the handle—it wouldn't budge. She leaned to one side of the landing, but the windows' slatted blinds and inner darkness hid Bouquet's secrets. Niki's screaming grew hoarse and long, a pain stretched to gooey strands.

Lightning flashed again, and with the matchstick jutting up from her fingers, Kate noticed what she couldn't have seen while tape had hugged the match to the door. A fingernail or fine knife had scratched tiny crude letters into each side. Kate had to spin it a couple of times to understand the whole message.

IF I TOLD YOU
SHE WOULD KNOW
SORRY

One last scream wavered through the door and then died in darkness. Kate's heart sank with it. What the fuck had just happened?

"Add the pieces," Kate whispered to herself, pacing outside the door. "Figure it out."

The figuring did not take long. Hadn't she already sorted some of it in the Eastlight Club—that Bouquet had only taken her to bed for this exact purpose? Catching Niki had been the game from the start, with Bouquet only using Kate to get this far, a secret kept even from the errand lady lest the fortune teller learn of trouble ahead.

Kate hadn't persuaded her way between Bouquet's sheets. She had accepted an invitation from the pretty woman filled with dragons.

Or worms.

And what now? What had Niki said? *The future must be tasted.* No matter how good a lookout she kept for a special kind of predator, fortune tellers couldn't see their own futures, and Niki had a skull full of taffy. Blood was the stuff the gods wove into dreams and nightmares, but Bouquet had already shown a talent for playing with the stuff herself.

Hadn't Niki mentioned sensitives were going missing? Kate had known they were vanishing from the city, but Niki hinted at malevolence, and now she'd found it. Doubtful Kate was the first pawn in Bouquet's machinations, either.

What next? Would she slit Niki's throat? Crack open

her skull and pick through the pieces? Kate hadn't seen any instruments of slaughter in the apartment, but she'd been too lost in sweet touch and thick darkness to notice. Bouquet had many reasons to keep her lights off. Her dragons or worms, whatever they were, had built a hoard of flavorful futures within Bouquet's blood. Sensitives down a god-cursed throat.

Kate pounded her fist again at the door. She wanted to shout some accusation. *You're a monster!* or *You used me!* or *This wasn't the deal!*

But for what purpose? Kate might as well shout to the long-gone gods for all the good it would do. Bouquet already knew what she was.

And what she'd done.

Silence loomed through the door as Kate drew a green pack from inside her coat and struck the match across her shoe. A gray cloud puffed from her minty smoke, and she let the burning match drop from the landing. Its fire sputtered on the pavement below.

How many sensitives had Bouquet taken? When might any future be good enough? She would certainly taste more until the city emptied, grabbing sensitives to keep ahead of Big-Heart Cressida, as if enough fortune gathered inside her body could warn of all coming danger.

That clairvoyance hadn't saved Niki. There would be no getting while the getting was good, no travel to less stormy pastures, none of it. She was gone.

The clouds opened in a light drizzle, and a raindrop hissed at the end of Kate's smoke. She made to stuff her pack into her coat pocket before the rain drenched them all.

Her fingers brushed against paper. She let go of the pack, pinched the paper's corner, and drew it into the open air.

Bouquet's invitation to the Eastlight Club tonight.

Kate studied the name, the directions, and the dark red-brown patch where Bouquet must have smeared her blood and intent to grant Kate entry. She leaned her smoke away and sniffed. Past the minty scent already filling her mouth and nose, she couldn't detect any curse or miracle upon the paper.

But that wasn't the case for Big-Heart Cressida. *You should have burned the paper*, she'd said. *One sniff led me right to it.*

She might be following the trail now through the city's streets and alleys. Kate should have burned the invitation, or at least left it rotting in the Eastlight Club's back-alley garbage, but she had already come this far and used up her only match. Should have burned the paper but didn't. Still hadn't. Couldn't.

And she wouldn't try.

She braced one arm against the brick wall beside Bouquet's door and wedged the paper into the doorframe. Unless a harsh wind blew the rain against the building's front, the invitation should hold in place.

How many worms crawled inside Bouquet? How many hearts did they have together? Plenty, Kate reasoned. A juicy prize for Big-Heart Cressida. Kate didn't have the muscle to break down this door or these windows.

But Cressida and her goons—they were another story. And they might bring Bouquet's tale to an end.

Kate slumped from the apartment doorstep and down the stairway. Her heels clicked across the narrow street and into an alley, where she smoked among crumpled newspaper pages. Mint flavoring took on some of the night's heaviness before she turned to watch the stairs, the landing, and the other alleys for signs of a cursed woman in a crimson hood.

Cressida might show soon. Or she might not find her way at all if she'd lost the scent. Kate had never been in much control of tonight, couldn't tell anyone's fortune, and maybe her patience wasn't the best plan for comeuppance on Niki's behalf. That was fine. Kate didn't need the best fortune here.

She only needed the one Bouquet wouldn't see coming.

She Was the First; A Dani Story

Angelique Jordonna

"Tell me a story, beautiful."

I feel her breath on me. The hot air drifts down my neck to my shoulder and disappears. I take a deep breath and slowly release it. "What do you want to hear?" I ask Lyric as I stretch my limbs and push my head into the pillow.

My body is tense. I need a night to myself, away from everything, though her voice soothes me a little. Her finger outlines small circles on my skin while she rests her head on my shoulder, her hot flesh pressed against mine.

"I don't know. Maybe tell me about your first time."

I shiver as she hits a sensitive area near my hip with the tip of her index finger. She laughs as I squirm.

"My first time? What do you mean?" I respond, shifting my body as my flesh tingles under her touch.

Lyric props herself up on an elbow, and her eyes fall on mine. "You know, the first time you killed someone. How did it happen?"

I think about her question for some time, not knowing if I really want to share. These are my personal moments, my special times, my getaway from the monotony of life. Does she really need to know everything about me? Is that how this whole relationship thing works?

"I don't remember," I whisper to her. Of course, I remember. I remember every little detail of it. No one ever forgets their first time of anything.

"Dani, don't do that. Seriously, do you think I'm stupid?" Lyric's voice raises a few octaves. She appears to be insulted by my unwillingness to let her completely into my world. "If you don't want to tell me, that's fine. I know you remember, though; no one forgets something like that. I know I wouldn't." There's a moment of silence, and her eyes dart away from me. "I mean, I won't forget Emma. There's no way I can ever push that out of my mind. Sometimes I even dream about how it felt, the knife on her neck. Every day, it's there."

"I'm sorry, Lyric. You shouldn't have been put in that position."

"I'm not sorry. She tried to control me for a long time. She wasn't a good person."

"Well, I'm not used to…" I pause, trying to find the right words, not wanting to offend her again. "I don't like talking about these things with people. Some things are better not talked about. I would like to keep you around a little longer, and if I tell you these things, it may scare you off."

"If I scared easily, don't you think I would have left already? And what do you mean by a *little* longer? You should want to spend forever with me by now."

I give her a little grin. She really is something special. I inhale a deep breath again and try to decide where to start. "Is there ever a good place to start when you're trying to explain a kill?" I say, not meaning to speak it aloud.

"Always start from the beginning," she says as she lays her head back on my shoulder, wrapping her arm around me. She gives me a little squeeze as if that will make talking about things easier.

My parents had been gone for about a year. At that point, everything in my life had improved. I didn't have anyone looming over me, telling me everything I did was wrong. No more beatings or pain; I was finally able to just be me. It was nice. I spent most of my time by the dock enjoying the water or working on an art piece in the backyard. I liked being alone. It worked for me.

The day it happened…it was so hot outside. There was no breeze, just the sun beating down. I was drenched in sweat as I tried to relax out by the dock. I lay on my back, facing that giant burning ball of torture. My arm dangled over the edge of the wooden planks so I could occasionally splash some cool water on my skin. Even though I could feel myself melting into that old wood, I thought, at that moment, life was perfect.

I listened as boats sped by, hearing the summer people laugh as they enjoyed themselves…

"God, I didn't ask for your whole day. I just wanted the details of the kill," Lyric interrupted. "Give me the short story version, Dani, not the whole novel."

"Fine. I don't have to tell you anything," I reply.

She rolls her eyes, and a little huff of air escapes her full lips.

"Hey, you're the one who said to start at the beginning. This *is* the beginning."

"I get that. I just meant you should start at the beginning of the good part."

"To me, it's all good, but okay…"

After being out there for a while, I was about to head back into the cool air of the house. But before I could move, a face appeared above me. It was a girl, and she was smiling. She had wild hair that flowed to her shoulders in hues of pinks and reds. At that point, I couldn't make out anything else because of the blinding sun.

'Hey, I'm Corrina. Mind if I join you?' she asked me. Her voice had a rasp.

'Where did you come from?' The words escaped my mouth before I could stop them. She'd caught me off guard; no one ever just popped up out of nowhere.

'Sorry. I was just walking through the woods. I got lost and wandered aimlessly until I noticed you here. I'm kind of new to the area. I'm not sure how far from my house I am now.'

'W-well, I was a-actually getting ready to go home,' I stuttered as I splashed more water on myself to cool down. I sat up and looked at her.

She was tomboyish, with tattoos all over, probably in her mid-twenties. She just stood there smiling at me for a while, not saying anything. It made me nervous.

'Well, are you going to tell me your name before you run away?' she asked. The expression on her face was playful, and she had this gleam in her eyes that caught my attention.

'I'm Rebecca,' I said softly. 'Everyone calls me Dani, though.'

"Wait, you never told me your name isn't really Dani. What the fuck?"

"Lyric, stop interrupting me, or I'm just going to stop there."

"No, I'll shut up. Go on."

"I don't even remember where I was. It's alright."

"You just told her your name," Lyric growls. "Now continue."

'How do you go from Rebecca to Dani?' she questioned.

'Umm, my middle name is Danielle. Rebecca Danielle. My mother's name was Rebecca too, so they called me Dani for short.'

I grabbed my towel and wrapped it around myself. 'It's very nice to meet you, Dani. I was afraid I wasn't going to find anyone out here.' She reached out her hand to me, and I just stared at it awkwardly for a moment before standing. 'Not a people person, are you?' she asked.

'I'm sorry. I don't really talk to many people.'

'That's all right. I think the shyness makes you even cuter.'

I could feel my face turning red. 'I really should get home. I still have a lot to do. It was nice to meet you.'

'Maybe I can come along and help you, and then you can help me find my way home. I don't have anything else to do today. And you can pay me back with some directions, maybe even have dinner with me.'

'I don't know. I really have a lot to do. Maybe some other time. The woods are pretty simple to navigate. You'll find your way back.'

She smiles really big. 'But you have to eat, right? So, why not eat with me? Then you can do whatever you need to do, and I can help.'

She was right. I hadn't eaten anything so far that day and was pretty hungry. I'd planned on cooking some chicken on the grill. I had enough for two. It wouldn't be so bad having company for a little while. Or so I thought. I looked at her again. She seemed harmless enough, even friendly.

'Maybe. I guess you could come up to my house and I'll cook for us. I was going to make some chicken,' I offered, still not fully trusting the situation.

'Sounds like a plan.' She grabbed my hand and pulled me toward the trail.

I pulled my hand away. It looked like she spent more time in the gym than on the beach.

'Shall we?' She walked up the dock, then turned to look at me, still standing in the same spot. 'I promise, I'm not going to bite. Not right away.'

I grin nervously at her and begin to walk her way.

"I hope this is good because you sure are dragging this story out," Lyric says.

"Can't you be patient?" I ask.

"Patience is not something I have. I know what I want when I want it. I don't like waiting."

"Well, we have nothing else to do. So, either shut it and listen or…"

"I don't do well with ultimatums either, so be careful where you're going with this statement, Dani."

Lyric seems to get a little more aggressive the more comfortable she gets with me. I don't fear her, but I wonder what wicked things shroud her mind. "I have some journals hidden if you'd prefer just reading about it," I reply. "There may be too much detail for you in there as well, though.

She gives me a look that lets me know I should stop teasing and just continue the story.

'Why do you have so many tattoos?' I asked her while we walked the trail.

'I just enjoy art.'

'Art belongs on a canvas.'

'My skin in my canvas,' she replied.

My mind plays with this comment, even during dinner. I was told tattoos were a bad thing. Your body is a temple, and you should not allow such things on it. I could see this human canvas's point, though.

We had a good dinner. Talking more about her tattoos, she explained the reason behind getting each piece and how it meant something to her. I was finally starting to feel comfortable with her when things changed quickly. Just as we finished dinner.

Corrina became aggressive. She pushed herself against me, kissing me hard. I tried to push her away, but she grabbed my wrists and pinned my hands to the kitchen counter. I'm not all right with being confined, not after my parents. She pressed hard, making my wrists burn with pain. I started to have flashbacks to when my parents would chain me up. The beatings they inflicted. I couldn't go through that again.

'You're hurting me. Please stop.' I was becoming anxious. 'You have the wrong idea. I'm not interested in doing this.'

'I don't think you understand, Dani; I don't get turned down.' She smiled at me with a devilish look in her eyes.

She had plans, and what I said wasn't going to change them. I knew it was going to be her or me. I'd lived through too much to let it be me. My mind raced, trying to figure out what to do. My eyes searched the room for anything I could use to stop her.

She pressed herself against me again. Her lips lashed at my neck, and her teeth bit down. She tangled her hand up in my hair and yanked. I could feel the strands detach from my head. In a matter of moments, it was just like when my parents were alive. I was scared she would hurt me more if I didn't stop it.

Without another thought, I grabbed the cheese grater from the counter, placed it against her face, and dragged it down toward her neck. Little pieces of raw flesh dropped from the grater, hitting my skin on the way down, leaving small speckles of red where they landed. My eyes focused on those little spots. A calmness I could have only dreamed of welcomed me. The warmth of those drops of crimson sent a wave of electricity through me. I wanted more.

Corrina let out a howl and released me. Confusion clouded her eyes, and she finally realized I was serious. I dropped the grater to the floor, my eyes focusing on the blood dripping from her torn flesh. The jagged rips leaked fluid, and I felt the slick wetness on my hand from the droplets that fell on me during the act. I traced my fingers through it.

'Are you fucking crazy?' she screamed at me. She grabbed a small towel that hung from the stove and stuck it to her face.

I panicked. I knew if anyone found out, I would get in trouble, so I had to do something to fix the situation. 'I'm sorry. You were hurting me. I didn't know what else to do.'

'You're going to be fucking sorry.'

'Wait, just wait. We can talk this out.'

She started to come at me again, only this time her eyes flashed pure anger, promising punishment. She would punish me for being bad. I couldn't handle that again.

I quickly grabbed one of the metal skewers from the dish rack and jabbed it into her neck. When I yanked it back out, a spray of blood landed on my face. I think we were both shocked by what I had done.

She took a few steps, reaching toward me, gasping for air. Before she dropped to her knees, she covered the wound with one of her hands while the other grabbed hold of my neck and squeezed. I grabbed for her hand, trying to get her to release me from her grip, but she tightened it and dragged me to the floor with her. She was on top of me, and I felt a few blows land on my face. Despite being so close to death, she sure put up a fight.

I still had the skewer in my hand, so I jabbed it at any piece of her I could hit. I hoped one of those strikes would get her off me. The last one landed in her eye. I released the skewer as she fell backward, then quickly got to my feet. My mind was racing. I walked around her, trying to decide what to do next.

She rocked back and forth, both hands trying to put pressure on her wounds. A puddle of blood gathered in front of her.

From behind, I took the skewer and ripped it from her eye. When I pulled the tool back, her eye came out with it. I found myself mesmerized by the long, pink, stringy part attached to the useless orb. I dug my fingers into the socket, looking for the other end of it, then ripped it from its place in her head. When I pulled my fingers out, there was a spongy chunk stuck to the other end.

With the last of her strength, she grabbed hold of my hand to stop me, but I lost control. All the years of being beaten and abused took over, and I couldn't stop myself.

For once, I had to protect me. I dropped the skewer and picked up a butcher knife from the counter. Her dulling eyes stared up at me from the floor, and I dropped to my knees, straddling her body. At first, I didn't pay attention to where the blade was going; I just knew there was this feeling radiating through me every time the blade sliced through her skin. It slid effortlessly through her flesh, and I became fascinated with the sound. Just a slight little wisp that filled my ears and brought pleasure to me.

I was surprised at how long she clung to life after losing so much blood. It was all over me, all over the floor, everywhere. Her body twitched slightly, fingers shaking.

Her single eye held terror in it but slowly changed to a look of dull lifelessness. It was that look that intrigued me the most. The fear, the pain, the way the eyes—or, in this case, the one eye—finally dimmed when life slipped from the body. I had Corrina to thank for my passion, my need, my desire. She put up a good fight, but I wanted to live more than she did.

Once she was dead, I undressed her and lay in the middle of the kitchen floor with her for hours in pure bliss. My fingers caressed her skin as it slowly cooled. I watched in silence as she turned a ghostly white. Her lips were painted a bluish color in the absence of breath. I paid attention to every detail as she changed.

It was my least artful kill, but I didn't know what I was doing at the time. It taught me a lot. It brought calm to my head. I'd never felt anything so serene in my life. It was like everything had fallen into place for me. I knew, at that moment, that was what I was meant to do.

I laid there with her until my back ached, and I was forced to move. If she were still alive, I could have made love to her right then. She had freed me.

I forced myself away from her. I went to the garage and opened the freezer. It would be her tomb until I could get my head together and figure out what to do with her body.

Before stuffing her in the chest freezer, I removed the tattoos from her legs. I thought they would make a beautiful art piece she would have enjoyed... if she could have.

I took a carving knife to her skin, slowly cutting around the colorful abstract pieces and pulling them from her body. They were absolutely beautiful. I placed each piece on the kitchen counter, stretching them out so they could dry. When I collected all of the art, I dragged her body into the garage and put her in that dark, cold grave.

I think she would have appreciated the way my piece of art turned out. Once the flesh was almost dry, I took it to my drawing room. I pulled out a larger canvas piece and painted it a skin tone, moving quickly so it wouldn't dry before I could place her art pieces on it. One by one, I stretched the marked flesh across the canvas, using the wet paint to make it stick. When it was arranged the way I wanted, I placed a lacquer over it to preserve it.

I hung it on the wall over my fireplace for a while, but it eventually started to smell. At first, it was faint, and I thought I could live with it. But it became too much, and I had to get rid of the thing. It took a few years, but I've gotten better at finding ways to preserve flesh. I wish I had known all of that then, but I guess we learn as we go.

"That's the only story I'm going to tell you. If you want to know anything else, you'll have to find those journals."

"That's not fair!" Lyric squeals. "I enjoy story time. We should do this once a week. You know, make it a thing."

I shrug my shoulders. "It's not really my thing. We could have spent that time doing other things," I say as I crawl on top of her, placing a kiss on her lips. "Find my journals. I promise, there's interesting stuff in there."

Lyric just smiles at me. "I like when you tell me the stories, though."

THE DENOUEMENT OF FREEZE-DRIED COFFEE

SUMIKO SAULSON

We both called out at once.

"Rock!" Lala cried, a beaded pink, white, and powder-blue bracelet jangling from their wrist as they threw their fist before them.

"Scissors!" I yelled, sticking out two lilac-nailed fingers as I slapped the air. Seeing I'd lost, I frowned. "Fine, I guess I'll go."

"Don't forget the freeze-dried coffee, bae!" Lala laughed, shaking their burgundy curls. I gazed off over the water at the dilapidated roof of the mostly submerged Safeway, its red and white logo running gray and pink from the acid rain. In the distance, an old woman waved from her porch. She was staring into the water and pointed directly ahead. I watched as an arched form slithered through the water.

"Be careful," Lala said, grasping me tightly around the waist.

"I'll be fine," I sighed, tossing my glitter unicorn fanny pack onto a nearby shopping cart and stripping out of my green floral-print dress. "It's just some kind of fish, right?"

Lala shrugged and released me from their embrace. Once down to my red bikini, I resecured the fanny pack to my waist and trotted off into the water.

As I hit the surface, my skin broke out in gooseflesh. I wrinkled my nose and jumped up and down a few times. It felt like someone had dumped a tray of ice over the top of my feet. Popping the snorkel into my mouth and pulling plastic swim goggles over my eyes, I prepared to dive.

Coffee was one of the first things people started hoarding back when you could still walk into the store, before the Pacific Ocean swallowed most of the Bay in August. I took a deep breath and dove in. Overhead, the bloated remains of fish that died in the sudden climate change floated, rotting in the sun. The stripped bones of cats and dogs littered the scummy ground below, and occasionally, the waterlogged corpses of human beings who had not escaped the sudden flood.

Something slimy nibbled salt from my toes as I swam toward the submerged Safeway. I turned around to see sharp rows of teeth and the powerful jaws of an enormous mutant wolf eel in hot pursuit. Surfacing, I inhaled deeply before dropping underwater again and pushing a sunken shopping cart between myself and the chomping beast. It slithered over the metal grate unperturbed. I flinched as a gray shark with black-tipped fins the size of a pit bull brushed against my arm. I ducked away to evade it and watched as the wolf eel tore into its torso, leaving large chunks of bloody flesh in its wake. I swam away quickly before the blood invited still more hostile ocean life.

I needed to get to the pharmacy first. Then, the coffee.

Something clingy and gelatinous slid down my arm. My eyes darted around in alarm, looking for a jellyfish of some kind. Instead, I saw drifting waterlogged teabags sticking briefly to my skin before they sunk to the floor. Coming up for air again, I collided with plastic jugs of putrid milk floating up from the murky depths. Diving under, I finally found them: soggy cardboard boxes containing eight patches each. I pulled a plastic bag from my fanny pack and shoved in as many as possible before securing the haul to the belt around my waist. Once I was done, I pulled a second bag out and filled it with other things we needed. Lastly, I grabbed a jar of freeze-dried coffee for Lala.

A cold chill ran over my skin as I surfaced to see a man near the water's edge, shoving a rowboat in as he chatted casually with an anxious-looking Lala.

"Gotta catch the fish before the acid rain kills 'em all," he bellowed, bundled in a slick windbreaker, baggy cargo pants, and a black woolen hat.

Lala nodded without speaking, scooting away from him and the water, looking at me with wary eyes.

I stood in the shallows just as the monstrous, deformed wolf eel leaped forth, latching itself onto the screaming man's face. Although they were about twenty feet away, I could see blood gushing from his wounds, a rusty-red geyser from his severed lower lip spitting out into the water below. Ducking my head under, I saw the sharks as they swam toward his feet. Adrenaline kicked in, and I found myself running through the chin-high water until it lowered to my waist, then my knees, and I finally found myself on the shore.

"We gotta get out of here," Lala said breathlessly, shoving the shopping cart down the path.

Humans were not the only monsters we might run into out here. I pulled my green dress out of the cart and pulled it over my wet skin. Then I grabbed a warm fleece-lined windbreaker and pulled it over me. I snatched the plastic bag full of estrogen patches and slipped it into my jacket pocket as we walked away.

"I found it!" Lala said, fishing a cellophane package out of their gaudily sequined purse. They tore the little bag open with their teeth and dumped it into their lap. A plastic spork and knife fell out, followed by salt, pepper, sugar, and powdered creamer packets. A neatly folded napkin clung to the inside of the cellophane. They shoved it back into their handbag, along with the cutlery. Then they handed me the seasonings.

"Thank you, love!" I bowed with a flourish, accepting their contribution to the feast. Two hand-plucked pigeons roasted on a homemade spit before us. I'd fashioned it from a car jack, two clips, and the metal rod and handle of an old, busted umbrella. Opening the salt and pepper, I dusted it across our dinner as they rotated the handle.

"This will go well with the freeze-dried coffee," I said, pocketing the sugar and cream. "We better save this for the morning."

Lala grinned. "Mornings without coffee are *no*."

"Any morning with you is a lovely morning," I said with a smile.

"Squab, m'lady?" they asked with a wink as they pulled the birds off the fire and lay them across our two plates, sitting side by side.

"And a fine salad, my liege," I added, carefully arranging dandelion greens on our mottled blue stainless-steel plates next to the meat. I drizzled hot pigeon fat over the greens, which released an intoxicating aroma, then topped them with fennel and wild blackberries. When I was done, I produced my pocketknife, cut open a lemon, and squeezed its juice over the entire meal. I used the serrated tip of my blade to grate the rind onto the salad and the birds and finally cut a little curl of it as a garnish to drop on each plate. Now that they'd cooled some, I steadied the squab with my fingers while Lala pulled the metal rod out of their centers.

"I would like to give thanks to the Transcestors that we were able to gather together today," I said, using our campfire to light a single rainbow-colored dinner candle. I dripped wax onto a rock on the ground between us and then stuck the base of the candle into the puddle it left. Lala arranged smaller rocks around it to hold it up and blew at the base until it cooled. Then we picked up our plates and ate.

When we were done, I pulled a scrap of paper from my pocket. I unfolded it in preparation for reading off the names.

"Wait, Wendy!" Lala said, suddenly standing and looking around anxiously.

"What is it?" I asked.

"I should do the Land Acknowledgement first," they said. "San Francisco is occupied Ohlone land." Lala went on to give a moving speech about the struggles of the Muwekma Ohlone Tribe to gain federal recognition from a government that might no longer exist. They talked about the stewardship of this land and how the colonizers failed to return it to its rightful owners and care for the land itself. They said we all needed to acknowledge that we were uninvited guests on this land, even those like myself, an African American Transgender Woman whose ancestors were brought here in chains. Finally, they exhorted me and anyone else who might be listening to take seriously our obligations to care for the land.

I gazed out over the water surrounding us on all sides, my eyes taking in all 977 ft. of Sutro Tower looming uselessly over our heads. I would have needed internet access to connect with half the information in Lala's head. An Indigenous person of Mexico, who spoke

Nahuatl and was very well educated on the subject of Land Acknowledgements, Lala didn't need the internet for this any more than I needed it to talk about Transgender Day of Remembrance.

I heard a rustling in the trees behind us and looked over my shoulder. "That you, Marco?"

"Who else?" snickered the mulleted nineteen-year-old through a lopsided grin. His pudgy brown body was clad in long johns that peeked through the torn knees of tattered jeans, a crisp sweatshirt sporting a Transgender flag under a faded old black hoodie. Mud caked both bare ankles and classic checkered Vans. He held a pile of blankets, extended like an offering. "Mama said to send these blankets out to you. Nice Land Acknowledgement, by the way."

Lala shook their head. "You better go back where you came from. Your dad threatened to shoot us if he caught us hanging out with you again."

I shuddered. "He doesn't want you influenced by the so-called Trans Agenda. Transphobia at the end of the world. Just what we all don't need."

"It's Transgender Day of Remembrance," Marco said, staring me down. "I should be here. Lala knew I was here. I mean, what else could they mean, talking about anyone else here who might be listening?"

"I wonder if our calendars are still accurate?" Lala asked, gazing off into the distance.

"We both knew it was Trangender Day of Remembrance. If we lost track of the days, then your calendar and my calendar saying the same thing would be quite a coincidence," Marco remarked, raising his eyebrows with a comic grin.

"Come on, Wendy! I rowed the boat all the way out here. Don't make me go back over there. I don't feel like

being deadnamed and misgendered all day on TDOR."
He pronounced it "tee-door," as most members of the
Trans community did, making a word out of the initials
of "Trangender Day of Remembrance."

"What does your dad think you're doing right now?" I
asked, giving Lala the side-eye for encouraging this.

"We're out of water…" he said, looking down at his
shoes. "He didn't have enough to make his coffee. He
likes the home drip kind. Has all of this fancy gear to
make it with. Mom sent the last of the freeze-dried if you
want it." He tilted his head toward his front hoodie
pocket, which held the goods.

Lala swooped down like a vulture and plucked the
precious brown gold from his pocket before accepting the
pile of blankets.

A chill came over me, and I gave Lala a frightened
glance. "The ocean took Stanford Heights Reservoir?"

"Dad says it's probably actually the Bay flooding."
Marco somberly shrugged. "The tectonic plates probably
shifted with all the earthquake activity along the Ring of
Fire after the initial hit."

"So, the water's still rising, then?" I asked, steadying
my voice so the kid wouldn't know how bad things were.

"Yeah…" Marco nodded, kicking at the dirt. "All the
houses at the same elevation flooded, like a two-block
circle around the mountain. Folks evacuated and moved
up the hill. Dad let some work friends move into our
garage. They're, well, pretty transphobic. And Mom
thought it would be best for me to come out here for
TDOR, no matter what Dad thinks about it, with, you
know, the whole world getting flushed down the shitter
right now. Or at least the parts of it that are anywhere near
sea level. Kinda wish I'd taken that internship in Denver
last year."

"No guarantee Denver's doing any better after two months straight of acid rain." I shrugged.

Marco looked less certain, though. As if Denver were a magical unicorn one could ride out of the apocalypse and into a glorious paradise of dry land, sunshine, and rainbows. I'd been grateful for the past month of dry weather. I'd thought it was the usual October heatwave until the grass began to die.

The smile on Lala's face evaporated. They dropped the glass jar full of coffee into their gaudy handbag, retrieved a map from within, and unfolded it across the stone picnic table. When they looked up, the color had drained from their face. "Twin Peaks Reservoir is only 150 feet higher than Stanford Heights Reservoir. When did it go underwater?"

"The water has been slowly rising ever since the asteroid," Marco said, head cocked to one side as he nervously shuffled his weight from foot to foot. "Mom noticed it first. She usually goes down the hill to fetch water. She saw people evacuating their homes. Some with motorhomes drove higher up the summit to set up camp. Houses were flooding downhill."

"After the rain stopped?" Lala asked.

"For about two weeks, the flooding stopped, and the water receded. Then it slowly flooded again. We stashed as much water as we could in our bathtubs before it went all the way under. The water in our house won't last. Folks from downhill keep breaking into backyards, setting up tents, or moving into people's sheds. Fights have broken out. Some folks have guns."

"How long do we have?" I asked.

"Who knows?" Lala shrugged, looking down dejectedly at her freeze-dried coffee. "It's been four months since the asteroid. Kinda wish I had the internet now."

At the tail end of summer, a massive asteroid smashed into the Antarctic, obliterating the ice cap and vaporizing so much of it that the sea level instantaneously rose more than fifty feet, flooding coastal cities around the globe. On the Pacific Coast, the disaster quickly compounded as Apophis struck the Antarctandes, a series of volcanoes in the Antarctic geologically linked to the Andes mountains of South America, popping off seismic activity along the Ring of Fire. The resultant tsunamis further decimated the coast.

A dark haze of fog covered the planet as the atmosphere filled with evaporated water particles, wreaking havoc on weather patterns. The city was cloaked in it all autumn, blocking the sun and causing frigid drops in temperature. Newborn animals (and humans) began to mutate due to radiation exposure. Eventually, most of the fog rained back down on us, flooding us further. Then things started to get really hot for a while.

I wish I'd paid more attention to the reports on NPR about greenhouse gases before all the radios stopped working.

"So, we're screwed, then?" I asked, thumbing the folded piece of paper in my pocket.

"We're not dead yet," Marco said nervously. "Mom… she told me she thinks it won't be safe anymore. Not with all of the neighbors crowding in. She thought I'd be safer over here with you."

"So, you lied…" Lala said accusingly.

"We've all lied," I said sympathetically, patting the boy on the shoulder. "If there were no need for us to lie to protect ourselves, there'd be no Transgender Day of Remembrance."

"You're right, Wendy," Lala said. "I'm glad you kept the names."

Marco nodded. "We should read them."

The three of us stood in a circle, passing around a handwritten list. I'd written down every name I could remember from the news reports and word of mouth from the year's first half. We read their names and told their stories. Like every year before us, the names of Black and Brown Trans Women topped the list.

At first, the most common method of murder was gunfire, like every other year before. Then we got to the part of the list we'd written after Apophis struck the Earth and Death became up close and personal.

The world was drowning; stabbings and strangulations were on the rise. After broadcast television and radio had shut down, Lala and I began to write down the names of friends and chosen family we learned through the grapevine had died violently when the world fell apart. There were riots after the news reported Apophis' impending impact. Then the End of the World religious cults arose. Some of them blamed the asteroid on Trans people.

"... her best friend said she was a sweet and gentle person who always had a kind word for everyone. Pebbles was trampled to death in the Apophis Riots." Marcus frowned as he read off the first name of those who died in the apocalypse.

And it went on from there. I read the next one, ending with "... a community activist for Transgender rights, they were always there to help others in need. Jo was shot during a carjacking during the evacuation of San Francisco."

The sun was dipping low in the sky by the time we reached the part of the list with only people we personally knew because it was harder and harder to get news.

"... ze was a bright light in a dark world, and I was honored to know zir. Mystika was murdered by a religious extremist who intentionally drove his car into a group of marchers at the last San Francisco Pride Parade."

It was dark, so we read by the campfire's light when we got to the last name on the list. I started to fold it and return it to my pocket when Marcus grabbed it from my hand, pulled a pen out of his hoodie pocket, and wrote down another name.

"Raindrop was a friend of mine from high school," he said shakily, tears welling in the corners of his eyes. "She was walking up the hill from her house, which had just flooded. She was jumped by three guys from school who used to hassle us. My mom was getting water and saw it all. Raindrop was the most talented singer and actress in our musical theater class. She was barely nineteen years old."

"That's why your mom wants you to leave," Lala said, leaning over to give the kid a great big hug. "I'm so sorry, sweetie. I didn't know."

"It's been really hard for all of us," I said, putting my arms around both of them. "But at least we have each other. And coffee for the morning!"

Lala tilted their head toward an old SUV that stood alone in the parking lot. "You can put the blankets in there. Picked the lock a while back. Now we keep our extra gear inside."

Lala walked him over to the vehicle by the light of the campfire. Marcus went to his boat and grabbed a tent out of it. He set it up far away to give us some privacy but close enough to make it clear that we were now part of the same tribe. After that, the three of us piled the boat onto the top of the SUV and strapped it down in anticipation of driving to the shore one day. Afterward, we sat around the fire.

"Mom said that if the water keeps rising, the smartest thing would be to hop in a boat and sail out to San Bruno Mountain. It's four hundred feet higher than Mount Sutro and three hundred fifty higher than Mount Davidson. We'd be safe there for a while. That's what she said she and Dad plan to do. His friend Max has a sailboat in the garage."

"Transphobic Max?" I asked.

"Yup!" Marcus shrugged. "The less land there is, the harder it is for us to avoid them."

"I'm not sure if we three could get there in your paddle boat," Lala said. "It's nine miles away. That's almost four times as far as Mount Davidson."

"It took me like an hour and a half to get here," Marcus said uncertainly. "Two people can fit in the kayak. But Dad said its weight limit is three hundred fifty pounds, so I don't think three people could fit."

"Desperate times, desperate measures..." Lala muttered as Marcus shuffled his feet, looking uneasy.

"We don't have to make up our minds tonight," I said, strolling over to the island's edge and glancing at the rough waves pounding the recently formed shore.

"Sutro Island, Davidson Island," I said, looking around us, pointing out each island in turn as I said its name. "San Bruno Isle, Forest Hill Islet, Twin Peaks Atoll. That's what we should be calling them."

I frowned when I saw how low to the ground the disappearing Forest Hill Islet was. It was only 50 feet higher than our reservoir. I wondered—not for the first time—if all the acid rain we had this fall had tainted the water we drank. Apprehension overcame me, a heavy mantle of impending doom. I didn't think there was any sense in letting my partner, or the young man who'd seemingly adopted us as his Trans parental figures, know how I felt.

"I think Isla de Los Pechos de la Choca is better than Twin Peaks Atoll," Lala said with a wink.

I laughed.

"What's so funny? I don't get it," Marcus said.

"Los Pechos de la Choca, Spanish for 'Breasts of the Maiden,' was the original name of Twin Peaks. Why not revert to that now that the place has really gone tits-up? Let that sink in."

The three of us broke out in cathartic laughter. Then I felt a cold breeze caress my shoulder. Suddenly, the sky turned gray, and the clouds gave way to rain. Heavy, filthy, poisoned rain that burned the skin. Mercurial weather pelted us with hail, rough and caustic, stinging my eyes and tearing open my cheek. Peals of thunder, bolts of lightning.

We ran into our tent. Wind began to blow, threatening to rip our tent stakes out of the ground. A frightened Marco stared in horror as his smaller, lighter tent was uprooted and blown away by the wind. He veered toward our tent, running quickly as the hail gave way to the snow. Clumps of frozen sod and broken boards from ruined wooden houses peppered the ground.

We watch him through our tiny tent window, running to the only safe place remaining: the SUV in the nearby parking lot. We watched as he crawled into the back of the old Range Rover.

"He's got the right idea," Lala said as the powerful gusts shook the sides of our tent. We abandoned it just before an uprooted park bench slammed down, smashing it into the ground. We crawled into the front seat, shivering. I watched in horror as the water continued to rise.

I saw something leap from the ocean that rose around us, arching its back in the distance. Was it a breaching whale or something new, something terrifying? I remembered the wolf eel from this morning and wondered what other kinds of malignant life might live in the sea now, poised and ready to destroy us.

"Let's just wait out the storm," Lala said as Marco handed them a blanket. They threw it across their lap. "Let's stay out of this weather until things calm down. Let tomorrow take care of tomorrow."

"At least California doesn't have to worry about a drought anymore," Marco quipped.

"Y-yeah…" I stammered breathlessly, my thoughts chilling me more than the snow, hail, or rain. Lala caught me in the rearview mirror just then, a serious look on their face as if they'd just read my mind. Silently, they handed me a cool thermos.

"The coffee's still warm inside from last night's fire," she said, unscrewing the cap and patiently waiting as I poured some into the cup. "Keep you warm 'til the storm passes."

"If the storm passes," I said gloomily. Looking up at Sutro Tower, I remembered thinking it was useless not so long ago. Now, I imagined climbing it to escape the rising waters.

"When," Lala said, looking over at the terrified teenager to whom we'd become ad hoc guardians, letting me know I needed to keep it together.

At that moment, I remembered it was still TDOR. I remembered all the years before this, sitting around in cafeterias, town halls, or dusty old bars, remembering our dead. I thought of the Compton Cafeteria Riots that took place a year and a half before the better-known Stonewall. Local Trans Women in the Tenderloin had been told that they could not sit around and talk to each other while drinking coffee.

So I smiled and poured a cuppa joe. Then I poured one for Lala and Marco. Moments later, I drank my lukewarm coffee, wondering if it had always been this way. Perhaps the only difference now was the monsters. They weren't men with billy sticks beating us and keeping us out of our safe spaces. They were animals trying to escape a natural disaster and reinvent the food chain. Even so…

Perhaps we'd always just moved from one cup of coffee to the next while ignoring the whole of the world collapsing all around us.

THE SIN-EATERS

MICHAEL R. COLLINS

Della's hands shook as she sat on the mossy stump. She knew the green would stain the light yellow of her dress, but what was one more grievance to add to the list? They had so many lined up against her; it ran longer than one of Momma's weekly grocery lists. Her family didn't understand her, and Della wasn't sure if she understood herself.

"Della!"

She jumped at the sound of her name, nearly sliding off the stump.

"They're here. It's time." Janey approached her like one might approach a leper. The slight girl refused to get any closer than she had to.

Della stood, brushing off the back of her dress.

Janey stepped back when Della approached.

"Why are you running from me?" Della asked.

Janey had no problems with her before. In fact, it was their close proximity that started this entire mess.

"I-I can't. I'm sorry, but I can't. I don't want those people turning their eyes on me. What we did is wrong. I mean, it wasn't, but it was. I don't know." Janey hung her head, tears welling in the corners of her eyes.

"Why was it wrong, though, you and I—" Della started, but Janey cut her off.

"It don't matter! They've come for you, and I don't want them coming for me. I got my own soul to worry 'bout." Janey turned and ran off, stumbling over roots in her path.

Della stood there with one phrase burning on her tongue. "But I love you." She whispered it so a passing breeze could take the words away. Take them away so no one else heard them. But no breeze came to collect. The low overcast sky kept the thick humid air from escaping. She wiped a hand across her damp brow.

Trying to build up enough resolve to walk back to the house, she reminded herself that she'd said the same thing to Jonathan Brubaker last year and was told she was being a silly little girl. Later on, she reluctantly agreed she *was* being silly. She liked Jonathan and enjoyed kissing him, but it wasn't love. Maybe by the time she reached the house, she could convince herself she didn't love Janey, and the strangers would leave.

Not just any strangers. Sin-Eaters.

Her parents sent a letter asking them to come and take away her sins. She had heard of bereaved folks calling on them for the dead, so the soul could be light enough to make it to heaven, but not for the living. Life was still so new to her sometimes, and there were so many things she didn't know.

Pastor James voiced his protests against calling in the outsiders, claiming they were shysters and charlatans. For a moment, Della thought Pastor James might show compassion for her plight. Instead, he suggested severe physical punishments and endless praying on her knees until she escaped temptation. Days and weeks of non-stop prayer if need be. She had no allies. Even Jesus felt too far away.

She didn't want to be a sinner, and she didn't want to go to Hell. Everyone convinced her she was on her way. Momma did everything but throw the bible across the room at her. Daddy actually did once. What did she do that was so wrong?

Della smelled the house before reaching it. The intoxicating aroma of food enticed her as much as the aroma of Janey's neck when they nuzzled alone in the woods. Only during holidays, births, and deaths did the scent of such a feast float over the clutch of houses and barns making up their little community.

This feast, the cost of which far exceeded the family's budget, was supplemented by neighbors and family. A feast none of them would eat. A feast for the Sin-Eaters.

Her stomach growled and gurgled from the savory aroma. She hadn't eaten since early yesterday, and it smelled so good. Calling on Jesus and cooking meals were Momma's specialties. Perfect for Daddy, who only cared about those two things.

Three days ago, the Sin-Eaters' letter arrived with an acceptance to come, as well as instructions. They seemed simple enough. A thorough bath the night before. Prayers said at sunrise, high noon, and sunset for two days before their arrival. And a fast. *If the intended is unwilling or resistant, it is acceptable,* the letter said in beautiful scrawling script. *Be aware, however, that it may make the task at hand harder. Please ensure the fasting, though. It is a must.*

Della had missed meals before without much issue. But the smells were too much for her this time, and her mouth watered. Each step closer to the house became heavier than the last. Voices buzzed inside. They were talking about her, she was sure.

The moment her foot hit the worn wooden step of her house, a voice called out from inside.

"Ah, our intended has arrived. Please come in."

Della stopped. She didn't move a muscle. She didn't dare breathe.

"Don't worry, dear. Now please, come so we may see you." The voice was deep but not timorous. The accent thick and drawling. It calmed and soothed, taking the slightest edge of her mounting anxiety.

If she entered the house now, she irrevocably agreed to proceed. She could run, she knew. Head out toward the highway, moving in the direction of the city. The city frightened her, though. Almost as much as the guests inside her house.

After a deep breath, she continued.

All the curtains were closed, making the house full of shadow. Soaking up those shadows were all her neighbors. They crammed in along the walls and corners. Despite the crowd, her eyes were drawn to the two. There were so few strangers in her life. How could she not?

The Sin-Eaters rested in the far corner of the living room. One sat in a wingback chair while the other stood beside him. Everyone in the room kept their distance. She wondered how he knew she was outside. Neither one could see the porch from where they sat.

They were an odd duo. The seated one was clothed in a suit, worn but in good condition. His widows peak as sharp as the rest of his features. His eyes were dark yet comforting. He was not a big man, but he filled the corner of the house with his presence.

His companion stood in stark difference. Their hair hung longer and less kempt. Hooded eyes looked only at her or the floor. They were rail thin, worryingly so. Given the facial structure, Della wondered if she had misjudged, and they might be a woman in men's clothing. It didn't matter—male or female—the two were here to expunge her of sin, for better or worse. For a moment, she imagined them towering over her, high as angels, dark as demons, and vast as the night sky. She blinked away the mental image.

"Please excuse if I don't get up. We had quite a walk to get here. It seems the neighborly spirit does not extend past your borders. No one wanted to give us a ride to your lovely home." The strange pair watched her, and she knew they were reading her like she read the bawdy books Jonathan kept hidden in his room. She and Jonathan read them and laughed. She sucked up every detail and came dangerously close to proving the accusations against her correct.

"I am Daniel, and this is Uriel. I trust you have been told why we are here."

Della nodded.

"Good. You have nothing to worry about. I won't lie to you, hon, this will not be the most pleasant of experiences. But in the end, you'll be better for it."

"And if she ain't?" Daddy, a big bluster of a human, barked from across the room.

Della's little sister cowered next to him. She looked afraid, but for whom?

"Then it will be very grim. And at least we're already dressed for a funeral."

"So, how does this work?" Momma asked, hands wringing and voice shaking. "The meal's prepared. At great expense, I might add."

Uriel raised their head and looked at the work-creased woman. In a high, quiet lilt, they said, "Only a meal? Such a sacrifice for the eradication of sins."

Momma recoiled as if slapped. Her eyes widened in fear and worry for herself.

"Now, now, Uriel." Daniel patted the hand of his companion. "These folks are worried about their youngster here. And you can't blame them for it. Our methods aren't exactly orthodox."

Janey's father asked him what he meant, but Daniel offered no explanation. Though Janey somehow sidestepped the castigation Della now endured, Della found it hard to hate her for it. Maybe if she had beaten Janey to the blame, this entire ordeal would be at her house, and Della would be the observer, not the focus. But she couldn't. Dishonesty was a worse sin than what they did.

Despite the risk, Janey came to watch the proceedings. The young woman stood plastered in a far corner, trying to be as invisible as possible. She refused to meet Della's gaze and that of the visitors, instead studying her shoes.

The adults asked the visitors questions and murmured amongst themselves. No one made eye contact with them. *What do they fear,* she wondered, *revealing their own sins?*

Uriel's dark eyes followed each person in the room as Daniel answered their questions. Occasionally a smirk would touch the corner of his mouth as if he sensed Uriel's thoughts about what they saw.

Daniel played the role of the slick southern gentleman, but Della sensed something more to him. Less than a snake-oil salesman, more than a holy man. Uriel scared her. The way they stood there, she felt they were out of proportion. Not so much physically, but rather their entire presence. Something hungry shone in their eyes as they watched the gathered crowd in her living room.

"I think it's time we talk with Della," Daniel announced, cutting off her neighbor John Daramond's question about their biblical authority. He made it well known he thought the pair were scam artists. Della overheard him tell her poppa that even if he didn't believe it, he hoped the experience scared her to see the right path. She hated him just a little for it.

"Do you need privacy? We have a room—" Momma started before Daniel cut her off.

"Our instructions to you were clear. We let the sins out in the open. And besides, we would hate to deny you the salacious curiosity bringing you to crowd this tiny house today." The silence following his statement was not kind. "Let us begin."

Della shook and held her hands against her stomach to keep her fear from being too obvious. The attendees turned their attention to her. She didn't like attention on the best of days. This level of scrutiny incited a level of nausea to rise from the empty pit of her stomach. The worst gaze came from the strange pair, their eyes on her, flaying her alive and baring her deepest secrets and desires. She knew she couldn't lie to them, no matter how hard she wanted to.

"Child," Daniel oozed reassuringly, "please tell us, did you go akissing on your friend there?" He nodded to Janey, who turned fourteen different shades of red and tried to melt into the wall.

"Y-yes, I did," Della stuttered, hating the confession even as it left her mouth. "On more than one occasion."

"I see," Daniel put his fingertips together under his chin. "You have impure thoughts about her or any other girls?"

"I…I have." Della hung her head.

Her momma gasped, and poppa shook his head.

"You pictured yourself kissing them up and down their neck? A hand on a soft bosom? Slipping your hand into the moist, wanton warmth between her legs?" Daniel purred the questions, and Della's temperature rose.

"Now that's too much," Uncle Frank called out from the back. "There's no reason to be obscene."

Daniel ignored him. "Answer the question."

"I have." Della might as well have stood there with no clothes on. These visitors might as well strip her, not just clothes but flesh. Expose her meat and bones. Her very soul.

"You think the images you conjured of taking a certain young man behind the barn and dropping his trousers is as sinful?" Daniel asked, and a few people gasped, though Della wasn't sure why. Isn't it the sort of thing they wanted? For her to want a man instead? Jonathan, who stood near the dining room door, stepped back through it and out of sight of the others.

"I do." Hot tears well up in her eyes. "It's all a sin. I can't help but like girls and boys. I wish it weren't so. It'd be better if I only liked boys and didn't have the thoughts I do." She looked at the two strangers. "Tell me, is the Devil in my head?"

"No devils in *your* head." Uriel said this so softly that Della barely heard it.

A moment of uncomfortable silence made everyone fidget. Awkward anticipation filled the room.

"Well," Daniel said, standing and brushing wrinkles from his clothes, "I say we get started then. There is certainly plenty of sin to be eaten, isn't there?" He walked past Della and gave her a wink.

Confused, she watched him part the crowd to the dining room.

Daniel sat at one end of the table, Uriel at the other. They faced each other, holding a look, speaking without words. Their attention shifted to the spread in front of them. Plain fare, granted, but it smelled no less delicious. Ham, chicken, and beef rested on platters, carving knife at the ready. Large serving bowls of boiled potatoes, green beans, beets, corn, and carrots lay next to pots of butter and gravy. Bread and rolls filled baskets. Per request, each seat had a setting in front of it, but they expected only two to be used.

"This looks wonderful," Daniel said, making a show of taking in the aromas. "Doesn't it, Uriel?"

"Yes, it does," Uriel said in a small voice, paying more attention to the crowd huddled around the doorway. "Please, come in." With a vague wave of the hand, they invited the audience to join them.

The group lined the walls of the small dining room, putting as much distance between them and the Eaters as possible. Only Della remained in the doorway, unsure what to do, her fear rising.

"So, now what?" Poppa asked, his voice hoarse and angry.

"Now, you will all stand there and be quiet," Daniel instructed him with barbed words. "Della, dear, please come in here."

She entered the room with light steps, wishing she would have run when she'd had the chance. Standing next to Daniel, she waited for further instructions. Uriel ordered her to serve them. Della jumped and grabbed at Daniel's plate. She knocked a drinking glass over and rattled a few forks.

"Take your time, lamb. You must fill everyone's plate, not only ours," Daniel instructed her gently.

"Make sure you give them all the best parts," Momma interjected.

"Of course."

Daniel gave her a wide smile that made Momma blush. Poppa caught it and grew red in the face. Daniel leaned into Della's ear and whispered, "As you serve Uriel and me, think about your sin. Envision it. Make it real in your mind—taste, touch, and smell. Even the passions of those moments. And if you get excited, all the better. Maybe add a little of your own juices to what you serve."

Della stood up, her entire body burning a brighter red than ever before. Concern washed over her family's faces. Jane looked away, and a few of the neighbors whispered. The rest were quiet as Della dutifully filled the plates. She heaped food on Daniel's plate before clumsily serving the others. When she reached Uriel, her hands shook so badly she couldn't keep the peas in the spoon long enough to deposit them. Uriel put a cool hand on hers. She jumped, flinging little green orbs everywhere, but the lingering touch calmed her.

"Take your time," Uriel told her, the low voice continuing to quell her fear. "Remember what you did." And she did remember. Like how Janey's lips had felt on her own and how Jonathan's rough hands had pawed at her. Even the bliss she gave herself in the moments alone, creating her own pleasure. She knew she was wet now and remembered Daniel's suggestion. She dared not do it. Not in front of everybody.

"This will be fine then," Uriel stopped her hand, which began to shake again.

Putting the plate down, she continued around the table, hurrying to fill the rest. Once finished, she stood beside Daniel, unsure where else to be.

The two dug into their meal with vigor. Daniel ate with some grace and manners, though no less voracious. Uriel made a mess as they shoveled food down, staining their suit and the tablecloth. Bits of gravy and meat freckled their chin and cheeks. It was a grotesque spectacle. Crumbs and morsels fell to the floor and littered the room. Despite the hunger from her fast, Della's nausea returned because of it. A number of the spectators had to turn away.

Once his plate was clean, Daniel looked up at Della. "Child, did you conjure up your sin while serving any of these other plates?" Della nodded.

Uriel eyed the nearest plates like prey would a wounded animal. The Sin-Eaters took an extra plate each and repeated the process.

Meanwhile, the audience grew restless. "Are you sure they ain't here for a free meal?" Jed Turnbridge, the neighbor who donated the carrots, asked Poppa.

Uriel took a forkful of potato and flung it at him. "You've got sin on you now." With a giggle, they returned to eating.

Finally, they finished. Two plates each, practically licked clean. The Eaters sat back with a burp to signify they were done. The audience grew pensive again, waiting to see what would happen next.

"Well?" Jonathan asked.

Della shot him a dirty look. He had no right to be impatient.

With another burp, Daniel dabbed the corners of his mouth and said, "One more thing, and this part of the ritual will be complete." He turned to the young woman.

103

"Della, sweetness, have you done what we've asked and fasted?" She nodded. "Good, see that plate there. Go ahead and eat."

"Really? I mean…I thought…" Della hesitated.

"This food is for you. You're the ones supposed to take all the evil from her," Uncle Frank chirped from his place behind Uriel.

The food-spattered guest responded with a small chuckle. "We could just as easily be eating this meal for you." Uncle Frank had no follow-up.

Della sat at the table and picked up the fork. It wasn't right. Weren't these two supposed to take away her badness by eating the food? Wouldn't this give her back what she tried to be rid of?

Looking around, her momma lifted her hands, indicating she should follow instructions. The others kept their emotions behind their eyes. Her gaze fell on Janey's wide-eyed and frightened expression. Della's confusion returned as she watched Janey. Why was it so bad to feel what she felt?

"I can't. I'm sorry." She hung her head, feeling as if she had let everyone down.

Daniel clapped his hands once, immensely pleased.

"I don't understand," Della said. "Was it the right thing to do? Did it work?"

"Yeah, did it work?" Poppa stepped away from the wall, his patience at an end. "Do we have our daughter back, or does she still cavort with the Devil?" None of this sat right with him.

"You did the right thing, my dear. We are almost done, I assure you. When we responded to your summons, we explained that our methods might differ somewhat from most, but they still achieved the same results." Daniel tossed a worn yellowed napkin on the table. "Now, the last instruction was for a pot of coffee at the end."

"Oh!" Momma jumped from where she stood. "I forgot to put it on the burner." She rushed out of the room.

Uriel let out a loud, long fart, then resumed looking at nothing.

After a rather awkward silence, Momma returned. "I'm so sorry. It will only be a few minutes."

"That'll be fine," Daniel assured her and stood up. "Let's adjourn to the front room again. I would like each of you to make yourself comfortable. We will finish the ritual and enjoy an after-dinner coffee.

Grumbling, they all followed the two out. The Eaters took their previous spot in the corner. They instructed Della to stand between them and the others. Uriel stood next to Daniel, their belly extended from the meal. The two shared looks, communicating without talking again.

Momma served as much coffee as the percolator could hold before disappearing into the kitchen to make more. She offered a cup to her daughter, but Della refused. She never cared for coffee, and the shakes had returned. A new fear arose as they adjourned to the front room: What if these two were con men looking for a meal? She feared for their safety. As much as they scared her, she didn't want them to get hurt.

Another fear followed: What if they were to get run out of town? What if she ran out with them? Follow them down the road and away from the heavy judgment weighing on her. She buried the thought far away, but Uriel smirked at her, and she knew she'd been caught.

The second round of coffee came as Daniel spoke, not in the voice of a pleasant southern gentleman but of a man backed by God.

"We are gathered together, family and friends of young Della, to see this young woman not stray from the righteous path. You each care for Della in your way. And some of you don't. Some of you are here out of an idea of obligation. Others, like Mr. Turnbull here, want to watch the show hoping to see something scandalous."

"I would never!" Jed Turnbull huffed.

"You would, and you are. Now please shut up." Daniel continued after a sip of coffee, "Uriel and I were called in because you wanted your child returned to the path of virtue. But that is not what we agreed to do."

The others murmured again.

Poppa's fist clenched.

"We agreed to come and take away sin, and we shall. No more, no less." Daniel took another sip of coffee. Uriel mimicked him, then sat the mug down on a nearby table. They both motioned for Della to face the assembly. Uriel put a hand on her arm. The lack of warmth from their touch surprised her.

"What are the sins?" Daniel asked.

The room went quiet.

He asked again.

"She fornicated with my son." Jonathan's father pointed at her.

"No, I didn't. I swear! I never!" She hadn't. Not once did they go that far, though she imagined it plenty of times.

"You have touched yourself in sin." Her sister called out.

She remained quiet and in hiding throughout the entire proceedings…until now. Della couldn't deny this accusation. She had left the sheets wet, and her body flushed, knowing it was wrong. But she'd done it anyway.

"We asked for sins. Not this trifle," Uriel said, his hand still on her. The touch produced a strange tingling on her skin, almost numbing her arm. Tendrils of the odd numbness invaded her brain.

"Tell us what the sins are. We are here to eat it," they hissed in her ear. The words wrapped around her mind. A lump formed in her throat. She coughed once as her mouth became an arid desert. Words forced their way to her tongue. Words she didn't want to say. And things she didn't even know about.

"Jed Turnbull killed the black man who used to work for him."

The room erupted in gasps.

She kept speaking as if compelled to do so. "He saw the man as 'getting uppity' because he always wanted to be home with his family before sundown. He got incredible satisfaction from the act of murder."

Della continued before anyone voiced more protest. "Janey, your sin isn't with me. You steal coins from your mother when she isn't looking. You lie and blame your little brother even though you know he'll get the belt every time. You got to where you look forward to his punishment." Della's trance broke long enough to look at her former crush with pity. Today was a day of heartbreak.

"Gregory Talbot, you take your own daughter out behind the woodshed. I'll not explain what you do because I cannot bring myself to utter the words," Della choked out, fighting the information. Jolts of pain shot up her arm as Uriel's grip tightened. The words vomited out before she could stop them. "She's pregnant, you know. She'll show soon. It wasn't the stomach flu from which she recently recovered."

Della continued before the group turned into a mob. "Nancy Talbot, you suspect your husband of what he does to your child and do nothing about it. All you've ever done is hope his eye might turn on some other poor girl, so he'll leave your daughter alone."

"Poppa." Her faraway gaze fell on her father. He stiffened, readying his protests. "You took advantage of a woman not long after marrying Momma. You and Jed, as young men, went to buy a prostitute, but they were all bought up for the night. Full of liquor, you found a woman alone and forced her to take your money while you took turns with her. She ended her life some years ago, unable to handle the shame of a broken life."

Momma buried her head in her hands and wept, "Please, child! Please stop!"

"I have feelings for men," Uncle Frank stepped up. "I'd rather say it myself than have these two devils rip it from my niece's mouth."

"Sir, we are here talking about actual *sins*," Daniel said. "Please, let her finish."

Confounded, Uncle Frank stepped back.

"Anybody else?" Uriel whispered in her ear like a lover. Like an enemy.

"Preacher James, who refused to join us because he disagreed with you two being here. He is sitting in the church praying right now. I can see him. He condemns everyone to Hell. When we assume he is praying with us, he's asking God to send our souls to fiery torment. He wishes Satan would crawl up from the pits of Hell someday to take us all away. He hates us so much he does not call on Christ for our forgiveness."

"And your own sins, child? Please tell us your sins." Daniel leaned forward.

Della opened her mouth to say them, but nothing came out. She tried again. Still nothing. The glaze of her eyes cleared, and she looked at him, confused.

"You see? You've done nothing wrong, only held true to your feelings, much as a young woman should." He stood up, and the gathering erupted in shouting and shoves. They were bent on tearing each other apart now that the secrets had all been laid out.

"WE ARE NOT FINISHED!" Uriel yelled over the din. The words shook the house. A picture of Jesus fell off the wall. A coffee cup hit the floor.

The arguing and threats stopped.

"We are still hungry. You gave us food, but now it is time to feast on the actual meal." A wide grin spread over Uriel's face, wider than one would think possible.

Della sensed what was coming and fell to the floor. She covered her ears and scrunched her eyes shut, praying to no one that it would soon end.

Around her, a horror of movement and muffled screams filled the air. She peeked through her fingers and wished she hadn't. A green mist flowed from Poppa's mouth. His eyes grew wide and rolled back into his head. He crinkled like paper, flattening as though deflated. The green mist pulled his organs out of his mouth in a knotted lump. A single glowing green orb, the size of a silver dollar, pulled out of the knot. Once freed, the clump of guts snapped back inside the man. He fell back against the wall and slid down, nothing more than dead weight.

The orb floated along the green mist to Uriel's waiting mouth. He gobbled it up while other tendrils of green mist flowed from the others' gathered sins.

She hid her head again, but the squish and snap of prolapsed organs, followed by Uriel's wet chewing, turned her stomach. After what might have been a minute or a year, the horror ended. All was quiet. A hand touched her shoulder. Carefully she sat up. Momma, her sister, Uncle Frank, and two others remained standing. The others did not. They lay on the floor or draped across the furniture. Their bodies misshapen from the rearrangement of their innards, their skin wrinkled like forgotten laundry. A final orb, no bigger than a penny, floated past her. It disappeared into Uriel's open mouth. They licked their lips.

"Come, child." Daniel helped her up. "It's over. We came to eat the sin, and so it has happened." He motioned for the remaining folks to follow him to the dining room.

"We have food here, and it's been a trying day. Please eat." He pulled a chair out for Della and then her mother. "Come, we've had our fill already. No sense letting it go to waste."

They all sat as if snakes hid under their seats. No one touched their plate. Della's stomach audibly protested her reluctance to pick up a fork.

"The others?" Momma's hoarse whisper hung in the air. "Poppa…?"

"We came for sin. Not once did we specifically say we were here only for Della's. There is a lesson here." Daniel's soft words were intentionally delicate. "We came to help your daughter, but the sin was around her, not in her. It happens that way sometimes."

"Eat," Uriel encouraged. "Letting it go to waste for nothing would be a sin."

The others grasped their forks and spoons and, in fear, shoveled the food into their mouths. Della hesitated, watching the others eat in desperation. She picked up her fork and knife with a satisfied smile, intent on enjoying every morsel.

TÉNÈBRES MON AMOUR

PIPPA BAILEY

I close my book as the sun descends; its last trailing fragments of gold, peach, and cerise slither away from my window frame and drift down the road outside my house. Orange light dances along candyfloss clouds and between wisps of sweet air. It tucks children into bed and bids farewell to a slowing world. It welcomes the night and all who dwell under its domain.

I slip my book onto my bedside table and undress. I shower and wash my hair, blowing bubbles from the white suds that cover my skin. My excitement bleeds into nerves; it spirals around my body, agitating my heart and making my ears ring.

I sit on my bed, legs crossed, quivering, and patiently wait for them to arrive, my lover and my dearest friend.

Love is a wonderful thing. It doesn't choose sides; it doesn't know how to. People will tell you that love hurts, that passion and pain must go hand in hand, which in most cases is true. Part of the human experience is to love and lose. Grief tastes like ash and old pennies, and lust like hot mulled wine, sherbet, and bloody steak. Most people who profess to know love haven't met them, but most will in time. What people fail to say is that love doesn't discriminate against who you are or what feels good. Love doesn't care what genitals you do or don't have. Love doesn't have straight lines or come with warning labels. Love is as immeasurable and twisted as Darkness.

I met Darkness when I had forgotten how to be alone.

I feel them; they are here. Ribbons of black caress my fingers and loop my arms in a delicate embrace. Their deep warmth saturates me, a silken shroud electrifying my skin. They draw lines of goosebumps along my flesh in aching arches. I let them carry me, Darkness. Like smoke, spindles of blackened thread, shadows shaping and twisting against my frame. I close the curtains and isolate us from the world.

We're supposed to hunt for our partners, like animals. We line up in bars, swipe apps, and compress ourselves into a socially measured scale of normality. We're bound by generations of those who never found their Darkness. Always looking beyond the important fragile moments, the ones that fall between the cracks of everyday life. We forget what it means not to consume, not to have it now, and the joy of sitting in silence. Silence is a long-forgotten friend.

We tumble between layers of what we want versus what we *should* want. Tradition dictates not only how we love but who we should love.

Darkness strokes me like fire licks at smouldering coals, like bubbling lava smothers rock, molten and all-consuming. They kiss my stomach and chest as if a flickering tongue, rippling the length of me. They move inside me, and I in them. We are one in this solitary moment. Our screams penetrate time, reshaping the world.

I'd bounced from dissatisfaction to melancholy and back again, constantly seeking something I didn't understand. We are supposed to love ourselves for who we are, but we spend so much time in masquerade that it's hard to tell where the fiction begins and ends.

A soft voice had called to me from beneath my bed. Melodic words drifting up through my mattress to rest beside me on the pillow. They knew me better than I knew myself.

They had been with me since the beginning, but I'd never taken the time to appreciate them. They'd played with me as an energetic child, Darkness' shadow running beneath my feet, my twin, mirroring me from below. Darkness cooled me on hot days as a teen, drifting below trees to wrap me in a cloak of dappled shade, lazily stroking my hair with ebony fingers. Hiding me from sight as I stole my first kiss, smoked my first cigarette, and the many times I ran away from home. Now Darkness arrives at night, hot, sticky, and saccharine. Steeped in rosewood and liquorice.

Ténèbres mon amour, entre.

We weave a magic of flesh and shadow atop my bed, white-knuckled and wood-splintered. I taste them, a heady aged rum. Fire fills my body, my stomach knots, a twisting, writhing mamba dance.

Darkness is not silent as many would have you believe. They are deep breaths and jaws snapping shut, the scrape of branches against glass on stormy nights, and gentle sighs. They are the whimper and scream of torn flesh and the shattering of bone. They are a baby's first and last tear-streaked cry.

I learned that it's not who we love but how we love that matters.

My Darkness holds no form: no breasts to cup, no cock to stroke, or pussy to tease. They are all and nothing. They offer themselves to me each and every night. They are lust and rippling heat. They are consent, the throb of a new wound, blood-streaked limbs, and severed arteries. They bring me autumn leaves and spring flowers caught in their wake, lining my face with blossoms. They teach me words, of new worlds, and what lies beyond the veil.

They show me horrors, the things that love Darkness as much as I. Darkness keeps their secrets, stories that have never seen the light of day. Tales of blistered flesh and stolen voices. Lives snuffed out for pleasure or pain. They tell me of the creatures I cannot see. Footsteps in the night, teeth that chatter inside closets, and holes in walls.

To love Darkness—its whipcrack sting, black coffee heat, and ever-changing form—is to love yourself.

We share hours of bliss, but Darkness cannot stay. For they no more belong to me than I to them. We lie entwined atop my twisted, sweat-streaked covers. The night calls to them, and I cannot deny the night its darkness. Darkness knows they must go.

I open my windows and doors, allowing the twilight air to penetrate my home; the night calls to Darkness again.

Darkness lingers longer than they should, writhing between my sheets, inhaling my musk. Amber and vanilla, a symphony to counter their own.

We say our goodbyes, my heart heavy.

I stand naked in the starlight as Darkness leaves me. I peer up to the heavens: those swirls of ancient flame, caustic and consuming. I wonder how many have burned bright and faded since Darkness came to be.

Darkness dances over rooftops, bouncing from satellite dishes and tv aerials. They tap-dance atop parked cars and along chain-link fences, catching in the loops and twists of rusted metal. They tease sleeping dogs, barking and snarling like wild animals. They rest in the smoke that plumes from chimney pots, twisting the charred air.

The night is a bitter, jealous friend. They warn Darkness that time is short, but Darkness doesn't listen. They splash in streams and follow oceans. They scale mountains and float high above the earth.

Midnight stars slice holes in Darkness's coat, piercing their flesh. Darkness howls and moans, their pain rupturing the sky. They tremble beneath the might of the moon. Effulgent beams grind Darkness like a millstone on dried grain, warping and corrupting them.

The night tosses Darkness around like a plaything. I cry, but I know Darkness. I know their strength. I know they were made for this.

Quivering holes appear in Darkness's body, aching tears from streetlights and cars that trundle by in sporadic bursts. Darkness cowers behind buildings and against walls; they sneak along with the animals of the night, rustling amid trash with rats, stroking the underbelly of fighting cats.

I watch Darkness wither as they hunt for safety, battered and bruised by the night. Darkness deserves better.

The sun begins to rise, tendrils of golden light piercing through Darkness, cleaving their form into fragments. They cling to the underhang of rooves and doorways. They crawl bare across the ground, whispering their farewells. Sunlight bathes the sky in an effulgent glow, rendering Darkness to dust, swept away by the waking world.

I close my door and go to the kitchen. I make myself tea and collapse back onto my bed. I dry my tears against my pillows and slip beneath the covers, watching the sky grow bright outside; blue replaces gold, and clouds evict stars. I turn onto my side and tuck the cover between my legs; my eyes focus on a dark patch in the corner of the room, where my bedside table blocks the window's blinding light. I watch for any movement.

A voice whispers to me from beneath my bed. They tell me that they've missed me and will return tonight. They have more to show me and new stories to tell. Darkness goes where I cannot, into the cracks between things, breaching the barriers between plains.

I will sleep now. I will dream of impossible things and patiently wait for Darkness to return, for they must rest too.

Ténèbres mon amour, dors bien.

Insurrection

Ruth Anna Evans

I listened to Lorraine sleep, her breath rasping into her clouded lungs. Today I would take her to the hospital for her chemotherapy. No matter what.

She'd said all week that it wasn't worth the risk. The hospital might not even open its doors. The last time the news was broadcasted, the official policy had been extreme emergency only. You had to be damn near dying to get in, and sometimes not even then. But Dr. Lilly had said he would be there. And Lorraine was damn near dying.

My wife rustled under the covers, taking quick, tiny breaths in her sleep. The oxygen tube had fallen from her face. I reached over and settled it into her nostrils again, my hand brushing her cheek. Her skin had become dry and gray, and a rash had started around her jawline. She had asked me to cover the mirrors weeks ago.

There was a sudden silence. The oxygen machine's whir had gone quiet. *Fuck!* The electricity was out again. They had been cutting it on and off several times a day to toy with us, to let us know they could. There was barely enough time to charge the battery between outages. Soon there wouldn't be any juice at all.

I threw my legs out from under the covers, smiling a little despite myself, amused at how hairy they were. At some point, I stopped shaving. It was one of the few things I didn't miss.

Billy the Beagle gave me a morose look and resettled himself on Lorraine's legs, where he had taken up permanent residence these days. When it got really bad, he'd snuggle his way under the covers, and she'd wrap her arms around his little body while she coughed. He'd just lick her face and wait for it to stop.

Lorraine stirred and opened her eyes as I fiddled around with the battery. "Power out again?"

"Yep."

"Figures."

"I wish we had gotten the solar charger."

"You couldn't get everything. It was expensive."

When the shortages began, I put every penny of extra money into supplies. Some of it was useless: the five-gallon bucket of dried beans we couldn't cook without power and the twenty-pack of batteries that didn't fit our flashlights. But I thanked past-Wren every day for buying the big rechargeable battery. If the power didn't come back on, we could charge it with the car and keep the oxygen machine running. As long as the gas lasted.

That was something I didn't want to think about. The image of my wife gasping for breath flashed before my eyes at odd moments throughout the day. When I was counting the cans of peanut butter or sharpening the butcher knives, I would imagine her dying in front of me, unable to catch her breath. I would feel complete helplessness, stop what I was doing, and just stand there, blown away by the fear.

We hadn't been anywhere for more than a month, eating dry cereal and canned fruit and letting the car sit, preserving its almost-full tank. That tank of gas was my peace of mind. Plus, there was nowhere safe to go.

But we had to go to the hospital today, and I wouldn't let Lorraine talk me out of it.

"Let's get you up," I said.

"It's okay. I can do it." She pulled the blanket back with a frail hand as though it was weighted down, exposing her swollen knees and wraith-thin legs. It was painful watching her turn her body and try to sit up. I reached out my hand. With a look, she grasped it and pulled herself to a sitting position.

"I hate that you have to help me so much," she said for the hundredth time.

"You would do it for me," I answered as I always did, and she gave a little nod. We both knew it was true, had always been true. When we had finally been allowed to marry, we went to the courthouse on the very first day and waited in line. People had stood outside with signs and jeers, but we hadn't felt anything but joy. We should have paid more attention to the faces in the crowd.

"We need to get a move on," I said.

She sighed. "You aren't going to give this up, are you?"

"No, I'm really not."

"Fiiiine. Jerk." Lorraine was still herself inside her cancer-filled frame. Goofy. Sweet. Mine. "You think he'll be there?" she asked, letting her nervousness poke through the facade.

"He said he would."

"Surely they'll let us in the hospital."

"I hope."

The "Insurs," as the talking heads had called them, had taken over all public spaces. Police had held the line at grocery stores and schools for a while, but their ranks kept dwindling as officers peeled off to join the insurrection or stopped showing up for fear their families would be targeted. The few who remained were soon killed, their bodies left to rot in the street as examples.

The Insurs had left the hospitals alone for longer. The doctors and nurses remained excruciatingly neutral in who they treated. Many had refused to work—at an incredibly high risk to themselves and their families—rather than turn people away. And the Insurs needed them. They were one of the few populations exempt from elimination.

When our substantial pocket of wackos first rose up, the National Guard sent a platoon out to keep the streets clear of roving men with AR-15s. But when the insurrectionists attacked the state Capitol, the governor called the Guard back to Indianapolis. Their ranks, too, dwindled quickly. The Capitol fell.

Then, one Tuesday, thousands of otherwise ordinary men and women stormed Congress, The White House, and the Supreme Court, shooting everyone on their list. The world watched the grainy security camera footage in horror as the Insurs piled the bodies up and lit them on fire. Any surviving left-leaning political figure went immediately into hiding.

Airports were overrun. Cruise ships were swarmed. People massed at the borders. We all knew we were fucked.

Black neighborhoods were put on lockdown, with anyone out of their home shot on sight. Young white men poured into inner cities, armed to the teeth.

The Insurs started broadcasting pictures of the naked dead bodies of trans and gay celebrities on social media.

They burned the few remaining abortion clinics. They didn't have a problem shooting those doctors.

It was *The Handmaid's Tale*, only real.

We couldn't sleep. Couldn't tear ourselves from the news until the networks stopped broadcasting. Couldn't talk of anything else. We'd whisper to each other when we realized we were both awake in the middle of the night, asking what would happen next.

All the while, Lorraine's cancer ate through her lungs.

We took our Pride flag down, locked the doors at all times, and only let Billy out in the backyard.

Our only long-term plan was hope.

Many people we knew had left in the dead of night, headlights off, tents in their trunks. With coolers filled with food, they headed north and talked of Canada. But Lorraine was sick and getting sicker. She couldn't travel, and we had a hair's breadth of hope that her chemo could continue, that the worst would stay away from our little town long enough for one last treatment.

"I want a shower," she said, returning me to the moment.

"I hope there's hot water," I said, knowing there probably wouldn't be.

"It doesn't matter; I'll be fine. You, though"—she paused for a breath—"I wish we had hot water for your stinky ass."

I laughed and helped her up. I had put a plastic yard chair in the shower, so all I had to do was help her get in and out. She managed the rest, though it left her exhausted.

"I'm good," she said, once on her feet. I followed her into the bathroom, where she slowly peeled off the pajamas she lived in now. All that was left of her seemed to be shoulder blades and hip bones and bruises.

This is love, I thought. *This part that hurts. This is my love for her.*

With her brittle body exposed, I helped my wife into the tub and turned the handle on the faucet.

Nothing came out. They had turned the water off.

Lorraine took a little breath, let it out, and looked at me. My heart twisted. She just wanted to bathe. Such a simple thing.

And now we had to worry about not having any water.

"How much do we have?" I could tell it took courage for her to ask.

"A good amount," I answered.

We had two five-gallon drums, a half-dozen gallon jugs, and six cases of bottled water. I had counted and recounted, fearing this was coming. The Insurs had been prepping their takeover for years. They had dug wells, for fuck's sake, and buried massive caches of supplies. And here I was with one closet half-full of water. I had been so proud of myself.

I imagined the panic some people were feeling now—those who couldn't afford to stock up. Or the people who had ignored the signs altogether.

I earned a living as a social worker for drug-addicted parents before Lorraine's illness forced me to take a leave of absence. My clients and their families had been living on the edge of survival long before any of this happened. And now no water.

What about their children? I could see their little faces asking for a drink. I imagined what it would be like to watch your child die of thirst.

I tried to stop thinking about it. My wife needed a bath.

I went to the closet, cracked open one of the cases of water, and removed a bottle. Straightening, I looked at my pile of water jugs and counted again. It wouldn't be enough.

I went back to the bathroom, soaked a washcloth, and handed it to Lorraine.

"We have to be so careful," she said, apologetic.

"We'll be fine," I said, trying to keep my voice cheerful. "Don't be a stinky ass."

She flicked the shower curtain at me. "Go away, you."

I smiled at her and left the bathroom.

In the kitchen, I stood in front of the coffee maker. Things used to be so easy. We used to make breakfast together every morning. She'd kick me until I got up. I'd put on the coffee and let Billy out. Then I'd go poke her until she rolled out of bed. And we'd cook breakfast together. Scrambled eggs, toast, sausage. Every morning. I had tried to do it on my own once she got sick. But it just felt too sad to make breakfast alone, and before long, we were out of everything except coffee. Now that was gone too.

I tried to quell the panic rising in my chest. *Handle it, Wren. Just handle it,* I told myself.

Lorraine coughed in the bathroom, and I resisted the urge to go to her. It sounded like her lungs were shredding. Raw and deep and echoey. Painful. But this was one thing for which she insisted on privacy. It drove me nuts, though I understood. Every time it happened, I felt like I might lose her. She would hack up her life's blood and die, and I wouldn't be there.

It took several long minutes for her to catch her breath. The silence that followed was pregnant with the thing we didn't talk about: the cancer had spread; she was worse. The first and second rounds of chemo hadn't worked.

"You okay, babe?"

"Yes," she lied.

"Ready for me?"

"Yeah, come get me."

I helped her out of the bathtub and into some clean, soft clothes. We would run out of clean laundry soon. We'd already run out of a lot of things.

"We should go ahead and go," I said. "Who knows how long it will take to get in?" *If they let us in at all.*

"It's not safe, and you know it." She dropped all joking, her face deadly serious. "We shouldn't be going out there. Two women? You think they aren't going to know we're gay if they stop us?"

"What are we going to do? Just not get your chemo? That's not safe either."

"You could dress like a man?"

"I'd just look twice as gay."

She sat in a kitchen chair, still recovering from her coughing fit. I knelt and started putting her socks on her feet.

"I can do that!" she insisted.

I sighed. "We're in a hurry, honey."

It was a mistake. Tears sprang to her eyes. She held her foot out.

With a lump in my throat, I eased on her socks, then her shoes.

"I'm sorry," I said.

"It's fine. We need to go."

I put my hand under her elbow and helped her up. Billy the Beagle nosed against my leg.

"Hey bud, we're going out for a bit. We'll be back."

He whined a little, his big eyes on my face. He was used to us being home all the time now and, like any dog, could tell we were leaving.

"Did you feed him?" Lorraine asked.

I didn't want to tell her we were almost out of food and that I now only fed him once a day. I had no plan for what we would do when the food was gone. "I'll feed him when we come back. He'll be okay."

Lorraine looked like she wanted to argue but thought better of it. She probably guessed about the food; she could see right through me on most things.

We peeked out the window by the side door. It looked clear. Most of our closest neighbors had left, and almost all the rest were hunkering down too. But the Maynards, two doors down, had been cruising up and down the street since this mess started. Confederate flag flying, gun barrels sticking out of their windows. Good, white, God-fearing people.

No one was around. We slipped out the door, keeping Billy back with our feet, and got in the car, a nearly new silver Toyota Corolla. We bought it back when Lorraine was still working at the bank.

Even having scraped the *Love is Love* bumper sticker off, we stood out from the Insurs. Badly. There was nothing we could do. At least the hospital wasn't far.

Having learned my lesson, I let Lorraine buckle herself in and started the car. I took a deep breath and pulled out of the driveway. No one was on the road. I remember when the pandemic first hit, and people stayed inside. The roads were almost this dead then, but not quite. Ironically, there was a lot of overlap between those out then and those patrolling the streets now. We should have tagged them somehow. We should have done a lot of things.

I pulled onto the bypass and zipped toward the exit for the hospital. I had been mapping the quickest way all week. We saw no one the whole way. Just one car: a red Volvo station wagon abandoned on the side of the exit, bullet holes in the windshield.

When we got off the highway, the road led through a neighborhood where the houses were marked with spray paint.

MT was scrawled on the houses in red. *MT? MT?* "Empty," I realized with a shudder. But some houses bore a blue snake, twisted like the one on the *Don't Tread on Me* flag. This marked the dwelling of an Insur. They had gotten more brazen. I bet the marking was to inform fellow Insurs not to loot that house. Or not to go there in the dead of night with their guns drawn, rousting the people from their beds.

What were they doing with the people from the now-empty homes?

I could see Lorraine watching the houses tick by, but neither of us spoke. The only words we had to say were filled with fear, and we didn't want to make the other's terror grow.

The hospital parking lot was dotted with cars, mostly Jeeps, pickup trucks, and big black SUVs. We pulled into an accessible parking space.

"Let me try to get a wheelchair," I said.

She shook her head with a frown. "We need to get in quick. Help me."

I darted around to her side of the car and began helping her out. I felt someone watching us and looked over the top of the car toward the hospital entrance.

A man in a tactical vest with a semi-automatic rifle was approaching.

"Don't freak out," I whispered to Lorraine.

"What?" She hadn't seen him.

"A man is coming over. Don't freak out."

She looked around and saw him, then looked back at me, her blue eyes wide. I held her gaze. She closed her eyes briefly as if saying a little prayer, then opened them again. "Okay. You've got this, babe. I'm right here."

I pulled her the rest of the way out and stepped toward the young man, leaving Lorraine holding onto the car for support.

I walked within speaking distance of our visitor and summoned all the courage my two decades as a social worker had instilled in me. The other women at work used to say I had a backbone of granite.

"Yes, sir?" I asked. "How can I help you?"

He stared at me, thrown, as though stunned that I wasn't afraid. I was scared shitless but didn't want this punk to know it. He was about twenty-five, a nice-looking kid except for a stubborn jut of his chin. White, of course. All of the Insurs were white.

"She has an appointment with her oncologist. It's time for her chemotherapy. We're here for her appointment."

"You should have stayed home. You aren't supposed to be here," he said. "This hospital is for Patriots only." His gaze was on my short hair.

"She has cancer," I said simply. "Her doctor is here." I stepped aside so he could see Lorraine, who was struggling without the oxygen I had left in the trunk. I had hoped she would be okay just for the drive, but she was holding her hand on her chest and taking long, determined breaths, trying to control her coughing enough to get some air in her lungs.

After a moment, the boy's stubborn chin relaxed.

"What's her doctor's name?"

Oh, thank God. "Lilly."

He hesitated, then raised his radio.

"This is Twelve. Come back."

"Go ahead, Twelve," the radio crackled.

"I have two civilians here for a Dr. Lilly."

"Civilians?"

"Yes, sir. I thought I'd check. It's for chemo."

A pause.

My heart beat harder … if that was even possible.

"There's no Dr. Lilly," the radio finally spat.

My fickle heart stopped beating for so long I thought I might die. He wasn't there. He had to be there. Lorraine…

"And Twelve, we aren't doing civilians anymore. Patriots only. Tell them to stay in their home until someone checks them in. You know this."

I didn't know what "checks them in" could possibly mean, but I was sure it wasn't as innocuous as it sounded.

"Yes, sir. Sorry, sir."

No answer. The young man lowered his radio, the irritation of a reprimanded inferior radiating toward us.

"I told you," he said. "Go home. Unless you want me to check you in here." He lifted his gun just a fraction.

"Come on, Wren," Lorraine said from behind me. "Let's go."

I stood stubborn for a moment, wanting to fight, to scream, to beat down the hospital doors. I wanted to find the chemo and put it in my wife's veins myself. I felt Lorraine's hand on my arm, like a whisper.

"Wren."

I turned toward her and away from the "patriot." Refusing to hurry, I pulled Lorraine's oxygen from the trunk and helped her raise the tube to her nose. The man watched, hand on gun. But I refused to look at him.

Something about us made him think. He was a little slow, but he wasn't that slow.

"Hey," he said dangerously. "How do you know each other?"

I wanted to tell the truth so badly. I wanted to proudly declare that this woman was my wife, whether that meant a bullet or not. I didn't want to be scared.

"I'm her cousin," I said, faking calm. "I moved in to take care of her."

"You don't look like cousins." He took a step toward us.

"We used to," Lorraine said in her softest voice, breaking the tension building between the wannabe soldier and me. "I've lost some weight."

He looked dubious but backed off.

"You guys need to go now. If one of them comes over here, you won't be leaving." He nodded back toward the building, where I hadn't noticed a huddle of black-clad men watching us. One of them was getting to his feet.

Lorraine and I didn't speak as we got into the car and pulled out of the parking lot. The group of Insurs watched us drive away from the only hope we had of Lorraine fighting off this cancer. They were like a pack of wolves, their heads pivoting to follow our car, their bodies ready to spring. I had never before seen something so menacing.

Once I had white-knuckled us far enough away, I cursed them loudly. I wept. I didn't want to do it in front of Lorraine, but I couldn't help it. The fear was gone. All I had left was rage, and the only thing I could do with that rage was cry.

"How could they do this to us?" I demanded.

"I don't know," she answered.

I looked at her. She was crying and shaking, her hands clasped together in her lap as though in prayer.

I reached over and gripped her two hands in mine.

"We'll figure something out."

"What? We're supposed to go home and wait to be 'checked in.' You know our marriage certificate is public record. They're coming, Wren."

"We'll have to leave and find another hospital."

"Where?"

"I don't know. I don't know!"

Neither of us spoke the rest of the way home. We entered the house still in silence. Billy sniffed Lorraine all over and then gave her a big lick on the neck to declare her okay. She chuckled, breaking the quiet.

"You're a good boy, Billy." She hugged him around the neck and looked up at me. "We have to take him."

"Of course."

"Can we be packed by tonight?"

"We need to be. We have to assume the Insurs got our license plate number."

"How can I help?" She looked so tired, streaks from her tears marking her cheeks.

"Just rest. I'll pack."

"I'll make a list," she said.

"That will help. Thank you."

It took hours for me to stuff everything I possibly could into the car, carefully making sure the street was clear before I hauled out each load, holding my breath the whole time I was out. Once in a while, the Maynards buzzed by, and I huddled behind the car, crouched to the ground.

Eventually, the car was packed. I left room for only Billy and ourselves. The rest was food, a few blankets, and the sundry survival supplies I had stocked. I had Mace. Mace, for crying out loud. How was that supposed to help us? But I packed it.

I stuffed the trunk full of as much water as I could. I was most anxious about water. Then again, I was anxious about everything.

As I made my trips in and out, I heard Lorraine crying—a quiet keening noise I could tell she was trying to muffle. She walked slowly around the house, touching things. The acrylic painting she had done of her six-year-old niece, Alex, whom we hadn't heard from in months. The Golden Pothos she had been training up from the cutting her boss had given her on her last day of work. It had been a little bit of life in our house while she fought through the stages of lung cancer.

The plant would die now, crinkle up slowly into a husk and eventually turn to dust.

We sat at the kitchen table for our last dinner in the house, forking bites of cold chili from the can. It tore me up how much food we were leaving behind, but I just couldn't fit it in the car. *Mistake*, my brain kept saying. *This is a mistake. Staying would be a graver mistake*, I argued back. There was no right thing to do. They had left us with no options, which had been their goal all along.

Chili is disgusting when it's cold. I forced myself to take a bite and resisted the urge to spit it out, letting my gaze wander through the kitchen. Normally when you move out, the walls are stripped. And the furniture leaves white rectangles in the carpet, surrounded by dog hair you should have vacuumed up but never did. But our home was intact. It was our lives that had been emptied out.

Lorraine wasn't eating.

"Eat, honey. It's protein."

She looked at me, miserable. "I'm sorry. I just can't. I don't want to waste food, but I can't."

"It's okay. It's alright. We'll save it for later." I reached out and touched her hair. The first two rounds of chemo hadn't stolen it completely. She had always had beautiful hair, long and blond and full of body. Model hair. Now I could see her scalp like a crown, and the remaining hair was mostly white. I had offered to shave it once, and she hadn't spoken to me for the rest of the day. I never mentioned it again. The third round of chemo would have taken care of it, anyway.

But she wasn't getting the third round. Her cancer would continue to spread. She would grow weaker, the oxygen would run out, she wouldn't be able to breathe, and she would die.

I put that thought in a closet in my mind and shut the door, locking it.

I looked at my chili and couldn't take another bite. Rummaging around under the sink, I found some Tupperware and scraped the chili into it. We'd eat it later.

"Are you ready?" I asked.

"No."

"It's dark out. We should go."

"Where are we going, Wren?"

I tamped down the aggravation that flared in my chest. I didn't sign up to make all the decisions in this crisis.

"We know Indianapolis is down," I said. Indiana was one of the first states north of the Mason-Dixon to fall, though the insurrection had taken root throughout the country, pitting neighbor against neighbor. And everywhere, they had more guns.

"I say we aim for Chicago. There will be a hospital. And I know how to get there." Having no cell service was like living in a completely different world. One where you had to know things. I felt like I didn't know anything.

"That's three hundred miles," she said.

"We have an almost full tank. I have cash. We just need to avoid getting stopped. So we need to go." I reached out both hands to her.

She gripped my fingers in hers and smiled at me, then pulled away and stood. "Okay. I'm ready. Let's go." She looked so fragile standing there, a sick woman who obviously should be in bed.

I grabbed the last bags.

"Here, Billy!"

He ran to me, wagging his tail, his nails clicking and clacking on the linoleum. I clipped his leash to his collar and went to peek out the window.

The Maynards were pulling into our driveway. Two black SUVs were parked on the side of the road in our front yard. They must have known all day that we were packing. They let us fill up the car, waiting until it was dark, letting us believe we were safe. And now they were coming for us.

"Put Billy out," Lorraine said instantly from behind me, her voice stronger than I'd heard it in months.

"What?" I was freaking out, trying to think what I could use as a weapon. The knives. Had I packed them all?

"Put Billy out. He'll try to bite them, and they'll kill him. He'll starve here alone. Put him in the backyard. Leave the gate unlatched so he can get out after we're gone. Do it."

She was right.

"Hide," I told her.

She looked at me, the knowledge of what was to come shining through her teary eyes. "There's nowhere to hide."

"Don't open the door, then. I'll be back."

I dragged Billy out the back door and tied him loosely to the clothesline. He could pull free, but it would take him a while to realize it. I unlatched the gate, focusing on what I was doing so I wouldn't think about running.

I could run. I could make it. They hadn't come around the back of the house yet. I could move fast, and I could be quiet. But Lorraine couldn't run. She could barely walk. She would be alone in there with those monsters.

I told Billy to sit and stay. He gazed at me with his brown eyes, confused but trusting. He wouldn't understand when we didn't come back for him.

With my hand on the doorknob, I braced myself for what was about to happen, then stepped back into the house.

Lorraine was right inside, waiting for me.

"They just knocked. I think we should answer," she whispered.

"Will it help if we comply?" I whispered back. "They may kill us anyway."

"It's all we can do!"

I thought of the few knives left in the kitchen and the useless Mace packed in the car. A cold sweat streamed down my back. Knives and Mace would get us killed that much faster. Lorraine was right.

"Go in the bedroom," I said, moving to unlock the door.

She hesitated.

"Go!" I insisted.

She went.

I blinked a few times, trying to control the adrenaline coursing through my veins, the metallic taste of panic in my mouth. Then I pulled the door open.

Mr. Maynard—I never knew his first name—stood at the door with a smile. Behind him were three black-clad, lightly armored men with heavy weapons. His wife and son looked on from the truck.

"Well, hello, Mrs. Peterson," he said pleasantly. "It seems you may be preparing for a trip, and we thought we'd stop by. We'd hate for you to go without saying goodbye. May we come in?"

I stood back from the door, and the four men filed in. One of them was very tall, ducking to get through the doorway. He looked through me like I wasn't there. That one scared me. They all scared me, but that one I knew would put a bullet in me, kick my body out of the way, and wonder aloud what was for lunch. I felt as though I might shit my pants.

"So," continued Maynard, "where were you going?"

I didn't know what to say. Usually, I have a story for everything, but I was at a loss. I stayed quiet.

"Where's your wife?" He said *wife* with a scoff. He had always been an asshole to us. We were pretty sure his son had stolen our Pride flag the first time we put it up. I knew he had waited for this day. Now that he was in my home, I wondered why he hadn't come sooner. Why we hadn't expected him. Why we hadn't prepared. It didn't matter; he was here now, and my hands were empty.

"She's sick."

"Where is she?"

Again, I didn't answer.

"Mrs. Peterson," he said clearly, though only slightly above a speaking voice. He winked at me and said as an aside, "Must be confusing—two missuses." Lorraine didn't have my last name, but he probably knew that and didn't care.

"Mrs. Peterson," he repeated in the louder tone, still pleasant, "come out here, or I'll shoot the other Mrs. Peterson in the head. You have thirty seconds." He raised his hand toward me, and I saw the glint of a handgun. He had probably babied the weapon for years, polishing it, cleaning it, just dreaming about putting a bullet in the neighborhood gay.

Lorraine walked into the room. She had her oxygen, a blanket, and two bottles of water. She was the bravest person I had ever met.

Maynard lowered his weapon. "Well, hello. There you are. Now we can have a proper conversation. Would you like to tell me where you were going?"

She didn't answer but kept her eyes on me.

"I see." His face looked a little gleeful now. "I will tell you that you *are* taking a trip. But you won't need your sweet little Toyota out there." He gestured with his head to the men. Two of them moved behind us, guns at our backs.

This was the moment when I should have fought. Later, I imagined I had swung around and grabbed the gun jutting into my back. Found the trigger and obliterated the man pushing a rifle into my wife's back. Put a hole in Maynard's smiling face. Quickly killed the vacant, frightening one and left a gooey mess of the other two. This was when I let someone make my wife and me prisoners, leaving us completely vulnerable to whatever they decided would happen next.

I did think of fighting at that moment. But the man holding a gun to my wife's back would have to move his finger only the tiniest fraction of an inch before she was gone.

If I were a man, I might have resisted. I would have been socialized not to be bested by another man, to protect my wife with my life. But I wasn't a man, and I was scared. And I didn't want to get us killed.

They walked us out to one of the SUVs and loaded us in. I lifted Lorraine's oxygen tank in behind her. They watched but didn't stop me. It would only function for mere hours, and then what would we do?

The next thing I knew, a bag was over my head. Harsh fabric that smelled like mold and clung to my mouth and nose. Someone cinched what must have been zip ties around my wrists, binding them. I heard Lorraine whimper next to me. I wanted to reach out and take her hand but couldn't. How was she going to breathe with a bag over her head?

I tried to block the terror I felt so I could think straight, but my only thought was that we were both going to die.

The two men in front murmured to each other, too low for me to make out the words from beneath my hood. I could tell, though, that Mr. Maynard wasn't one of them. As horrible as he was, being abducted by strangers was worse. He was someone with whom I might have reasoned. He knew us. We were his neighbors. It probably wouldn't have mattered, but I could have tried.

To these men, we were just two more gays going against God. I made an attempt anyway.

"Please, can you take her hood off?" I begged. "She has lung cancer. She's not going to be able to breathe."

I couldn't see, so I couldn't brace for the blow. My jaw exploded with pain, my teeth crunched, and my head snapped sharply back.

"Shut the fuck up," said one of the men calmly. "Fucking gays think they're entitled to breathe," he said to his partner. And they laughed.

Blood and broken teeth filled my mouth.

"Wren?" Lorraine said in a high, thin voice. "Wren?"

I shook my head vigorously to tell her not to talk. But, of course, she couldn't see me. Blood ran down my throat, and I gagged. I tried to spit the blood out, but there was too much.

"Wren!"

"Lady, you'd better shut the fuck up back there. I don't want to smash the face of a sick woman, but don't think I won't."

I tilted my head forward and opened my mouth, letting the blood and teeth fall from the hood. Closing my throat,

I breathed through my nose, hyperventilating. I felt Lorraine twist next to me, and her fingers grabbed mine. I curled my fingers around hers and held on.

So, talking had been a mistake.

We sat, clutching each other's fingers, both of us trying to breathe while the vehicle sped on. The men turned on the radio, and I was shocked to hear what sounded like a news broadcast. Our channels had gone out weeks ago.

I tried to make out what they were saying. It sounded like information on what to do with children when a family was taken.

"Children under the age of ten are to be transported by bus to the Tennessee Re-education Center. Elevens and twelves should be immediately evaluated for radicalization, and a determination should be made..."

The man turned down the radio, and I couldn't hear the rest.

The SUV made a turn. From the crunch of the tires, I could tell we had come to a gravel road. It went on and on. The bleeding in my mouth lessened but sweat stung my eyes and dripped down my back. Lorraine was gasping, and I could feel her fingers trembling.

Finally, the vehicle slowed and stopped. The front doors slammed, and a moment later, I felt rough hands grab me and pull me out of the car.

"Get up!" I heard the man on the other side of the vehicle shout. Then came the sound of a kick and a cry from Lorraine.

I jerked away from my captor, scuffling around the vehicle toward her voice, barreling through one of the men and falling onto her body, where she lay curled up in a ball. She was crying.

Something smashed into the back of my head, my skull blossomed with pain, and then there was nothing.

"Wake up." Lorraine's voice was a hoarse, desperate whisper. "Wake up, Wren, wake up!"

I blinked my eyes. The back of my head was on fire. My jaw ached, and my tongue found the places in my gums where sharp shards of teeth were still hanging on.

Lorraine was across from me, looking pale in the dark with black circles under her eyes. Her arms were still pulled behind her back, and her chest was heaving. She didn't have her oxygen.

I forced myself off the ground into a sitting position. A spike of pain shot through my head. I looked around. We were in a pen, a dog pen, with a cement slab beneath us.

In the moonlight, I could see identical pens all around us and hear muffled crying in the night. Woods surrounded us. Further away, someone was wailing. A shot rang out, and the cry was cut short.

"Lorraine," I said, then fell silent. I didn't know what to say. The fact that she was there and not dead was a momentary comfort in the night. I hadn't expected them to put us together.

"I think I have a broken rib," she wheezed, leaning her head against the chain link.

"Oh, sweetie," I breathed. I scooted toward her. "Lean on me."

She let her weight fall on me; it was like a feather settling. Her breath dragged in and out of her lungs. I could hear the crackling myself. There was nothing I could do to help her. She laid her head on my shoulder.

"Do you remember when we met?" she asked quietly.

140

"Yes." The pain in my face screamed at me as I smiled.

"I thought you were a boy."

"I thought I was a boy."

"Too bad. I would have liked a little dick before I died."

I couldn't help myself; I laughed despite the tears running down my face.

"Bisexuals," I pretended to scoff, as I always did at this part of the joke. But my voice broke. I was on the edge of hysteria.

"I love you," she said, her eyes drooping, her breath shallow.

I kissed the top of her head. "Sweetie, please stay with me. I can't do this without you."

She made a *hmmming* noise but didn't open her eyes.

"Help," I said softly. "Someone help." Then louder. "Help!" I couldn't stop myself. "Help!"

A flashlight came toward me in the dark.

I checked. Lorraine was still breathing. I had to try.

"My wife!" I shouted to whoever was coming. "My wife needs medical attention. She's not breathing. You have to help her!"

The flashlight's beam shone directly in my eyes, a dark shape holding a rifle behind it. The man walked close to the cage, stopping right behind us. I twisted toward him.

"Please," I begged, "she needs oxygen. There's some in the car we came in. Please, I'll do anything."

He laid the flashlight on the ground and lifted his gun. He put the barrel up to Lorraine's head, and she stirred a little.

The shot blew out my right eardrum.

Lorraine's flesh, blood, and brain matter exploded onto me.

"She doesn't need medical attention anymore," he said. "Now shut the fuck up." He walked away with a smirk.

Her body leaned forward, half draped over my lap, and I stared at her. I was numb. The top of her head was gone, pieces of skull glinting wet in the moonlight. The top half of her face wasn't there anymore. Some of it was on my face. I felt strands of her hair in my mouth. It tasted burnt. I couldn't raise my hand to wipe my cheek, so the gore just stayed there. Bits of her slipped from my skin and landed on the cement.

The bottom of her right ear remained intact. She was wearing an opal stud I had given her for her birthday last year. It shone and sparkled despite the darkness.

I sat there all night with my wife's splattered corpse in my lap. I couldn't move and leave her on the cold cement.

I had known Lorraine was going to die. I had known since the moment they told us she had stage-three lung cancer. It was in her lymph nodes, and they would do everything possible, but it didn't look good. My gut had realized that grim truth immediately, though I was determined to try to save her.

But I didn't expect this—for her to die in a cage.

In the morning, men swept between the pens, checking the locks. I could see the others around me. Huddled in the corner of their cages, they were as far back as they could get.

One of the men made eye contact with me, and his eyes flitted down to my lap, to Lorraine. He made a face, then shouted: "Hey, Mack! We've got a body needs clearing!"

"Aaggh, Fuck, Jordan," called back a nearby voice. "I hate doing that. Make Jer do it."

"You're right here, asshole. Come help me."

Mack walked toward the cage and looked at the mess. He sighed deeply. "You get the head," he said.

"Whatever. Let's get this done."

Pulling out a key, he opened the padlock and then the gate on my pen. My hands were still tightly secured behind my back, so I couldn't hold onto Lorraine's body. They lifted her off me as though I wasn't even there. Bits and pieces fell from her skull.

"What are you doing with her?" I asked.

They looked at me like a stuffed animal had just talked.

"We're adding her to the pile," Mack said as though it were obvious.

"Why don't you just kill me too?"

"The gays are special," he said, wiggling his eyebrows up and down. "We've got a big event planned for you."

"Shut up, Mack," Jordan said. "You're an idiot."

They carried her out swinging between them like a roll of carpeting. Mack dropped her feet with a thunk and turned to lock the gate.

"Her name is Lorraine," I called out.

"Not anymore," Jordan said with a laugh.

They took her away.

I think I slept, but I didn't dream. There was nothing to dream of now.

The day turned to twilight, then back to darkness. There were shots in the distance. I was dehydrated. I wondered if Lorraine was thirsty and then remembered that she was dead. I missed her. It was so profound—her absence. The permanence of it. I would miss her forever. Until the "big event." I could only imagine what that would be.

I heard rustling among the enclosures, the sounds of gates opening and hushed words of surprise, then footsteps. Running.

Someone was at my pen. It was a tiny young woman dressed all in green. I tensed, waiting for the worst.

"Hey, are you okay?" she whispered, turning a key in the lock and opening the gate, wincing when it creaked. "Come on. You need to go. There's not a lot of time."

"What?"

"I'm letting you out. Hurry." She moved to the next pen.

I almost didn't go. I almost stayed where I was, not wanting to leave the place where I was last with Lorraine. But that was ridiculous. She would be irate.

I pulled myself to my feet, gripping the chain link, and looked around, watching for the men with guns. I didn't see them. Only a stream of figures leaving the kennels, headed in one direction. I left the pen behind and followed the others.

We passed the SUVs in the large gravel parking lot. Young soldiers were slumped here and there in pools of their own blood. There had been an attack.

The gravel road stretched on and on through the woods. People around me talked in hushed voices, exchanging names and stories, but I didn't speak to anyone. I just walked.

We came to a large white house and heard yelling inside. Past the house was a road. People would approach the road, look left and right, then choose a direction. There was no sign of the tiny woman who had freed me or any others who might be responsible for our release. A guerilla resistance. *Cool*, my numb brain thought inanely.

Most of the people were choosing to go right. It felt like north to me, and my humble sense of direction told me our abductors might have taken us south. I set off, forcing my legs into a run. Every step took me farther from my love.

I wanted to go back, find her body, and bury her. What was left of her. I wanted her to have a gravestone I could visit and cry, and upon which I could lay flowers. I wanted to call her sister and break the news. I wanted to go through her closet and choose what to treasure and what to donate. I needed to grieve and for the world to be normal enough for me to grieve.

And if I couldn't do that, I at least wanted to go home.

I came to an on-ramp for a highway I recognized. Scattered around the on-ramp were various closed gas stations and fast-food restaurants. Someone had broken the doors and windows of a Shell station, and people were gathering what they could carry.

I approached. A blond woman who looked a little like Lorraine handed me a bottle of water through the window, then a bag of Chex Mix.

"You look rough," she said. "You should rest."

I nodded, thanked her, and turned toward the highway. At the top of the ramp, the stream of people sorted itself into east-going and west-going. I checked the exit number and turned east. I felt like a zombie in *Night of the Living Dead*, shuffling through a world of black and white, all color leached away. I gingerly touched my jaw, and it stung. My head still throbbed, yet I kept walking.

Up ahead, I heard a shriek. Suddenly, people were running back toward me.

"Insurs!" a man with long locks shouted at me as he raced by. I looked around for somewhere to hide. I knew I couldn't run far. There were no abandoned vehicles, and that part of the highway was raised, with cement guards on either side. I was stuck.

I heard a vehicle coming down the road and could see the beam of headlights cutting through the night. I dropped where I was and lay flat, hoping I looked dead. A black SUV cruised by, packed with Insurs pointing rifles and flashlights out the windows. I squeezed my eyes tight when I saw them and waited for the shots to ring out. But it worked. They continued past me on their hunt for live humans. And I heard a rattle of shots a few minutes later.

The pavement was rough against my face, and bits of gravel stuck to my cheek. I wanted to stay there, flat and unnoticed in the dark. But after I was sure they were gone, I rolled to a sitting position, then got to my feet mechanically. I continued walking east, my senses a little more alert.

My water and food were long gone by the time the sun came up. I had made it, though. I was at the exit for my little town. I ducked and peered down the exit. At the end of the ramp, a group of pickup trucks clustered. On one of the hoods was the teenage Maynard, hunting rifle balanced on his knees.

These weren't the black-clad professionals who had been drilling in basements for years, hovering in Parler and waiting for their chance, waiting for the right election, listening for the dog whistles. These were the regular-grade haters. The ones who cheered when their kid spit on the trans child in the bathroom, who thought all Black people were on welfare and drugs, and that Mexicans took their jobs away and needed to learn English. These were the people who talked about being "outnumbered" by minorities as if it was obvious what a bad thing that was. They thought that America had once been great. These assholes were everywhere, and it took no work for the Insurs to recruit them for their war. They, too, had been waiting for this. Their aim just wasn't quite as good. At least, I hoped not.

I left the road, something I would have done long ago but for fear of getting lost, and went into a crawl, trying to get past the posse before heading home. I wished again that I had grown up as a boy, playing war in the woods. I thought I was in the clear when a shout went up. I froze.

"There's one!"

"Shit, where?"

"There, across the road. It's a dyke. See her? She's on the ground."

"I got her!"

I leaped to my feet and ran, zigzagging like they taught little kids in elementary schools. The shots rang out, but they didn't hit me.

"Man, you suck," I heard young Maynard say. Then I heard a pop, and my calf felt as if simultaneously on fire and sliced with a razor blade. I dropped, but I kept going on my hands and knees. I was not going to fucking die at the hands of these rednecks.

I found myself at the opening of a little alleyway between rowhouses. They continued taking shots at me. I crawled out of range behind a garage, then gripped the side of the building and pulled myself to my feet, trying my leg. It was on fire and bleeding profusely, but the muscles and bones felt intact. Young Maynard wasn't a crack shot, after all.

I hobbled forward. The pickup engines revved toward me. I darted into a wooden-fenced backyard, then out through the front of that yard. Zigging and zagging, ignoring the pain in my leg, I crossed the little street ahead of me and went through several more yards. In a couple of houses, I saw scared eyes peeking through windows before the curtains were drawn. I didn't blame them. Helping me risked death. I understood wanting to keep your family safe no matter what, especially now that I had failed.

Somehow, I lost them. They shouted to each other a few streets over. I knew the Maynard boy likely recognized me. So I did the stupidest thing possible—I went home. It was all I had left.

My door stood open.

I should have prepared myself before walking in, but I was so tired, and I was bleeding. It hit me like a two-by-four. Lorraine was everywhere. Her smell: brown sugar and vanilla and medicine. Her Stephen King book left open on the table by her chair. Her plant drooping for lack of water.

I went to the closet, got a bottle of water, drank half, and gave the rest to the little plant. Its leaves quivered in gratitude.

I felt a cold touch on my wounded leg, a little lick. It was Billy. Sweet Billy the Beagle. He finished his greeting and went and stood in the doorway, looking out. He glanced back at me as if to ask, "Where is she?"

"I'm so sorry, bud. She's not here." My tears fell freely.

He returned and put his front paws on me, giving a little grumble. Then he turned and trotted toward the bedroom. I followed him, dreading the sight of our bed.

By the time I got there, he had hopped onto the mattress and curled up on Lorraine's side. His face seemed to say, "I'll just wait right here, and she'll come back."

I went to the bed and lay beside him, stroking his soft ears.

I heard heavy footsteps. The voices of young men called out, threatening.

I closed my eyes and let myself believe Lorraine was there next to me. In a moment, she would start kicking me to get up and make coffee. I would bring her coffee and lots of milk, and she would sit up and smile sleepily. Billy would whine to go on his walk. I'd grumble and take him while she started the sausage. Then I'd go to work, and so would she. I'd have a rough day, and in the evening, we'd go to dinner at the Chinese restaurant that was only okay. At the end of dinner, we'd read our fortunes.

You will have a long life with the one you love.

She'd roll her eyes and tell me she'd better find them soon, then. I'd laugh and eat her fortune cookie.

And when they shot me, I'd be smiling.

THE PARACHUTE

EVAN J. PETERSON

"…because the human body is unstable, right? Things erupt out of our skins, immune systems attack our own organs, vasectomies reverse themselves. The body is a strange and miraculous thing."

Glasses clinked, and silverware scraped against plates. Brandon's date blinked at him and sipped from his glass of craft cider. The kid didn't seem terribly bright so far. Maybe he hadn't heard Brandon clearly in the loud tavern. Maybe he was too polite or too bored to ask Brandon to repeat himself.

Brandon continued: "I mean, you're into tattoos. So many things can happen to the skin, and tattoos stay through most of it. Scrapes, minor burns, whatever." He had seen the inscriptions swirling across Abe's body in the pics on the dating app. Abe was a wiry thing, pulled lean by aerial silks and acrobatics.

Abe stared back. Brandon wasn't so bad, but Abe could tell that Brandon was judging him. Fair. Each sized the other up.

Abe forked some prosciutto chicken into his mouth and talked around it. "Mmhmm. I had a dream once…"

Just once, Brandon thought.

"You ever wake up in your dreams and think you're really awake? I woke up one day, and my skin had rejected all my ink, just like threw it up. There was ink everywhere on my sheets. In the dream, I mean. Not really. Ha!"

A few particles of food flew out of Abe's mouth. Brandon looked away, but he noticed a fleck land on his salad. He would eat around it. The kid wasn't perfect, but damn it, Brandon hadn't gone out with anyone since the accident. It took him a week to muster up the courage to message Abe. The profile said that he liked smart, chubby guys. Well, check and check.

Abe was staring at him again, not in a creepy way, but the way a dog cocks its head and stares.

"Do I have food stuck to my face?" Brandon asked, brushing here and there with his napkin.

"You have really nice teeth," Abe told him. "Rich people teeth. I love guys with nice teeth. Mine are fucked up."

"Thank you. My family isn't rich. Middle class, I'd say." Brandon looked down at his plate and picked at his pomegranate spinach salad. He'd finished the steak slices and now faced only the leaves and arils.

Abe relaxed. "I'm new to the whole online dating thing. Late bloomer, I guess. I like it so far. It's like a catalog or a menu. Hey! What a coincidence!"

He held up the wine list and waved it for effect. Brandon nodded and faked amusement.

The server came and went, promising more bread. Brandon stuffed another pile of raw spinach into his mouth. He wished he'd just starved himself instead of letting himself gain all the weight during the long bed rest. The painkillers weren't helping, either.

"I know what you mean about bodies. I'm also a contortionist, not just an aerialist. I can dislocate some of my joints without hurting myself. I can climb through a tennis racket!"

That was flirting, right? Brandon imagined what that flexibility might be like in bed.

Without segue, Abe said, "I was a shit kid."

"I'm sorry?"

"Don't be. I was a shit kid."

"No, I mean—I don't know what you mean. You were a shitty person, or you were into actual…?"

Abe laughed and danced in his seat. Brandon was grateful that the younger man's mouth wasn't full. Come to think of it, Abe's mouth was odd. Just a little too small for his face, something uncanny like that.

Abe explained himself. "I was a shitty person when I was a teenager. I got shithead tattoos and did shithead things. I mean, normal kids don't literally run away with the circus."

Brandon dropped his shoulders in relief. "Ah, okay. Because you never know, right? You could be into anything."

"I sure could, Brandon. Maybe you'll find out what I'm into."

The server returned with a third cider for Abe and a new basket of bread and butter. Brandon would just skip the butter, eat all the salad, and have some bread to make it go down more easily. He wouldn't order a second beer. Let Abe get drunk and loose.

He changed the subject. "So, Abe is short for Abraham, I'm assuming?" Brandon plucked a roll from the basket.

"Nope." Abe cut another hefty chunk of meat and ate it. They watched each other chew.

Brandon decided to play this game. "May I ask what it's short for?"

"Abelard." The boy took a roll and tore off a chunk with his teeth.

Brandon looked down and admired how much of his salad he'd made disappear. "Oh. That's an unusual name nowadays. Like Abelard and Heloise? Is it a family name?"

Abe narrowed his eyes and swallowed. "Not exactly." The educated ones like Brandon always pried. Abe could keep this up for hours, but he didn't need that long.

"Hey, Brandon, what do you call this again? Pro-shoo-toe? Is that French?"

Brandon laughed. "Italian. I'm glad you like it. It's one of my favorites."

It was a pretty April night, a little damp but not raining. They walked from the restaurant to a nearby park, making a pit stop for ice cream. Abe was more genteel now. He hadn't offered to split the check but had paid for their ice creams at the fancy organic creamery.

Brandon put his hand on Abe's lower back as they walked. Abe smiled. Brandon imagined how they'd fit together. Abe was so slim, with those long arms and legs. For a moment, Brandon wondered if Abe had Ehlers-Danlos Syndrome or Marfan or something like that. Maybe he was just malnourished as a kid. That would explain a few things.

They talked about circus life. Abe would be in town for another week, then move on to Portland, but he'd be back in a couple of months.

"A girl in every port, huh?" Brandon half-joked.

"Nah, too much work to keep track. I just meet who I meet. It's the life of a traveler."

"Yeah? A bit of a gypsy?"

"Nah, tramp and maybe thief, but I'm not a gypsy, I don't think. I thought we weren't supposed to say 'gypsy' anymore?"

Brandon laughed. "I don't know. Nice Cher reference, by the way. You a fan of hers?"

"Yeah, I guess I can relate to a lot of her early songs. 'Gypsies,' 'Halfbreed,' 'Dark Lady.' She would've been a queen at the circus."

Brandon decided to push a little into vulnerable territory. "Do you still have contact with your family?"

Abe didn't answer; he simply consumed his ice cream.

"I'll take that as a no. What happened there?"

Abe stopped but didn't look at him. The ginkgo tree above them dripped.

Abe decided to tell Brandon part of the truth. It probably wouldn't change things at this point.

"My family is in a cult, Brandon. My parents named me Abelard after one of the founders of their batshit religion, some guy who supposedly married a sea goddess. They used to make me drown little animals for their fucked-up rituals. I have scars on my body, under my tattoos, from all the shit they did to me. I ran away from home at fourteen and sucked and fucked my way across the country until I joined the circus. Is that enough background? Do you wanna know more?"

Brandon could feel how widely his eyes bugged, the hot blood at the surface of his cheeks. "Oh. I'm…so sorry. Sorry."

Dammit fuck shit, Brandon thought. He'd pushed too hard. Who would run away with the circus but someone escaping that level of crazy?

He studied Abe's face, and Abe looked like he was barely hiding his pain. Brandon didn't know what else to say, so he made his own confession.

"Abe, I had a car accident three years ago. I was so drunk that I hit a fucking tree. I was in the hospital for

154

weeks and had to drop out of my Ph.D. program. That's when I got fat; I used to be ripped."

Abe made that puppy dog head tilt again.

Brandon continued: "My brain injury makes it hard to read for very long now, which is the worst. I hate it. And I know that's not nearly as bad as the horrible things your family did to you. You were innocent, and this is my own fault, but I hope it makes up a little for me prying."

Abe's face held a distressing lack of expression. Then he said, "Hey, kiss me."

Brandon did. His heart raced. Abe wrapped his long arms around him, and they kissed like hungry things.

They did not go back to Brandon's. Abe invited Brandon back to his trailer at the circus, and Brandon figured, *Why the hell not?*

The dim illumination in the trailer came in pulses from the lights of the carnival fifty yards away. Red, blue, yellowish white. Now that they both stood naked, Brandon noticed other peculiarities to Abe's body. *Poor thing*, Brandon thought. *I bet he's inbred. Fucking cultist bullshit.*

Abe was a little too long, yet his chest seemed too short, the nipples too small, his abdomen stretching between the rib cage and the pelvis. His arms continued just an inch or two after they should've terminated in hands, but the hands were dainty. His feet were huge, but his cock seemed too small for the rest of the body. Somehow, it made him all the more fascinating.

Abe pulled away from Brandon's kiss and said, "You ready to fuck me, stud?"

Brandon blushed. "Can I rim you first? Do you like that?"

"Mmm … Go for it."

It was a beautiful little ass. Abe reclined while Brandon crouched between his legs, looking up at him.

"Here—" Abe flipped onto his hands and knees, facing the wood-paneled wall at the head of his bed. Brandon saw an elaborate tattoo on his lower back, some kind of pseudo-Japanese mural. But it proved difficult to make out in the faint light. Underneath that, he could feel scar tissue—a lot of it. He began licking at Abe again, but he stroked the man's back in an attempt to feel out what shape the scar suggested. It felt like a starfish. *Fuck*, Brandon thought. *This poor kid.*

Abe decided to enjoy it while it lasted, but after a few more minutes, he said, "Brandon? Hey, Brandon?"

Brandon stopped worshipping Abe's ass and said, "Yeah?"

Abe still looked at the wall a few inches from his face. This part always made him a little sad. "For what it's worth, I really do like you. And I'm sorry, but this is what I do."

"Huh?" Brandon said, but Abe's ass was already dilating. Scarlet tissue, slick like the skin inside a mouth, pushed out like a parachute.

"What the f—" Brandon began, but the tissue kept coming out and, in an instant, lurched forward and clung to his face, quieting him.

"Shhhh. Please. Just don't," Abe said, continuing to externalize his stomach, but Brandon could hardly hear him. The smooth muscle of Abe's gut surrounded Brandon's entire head, then jerked back and forth, snapping Brandon's neck. More smooth muscle came out, moving down past the shoulders to mid-torso, locking his arms against his body, but he was already paralyzed.

Like a sea serpent consuming prey larger than its own head, Abe's body cavity expanded tremendously, the pelvis and joints and limbs clicking apart. The starfish stomach sucked Brandon in, and he suffocated before he could feel the worst pains of digestion.

When it was done, Abe said the little prayer of thanks that his mother had taught him. Full now and lethargic, he'd sleep for a week, breaking down Brandon's soft tissue. Then he'd shit out the bones but keep those beautiful teeth.

Abelard always felt jealous of the ones with good teeth.

Take Me to Church

Dan B. Fierce

"What have they done to you?"

David couldn't stop the tears as he peered through the small window from the outside. It was the only light allowed into the dank, musty basement. He crouched down on all fours, still trying to get a good look through the textured glass pane.

"Get out of here," Gerald muttered weakly, his arms outstretched in the cuffs like a medieval prisoner. "If they see you talking to me, they'll throw you in here too." He chuckled a bit before it morphed into a slight cough. "Besides, you're blocking my sun."

Something was inviting about the sliver of light on the wall. It gave him a bit of hope in this dismal place. He heard David sniffle more before footsteps crunched on gravel in the distance. He couldn't bear to look at the pane while David was there. It would cause him to have *those* feelings again, the very emotions that got him in this position in the first place.

Neither of them deserved this. None of the kids at this so-called camp did. Torture in the name of religion was hardly a new concept. The supposed faithful simply had gotten better at disguising their motives.

A rat chittered in a corner. During the day, this basement had some semblance of illumination. At night, the darkness was engulfing and lonely. Gerald longed for the comfort of David's touch again. Even at a young age, he knew what love was. Too bad his mother disagreed.

As always, Gerald traced his chains while the sun faced the window. Each tether started at his wrists and was securely welded to a metal pillar upholding the Victorian-style house above, his arms perpetually outstretched. The restraints on his ankles looped through an arc of rebar set into the cement floor.

Locks rattled from above and behind. A new shank of artificial light hit the wall before him as the old cellar door creaked a chilling welcome. The old wooden steps groaned as two people lumbered down. Feet met concrete, drawing nearer. He couldn't see them with his back turned but knew who it was. He always knew.

"Hello, Pastor Daniels, Mrs. Whyte."

Their approach stopped in unison, the aged man drawing in a deep breath and letting it out as his eyes scanned the thirteen-year-old boy sprawled out before him. "How are you doing today, Gerald?"

"Oh"—Gerald flipped matted and filthy sandy blond hair from his forehead—"I'm hanging in there."

"It's good that you're keeping your humor, Gerald. Are you ready to give your body to the Lord and cease these impure thoughts?" The preacher slowly wrapped his hands around a horse whip as Evangeline Whyte offered it to him. "Belief in the Lord shall save your soul from Hell."

"Tell me, Pastor." Gerald steeled himself. He knew what his remark would bring. "Is Heaven filled with people like you? Because if it is, I'd rather go to Hell." A white flash of pain sang across his back as the whip cracked his skin.

"If a man lies with a man as with a woman," Pastor Daniels snorted as he swung again, causing Gerald to yelp in pain, "both have committed an abomination and shall surely be put to death."

"Leviticus? Well, never let it be said that originality is your forte." Gerald winced, sucking in air through his teeth, as a third swipe of the whip etched a bloody groove into his flesh. "Then kill me already. At least I wouldn't have to listen to your self-righteousness."

Gerald heard a huff of deep, seething anger from the pastor that made a curl of a smile bloom from the corner of his mouth. He stomped toward the front of the boy, rearing back once more. This time, Evangeline stopped him. Pastor Daniels leered at the woman, his lips pursed tightly, desiring the release of his fury. She silently nodded to the boy's bleeding back; the three lash marks glared red as they seeped a copper scent into the air. The preacher swallowed his ire down, lowering his arm to his side. "I've cracked tougher cases than you, Gerald. I haven't failed a soul yet. God works through my hands and will heal your sinful ways."

Gerald spat a thick, bloody wad of phlegm onto his tormentor's face, lightly cackling as it slid down. "We all know the impure thoughts you have, Pastor Daniels. That must be why I'm half-naked. Have you told Evangeline what you do when you sneak down here at night? The things I hear through the vents?"

"Lies!" Pastor Daniels arched his arm once more, bringing the whip down across Gerald's developing chest. He bared his teeth as he spoke one final warning. "I'll see you cured or dead. Either way, I'm doing God's good work, son. Your mother..."

"My mother is an absolute bitch for putting me in here with the likes of you. And you...both of you...you're cowards hiding behind a bible."

"Your mother is a saint for her sacrifice to bring you here," the minister huffed. "She knows the eternal torment your soul will endure." Evangeline proffered a handkerchief, beginning to dab at the blood dripping from the gaping wounds. Pastor Daniels disarmed her of the cloth, using it to wipe the spittle from his face instead. He sneered at the defiant kid strung up before him, cupping the boy's chin in his hand. "She'll be here tonight, your mother. Praying for you, along with the rest of the parents. Would you like to see her?"

"I hope you all choke on communion wafers," Gerald hissed as the assistant dabbed at his bloody gashes. "Please do bring her down here. She'd be interested to see your methods."

Pastor Daniels chuckled. "She's perfectly aware of our ways. I always make sure the parents know that sometimes…extreme measures need to be taken. If you'll excuse me, I have a sermon to rehearse." He released Gerald, a loathsome grimace on his face. "Evangeline?"

"Yes, Pastor?" Her voice trembled beneath her breath.

"Clean his wounds with lemon. We'll see if that takes some of the Devil's fire out of him. And don't stay here too long." Then he leaned into Gerald's ear and whispered. "You enjoy my nightly visits."

Evangeline lowered her head in silent obedience as the preacher gave the chain attached to Gerald's left arm a mighty tug. Gerald yowled in agony, his shoulder hanging at an odd angle. Heavy steps caused the boards to protest as the headmaster of the camp reemerged on the ground floor.

"J-just do as he says, Mrs. Whyte," Gerald stammered.

Quietly, Evangeline picked out the wedges of lemon from her tray. The years of doing this taught her that preparation was the key to the children's survival. "Renounce Satan's work in your heart, Gerald. I beg of you."

Gerald winced loudly as the woman squeezed the juice from one of the wedges over his opened skin. He sucked air through his teeth as she nursed him with the unsavory fruit. "Tell me, Mrs. Whyte, is God infallible?"

"He is."

"And He created us all, right?"

Again, the woman nodded while plying the painful liniment to his flesh.

"If His plan for us is written in stone and God is never wrong, how is it that being gay is truly so horrific?" Gerald twisted in a way that reminded him of his shoulder, bringing forth another yelp. "How does who I love hurt anyone?"

Evangeline stiffened as she finished wiping the last trickles of blood from Gerald's otherwise flawless skin. "It's unnatural." She nodded as if that were the only answer in the universe. "It's unhealthy for a young man to desire other young men and young women to desire other young women. I-It's," she stammered, "It's just not right." She leaned in, whispering into his ear, an act that would have aroused him had David been the one tending to his injuries. "Please, Gerald. Don't allow these demons to keep your soul. Give in to God." Gathering her tray, Evangeline brushed the dust from her long skirt, eyes watery with grief as she studied the boy. "Give in to the Lord, dear. We know what's best for your eternal soul." She ducked under the chains, giving the prisoner one final, tearful look of pity.

"Abuse is good for my soul?" Gerald growled as she crossed the room. "Torture is holy? If that's your God, you can have Him."

Gerald heard the last set of steps groan, the overhead bulb flashed off, and the darkness again enveloped him. All that remained was that fleeting sliver of sun that had now retreated to the wall to his left. He looked at the glow as if it had betrayed him. He glared at the daylight until the pain and tears made it blur. He wept, the sorrow fading away into another desperate, lonely night. Then exhaustion took him.

Gerald hung limply from the restraints, his knees not quite reaching the floor for support. He snorted awake, the sound of crickets pouring through the window. The blackness of the basement was always disorienting. The night's full moon offered little help through the meager portal. The trees outside danced as if mocking his torture. The corners were voids threatening to swallow him.

"Astonishing. You have an unbreakable spirit, boy."

The voice, low and gravelly, shocked Gerald into full alertness. His eyes flew wide as he peered around the room. "Who's there? Pastor Daniels? Admiring your handiwork?"

"Over here." The voice growled a hideous laugh, sending prickles dancing on Gerald's spine. He searched, never pinpointing its origin. "In the shadows."

Squinting, Gerald noticed a crack in the foundation reaching from the ground in the darkest corner. Tendrils of onyx shadow bloomed from the crevices. His eyes shot wide; his heart drummed in his chest. Still, he couldn't summon the energy to tense up his shackles and pull himself upright.

Two gleaming orbs the color of lava blinked at him from an impossible height. Whatever skull housed them seemed to have to duck to keep from striking the floor joists as it stepped out from nowhere.

"W-who..." Gerald stammered, his pulse quickening. "What are you?"

"I am many things." Hoofbeats thrummed on the concrete. "I have many names. For some, I am

163

damnation." Twin clouds of vapor snorted from unseen nostrils. "For others, salvation." It paused, those glowing crimson eyes boring into him. "I can be the answer to your prayers. Or to theirs."

"Wow. Evangeline must have slipped some serious drugs in with that lemon."

"I assure you, child, I am no illusion. You are always looking in the wrong place for your solutions. You look to the light for your hope. What does it give you in return?" Now the shadows congealed into a silhouette. Though still somewhat amorphous, whatever it was appeared to be substantial but not entirely man-shaped. The light broke again, this time lowering into a grin below the other two glints of sun. The more it spoke, the more precise the image became. "I could save you."

The darkness sharpened into a thing with the head and legs of a stallion and a muscular man's body Gerald had only imagined in fevered wet dreams. The being materialized from the wall, its cloven feet clopping thunder through the room. It radiated an impossible light from within, a perfect combination of man and horse, a rainbow mane flitting in an unseen breeze behind a single, scarlet horn atop its head.

Gerald blinked, attempting to clear the pain and grit from his vision and perhaps place his visitor firmly in the realm of delusion. Nothing changed. The magnificent beast still stood before him. Gerald's body reacted to the strange phenomenon in the only way adolescent boys' bodies knew how. He shook his head, the thoughts invading him in agony-driven spurts.

"Let me guess," Gerald slammed his eyes shut, hoping to ward off the invader. "If I give you my soul, you'll help me take out the pastor."

The creature grinned wide. Huge, sharp teeth shone in the blackness as it nodded. "That's the deal, yes. Did you know that they are planning a prayer vigil for you today? Right above this very spot. Pastor Daniels, Evangeline Whyte, and your mother will be there." It looked skyward at the wooden floor above. "I can help you with all of them. All you have to do is succumb to me."

The moans from the basement resounded through the house, pouring from the air vents like specters. Whenever Evangeline looked at the door leading to the basement, Pastor Daniels warned her gaze away. The preparations had been made for the vigil. All of the parents lined the pews. Some of the children still kept their distance from them. Others cuddled and wept, begging for forgiveness.

David sat in the back pew, alone, his spot ever since Gerald's punishment began. There was a vent where he and Gerald could talk when David believed Pastor Daniels wasn't paying attention.

Next to the French door entry to the church, Gerald's mother and Pastor Daniels stood by yet another vent, conversing.

"What is *he* doing here?" David looked back in time to see Maggie, Gerald's mother, motioning toward him with an accusatory glare. "He is why my Gerald is here, to begin with." The venom dripping from her voice was palpable, even from a distance. "If his brother Henry hadn't caught them…" She trailed off, the waterworks flowing heavily.

David suspected it was more for show than pity for her child. Still, his heart felt like it weighed a ton from the accusation. *She's right. If I hadn't…* His shoulders slumped as the heartache surfaced. The emotion-filled room was too much. David wanted to run. He wanted to hold Gerald. Mostly, he wanted to die.

Pastor Daniels held up a hand. "Both boys need God's guidance, Mrs. Carmichael. David has taken more to our teachings than your boy. That is why we're all here: to pray to God for him to come around, to pray for his soul." He held a hand toward the front of the congregation, silently directing her to take her seat.

Maggie cast a baleful glare at David as she passed by.

Evangeline sat at the organ, playing a soft hymn as Pastor Daniels glided down the aisle toward the pulpit.

The preacher raised his arms to the heavens, slowly bringing them down. The followers seated themselves as he began to speak.

"We are gathered here today to bring the love of the Lord to Gerald Carmichael. He needs our thoughts as he is set back on a righteous path."

Gerald and his dark visitor listened in on the tinny sermon as it slithered through the ventilation system. Gerald's ire blossomed within.

"Liar," Gerald grumbled weakly upon hearing the ceremony's opening.

"That's it, boy," soothed the creature beside him as it caressed him seductively. "Give in to your rage."

"We must pray for his soul to release him from this sinful torment."

"The only one tormenting me is you," shouted Gerald, this time with more enthusiasm.

A chorus of "Amens" echoed down the vent, drowning out Gerald's accusation. *"Please join me as we sing a fitting song: 'Jesus Loves the Little Children.'"*

"Jesus loves the little children."

"Bullshit," seethed Gerald. His breathing ratcheted up, the heat from his loathing warming the damp room.

"Do you hear how they taunt you, boy?" cooed the demon, running his hand over his captive victim. He traced the wounds, licking the blood from his hands with a shudder of ecstasy.

"All the little children of the world."

"Hypocrites!" Gerald screamed, his voice cracking.

The demon chuckled, a throaty guffaw that only fed into Gerald's rage. "Yes, child. But what will you do about it? Will you hang from your shackles or be free to get your vengeance?" The demon grabbed Gerald's face. A slender, black tongue shot from the creature's mouth, licking Gerald's lips. "Give me what I want, and you can have it."

"If I do this, will you spare David from this hell?"

The unicorn's grin grew menacing. "You have my word. I simply require your blessing."

Now Gerald's mouth split in a rictus grin, his hands wrapping around the cuffs and chains. "Have you ever heard the story of Samson?"

David cried harder with each response from the vent below his feet until, mercifully, it stopped as the song did.

"Run, David!" echoed up from below, snapping David from his sorrow. He wasn't even sure whether he had heard it.

"He said run, boy!" bellowed a deep voice in his ear, the smell of sulfur and brimstone wafting past.

David shot up from his pew and scrambled out of the church, wide-eyed and heart racing.

Before Pastor Daniels could utter another syllable, all the doors to the house slammed shut in unison, startling visitors and residents alike. The structure heaved mightily, banging sounds emanating from each side of the immense room.

"Now you'll pay the price, Pastor." The voice boomed through the walls, echoing in the church like the command of God Himself. *"Now you'll see what sins you have wrought upon your flock."*

The house boomed again, the floor heaving and cracking. Panic set in as people climbed from the hard wooden seats and rattled the doors to escape.

David closed his eyes, skittering to the front lawn. The house bucked one final time. Wood creaked and groaned. The middle of the house began to fold in upon itself, splintering like a felled tree.

The floor beneath the congregation yawned open like the mouth of a beast. An impossible hole belched the scent of hell unto the petrified masses. Gerald's mother was the first to be swallowed up. Jagged, wooden teeth tore at them as people fell screaming into the abyss. Pastor Daniels grasped at shattered planks, horror etched on his face.

"Come on down, Pastor," Gerald's voice taunted from deep below. "There's a special place for you here." Shadowy hands reached from the abyss, grasping at the minister's body. His clothes fell from him in shreds, bloody lash marks weeping life into the pit as he struggled.

The pulpit teetered toward Pastor Daniels, bounding off his slipping fingers before disappearing into the black. His grip failed, plunging him into the darkness below. Evangeline attempted to escape, the organ snagging her skirt as it careened down, dragging her, wailing, into the depths, swallowed by the obscurity.

David opened his eyes once the sounds had stopped. Fading sunlight drenched him as he sat up from the thick grass outside. Jaw agape, he watched a rainbow form over the house as the massive chasm consumed the final standing bit of the roof. Crawling to the ledge, David watched as the piece of the church fell forever into the black, never seeming to crash to the bottom.

A unicorn with a sandy blonde mane pranced beside David, reared back on its haunches, and urinated into the hole. The boy skittered back, startled by the majestic creature.

"Don't be afraid," it declared in Gerald's voice. "I'm free. I'm finally free."

David's face slackened as he shook his head, trying to will away the hallucination. Timidly, he approached the mythical being as it snorted lightly and clomped the ground.

"G-Gerald?" David extended a trembling arm, knowing that feeling the unicorn would decide reality or insanity. The soft fur and gentle gaze from the green eyes eased his doubts. "What happened?"

The Geraldicorn met David's hand with his head, whinnying softly, leaning into his unsure caress. "I made a deal to save you from this hell." A small tear poured from one of the large eyes.

David wiped away the tear, leaning into the stallion's neck. It even smelled like Gerald. "Is this real?"

The unicorn's face brightened. "Mount me."

David stepped back; an eyebrow playfully arched. "Ew."

The Geraldicorn rolled his eyes. "Get on my back, you perv." He kneeled to allow the boy on top of him.

David climbed the steed, using the horn for assistance. "Where are we going?"

"Far, far away from here."

David looked at the gaping maw in the ground, flipping his middle finger. "Fuck you! I'm mounting my demon boyfriend."

In a scene straight from a western, they strode away. It was the first time David had ever enjoyed a sunset in a good, long while.

A Song of Sorrow

James Lefebure

She missed her hair the most.

She would spend hours brushing and styling it. Every glace in the mirror was to check that it was still serving the purpose of the day. It had a natural bounce, and when the light caressed it, people would always comment on her golden locks. Callie knew she was an attractive woman. It was a natural beauty that she didn't have to enhance with much makeup. She never tired of telling people that fact. Secretly enjoying the slight envy it would invoke. Her hair was the cornerstone of her identity. She had learned to weaponize her blonde locks in a variety of hairstyles to achieve whatever dark desire she wished.

As the wind gently caressed her rough scale-covered skull, she wished that just once, her weapon had failed her. "It was all her fault" a dark thought whispered. Callie wanted to agree. "fucking dyke," hissed the thought. Her body crackled at the memory of her. She opened her mouth to scream, to let out the rage that had found a perfect nest inside her heart. Instead of the raw anger, she needed to release the song. The one she had been singing for over a year. A melody so sweet nobody could resist. This was her new weapon. Tears burned her blackened eyes as they fell. She missed her hair. Her melancholy melody carried across the gentle sea. Callie knew that food would soon arrive. Until then, as she did every day, she allowed her song to carry her back to the past.

"Tell Percy I can't meet him until at least four this afternoon. Cancel my appointment with Griffin and see if Deter can meet at lunch." Owen stopped for a moment and looked at Callie.

She smiled and nodded.

"I'll do it now. I've already sent apologies for your 10 am, so you have time to get the report ready for this afternoon." Owen's smile was less than professional, but she knew it had scored her a few points with him.

"That's my girl. What am I going to do when you leave me, eh?"

Callie performed a perfectly rehearsed "oh stop" motion with her hand while shaking her head just enough to have her hair bounce and catch the light in the office. She had performed this move enough times on Owen to know the result it would achieve.

"I've not got it *yet,*" she replied as she tucked a strategically positioned portion of hair behind her ear. "Besides, there's bound to be some strong candidates interviewing. They might be better than me." She knew what would come next. She had been training Owen for this answer since she had accepted the interview to become a Senior Administrator in the office.

"Nobody will be able to beat you, Cal. Two reasons. Numero uno: I'm on the panel. As much as I don't want to lose you, it wouldn't be fair for me to keep you. Numero two-o: The only other person is what's her face. You know, the Gorilla."

Callie performed her "shocked face" and clasped her hands to her mouth. "Owen!" she scolded. "You can't say that." Callie knew that was exactly what he was going to say. She started the nickname the minute she found out that Olivia had also dared to apply for the senior position.

"What?" Owen laughed. "She is. I mean, she looks like one." He did an impression of a gorilla banging its chest.

Callie allowed herself a mock laugh with him before shaking her head just enough to make her hair move and catch Owen's eye again. Another trick that she had spent months working on. His eyes rarely completed the journey up to her hair; they always got side-tracked by her chest. "I'll have you know that Olivia is very good at what she does." Callie put her best professional voice on. "She's *almost* as good as me." She let it hang there. This way, nobody could accuse her of being a bully. "She did bring in that whole new database thing." Callie waved her hand dismissively.

"Yeah. But, you know, she looks like a bloke, Cal."

"Oh stop. Now you're just being mean." She pouted and tucked an invisible bit of hair behind her ear. "She's good," she whispered.

"You're better. I know the others will think so as well."

This is exactly what she had wanted to hear.

"Thanks, Owen. I honestly got so lucky to have you as a mentor here." Before he could reply, she turned and walked to the door. "I'll have to think of a way to repay you sometime if I get the promotion." Leaving the words hanging in the air like her cheap perfume, she walked to the door and let it click behind her. Smiling to herself, she walked back to her desk.

Busying herself with Owen's diary and phone calls, she watched as the time passed. Her interview was at One. Olivia's was at two. Callie was confident that they would choose her. Admittedly Olivia was the better candidate, but as Owen had clearly stated. She looked like a man. A butch one at that. She was the only person in the office who was openly gay. Everyone knew about Craig from accounts, but nobody mentioned it to him. It wasn't that type of office. Olivia had a rainbow mug. She mentioned her girlfriend. She had this whole mantra of "Women Supporting Women." As if it needed to be said. Especially by *her*. All of the women in the office supported each other. She was a bit much for everyone. Especially the other admin. All the girls had agreed at lunch yesterday that Callie was the perfect one to be the head of the team. Not Olivia. With her short hair and shorter fingernails. She didn't even wear a skirt or heels. What self-respecting woman would come to work in an office in pants and a shirt? It just wasn't how things were done at Journey Inc.

She could hear laughter on the wind. Her talons clacked on the rock as she hefted her body to the water's edge. Her mouth began to water slightly as the sound of laughter got a little closer. She hadn't eaten in days. Winter wasn't usually a time for people to get on boats and travel around the loch if they could help it. Today's winter sun had brought a welcome warmth to it. It was the perfect day for a trip round to the water for tourists. Even now, she knew that money spoke. The rumor of the Lady of the Loch had been her meal ticket for the last year. It had been just enough for someone to start offering rowing boats to travel round the loch and see if they could catch sight of The Lady. Callie had played her part well. She often dove under the water and hid in one of the caves. "When life gives you lemons," her mind reminded her. Her rage bubbled again. She was hungry and needed

*to eat. Parting her dry lips, she allowed her soft melody
to escape. Her feathers bristled as the air filled with her
voice. The laughter stopped. She knew she had caught
breakfast.*

"Any questions?" Oliva paused. The silence was just
short of uncomfortable. "OK then. Well, my door is open
if anyone has anything they need."

The quiet conversations between colleagues quickly
filled the previous silence. Callie could barely think
straight; she was so angry. This... *thing* had taken *her* job.
She sulked her way back to her desk outside Owen's
office. He had at least been smart enough to have the
decency to keep to himself.

"The others were impressed with the database," he'd
offered meekly yesterday when she asked him to sign a
letter for sending.

"It's fine," she had replied, her smile barely moving
her mouth. "The best *woman* got the job, I guess."

"There will be other opportunities, Cal. She was just
the right fit for the team."

"Don't forget that you have to call your wife at four,"
Callie answered, bored of the conversation.

She was the right fit for the team. The others had all
agreed, but as soon as Olivia had been announced for the
role, they had clapped and offered congratulations. It
should have been her.

Instead of enjoying the congratulations of her co-
workers, she had to endure pity and mumbled apologies.
She watched as they flocked to Oliva over the coming
weeks. The stupid open-door policy Olivia had brought
into her management style meant she was invited to
lunches with the rest of the team. Olivia had even had the

nerve to correct her on a report that she'd run for Owen. So much for women looking out for women. Callie had raged as she ate her way through a lunch box with Tara stamped across it.

Over the next three months, Callie seethed and thundered silently. She watched people cross the battle line and praise Olivia. Even Owen—*her* Owen—had been complimenting the increase in productivity since Olivia's promotion. Through all of it, Callie kept her composure. She knew the promotion had belonged to her. It would be hers. She was confident there would be a way to get rid of Olivia and claim the position for herself. Until the moment was right, she watched. She waited. She schemed. She obsessed. She watched as Olivia's stupid mantra embedded itself in the office. "Women Supporting Women" was her battle cry. All Callie wanted was to support Olivia out of the office and into another company.

It was a snippet of an overheard conversation in the bathroom that birthed the plan. She had listened with mounting frustration as two receptionists talked about Owen. He was no longer *her* Owen. That right had been taken away the day he chose Olivia over her. Then they moved on to an involved discussion regarding Olivia and how amazing she was. How they felt supported by a manager and much happier in the office. Callie could have beaten them with her stapler.

She now hid in the bathroom cubicle for as much of the day as she could. Not only did she get peace from the idiots she was surrounded by; she found it was one of the best places to catch gossip. Nobody expected someone to be hiding in here. It's how she knew that Martin from finance was sleeping with Joy from the art department. It was where she learned that Karen the receptionist was struggling with money due to her son's drug problem. People let their guard down in the bathroom. She was about to leave the stall on an uninspired Wednesday when the door opened. Instinctively she lifted her feet off the floor.

"Don't be like that," pleaded the voice.

Callie's heart raced. It was Olivia.

"I know it's special." Olivia let out a sigh. "I'll be back for it. It's only going to be for a few drinks." Silence. "It's for work. I've got to go. It's a senior's thing."

Callie could hear the sensible shoes walking the space in frustration.

"Look, they asked me. I need to get them to know me. Babe. Please calm down." Another pause. "Listen, I need them to know I'm not The Gorilla, OK?"

Callie nearly burst out laughing then. She knew! Oh, that must have stung. This was turning into a good day. It must be the girlfriend on the phone.

"Jane. Honestly, it'll be a few drinks. No other women are going; it's one of those awful boy's club things. I *need* to go; I don't *want* to go." Another pause. "Jane, don't be like that. Come on, it won't be like last time. It won't." Olivia sighed deeply. "Look, it was one time. I've apologized a hundred times. Hello? Jane?"

It was at this moment Callie flushed the toilet and walked out.

"Oh. Sorry." Olivia was an enjoyable shade of red.

Callie put on her best sad face. "Sorry, I didn't mean to overhear," she offered.

"It's fine. Just my girlfriend."

"I'm sure it will work itself out," Callie said as she very slowly washed her hands. "You know what we women are like."

"All too well." Olivia sounded defeated.

Callie savored the moment. "Is this about the Senior Party tomorrow?"

Olivia nodded.

Callie knew all about the Senior Party. She had been so excited to attend. Something else Olivia had taken from her. "I've heard it's awful," she lied.

"Yeah, I'm not looking forward to it." It was clear Olivia regretted the admission as soon as she made it. "I mean, it's just different from what I would normally do."

"Honestly, don't worry about me. I get it. And I won't say a word." Callie smiled and ran a hand through her hair. She followed Olivia's eyes as they watched her hair. "You're right, though—it's a total boys club."

"Right?" Olivia relaxed visibly. "I hate that I'm the only woman that's going to be there."

"You know you're going to stink of cheap aftershave and cigars when you leave," Callie laughed.

"Oh don't."

"Listen, it'll be fine. I've spoken to Owen in the past. It's usually just them all sitting around drinking whiskey, smoking those awful cigars, and telling each other how they're the Kings of the world."

"That's the part I'm not looking forward to."

"The cigars or the drinking?" Callie probed.

"The drinking. I really don't mind a cigar," Olivia laughed.

Of course, you don't, Callie's mind hissed. She joined Olivia in the joke.

"But I'm a lightweight with a drink. Especially spirits. It just goes straight to my head."

"You need a wing woman," Callie casually mentioned. "Someone to keep you on track and take the attention away from your slower drinking."

178

"That would be ideal, but they'd never go for it. It's a seniors-only gathering."

"If it's in the office, I'm sure you could get one of the team to hang back late."

"I don't think that would work." Olivia paused, clearly thinking this plot twist through. "And who would even do it? It would need to be someone they wouldn't mind being there."

"What about Louise? She's gorgeous, and you know what men are like. They never say *no* to a pretty girl." Callie laughed and hoped the bitterness didn't come through. She hated Louise.

"You think Louise is pretty?" Olivia asked, slightly confused.

"Well, she's got those massive boobs," Callie laughed, putting her hand gently on Olivia's shoulder. "The boys love them," she added.

"I couldn't ask her. She's nice … But honestly, she spoke to me for twenty minutes about biscuits yesterday. I can only imagine what a glass of wine would do for her conversational skills." Olivia paused, looking at Callie. "What about you?"

"Me?" Callie asked innocently, taking her hand to her chest.

"Absolutely. I mean, you could have been the senior if things had gone a different way."

Callie bit her tongue.

"You would be doing me a massive favor. And I've seen the way Owen looks at you. He wouldn't mind at all if you were there. Especially if you wear that red blouse of yours."

Got you! Callie thought.

"I do love that blouse." Callie laughed to diffuse the tension. "And I know Owen does, as well. I'm a very good PA," she giggled.

"So it's settled? You'll save me?" Olivia's brown eyes pleaded.

"Oh, go on. Women supporting women—am I right?" Callie smiled with all her teeth.

The notes had stopped. Thankfully the screaming had stopped as well. Her taloned feet clicked and clacked on the rocky surface as she used her dark talon to pull the smaller of the two bodies toward her. She hated this part, but she needed to eat. Lowering her head, she bit into the fleshy stomach of the body below and pulled. Her transformation had given her the teeth she needed to complete the task of cutting through the flesh. Pulling back, she felt the skin stretch and tear. With a wet rip, it came loose. Tilting her head back, she swallowed greedily. Steam rose from her blood-covered face as she lowered her mouth for another bite. After the first tear, the meat was usually easier to rip. She had long since stopped crying over the meat. It didn't change things. As she sucked down a second mouthful, the sun glistened on something. Looking at the body below her talon, she allowed herself to find the source of the sparkle. It was a wedding ring. Callie did her best not to look at the body. It was easier to think of the food as something akin to sushi. "I'm sorry," she whispered, using her sharpened fangs to bite through the hand. The ring clinked lightly on the rock as she crunched the finger like a potato chip and swallowed.

"Tell them you lied," Olivia's voice screamed down her ear. "Tell them you fucking lied, or you'll regret it!"

With shaking hands, Callie pressed the red button on her mobile screen and sank into her bed. It wasn't supposed to have gone this way. She had convinced people with relative ease that Olivia had tried to sexually assault her that night. She wasn't the same as everyone in the office. Deep down, they *wanted* to believe that she was all the things they had heard about gay people. All the whispers from school and social media had become shouts in the minds of the office. Olivia wasn't like *them*.

She was a predator.

She was a pervert.

She was different.

One little cry in front of Martin, one of the senior partners, and a mini "panic attack" at lunch when Olivia came storming over, and the whole office was aware of her story. But when Martin had pushed for the police, Callie knew it was going too far. She couldn't back down, though. She had stuck through it to the end. Olivia had not only been arrested but fired. She had been removed from a company that didn't want different. Callie had been praised for her bravery, and she had been promoted. Callie had conformed; she was once again one of them. Nobody looked at her with pity anymore. They had nicknamed her Queen Callie for a few weeks as she took charge of the admin team. She had started to believe them, too. Until the phone calls started. Until her toenail fell off.

The calls were from an unknown number. The first one was Olivia calmly asking that she tell the truth of the night—that nothing had happened. Callie hung up. There were a lot of calls like this. Callie quickly learned to ignore them all. One evening a call had come from her work number. When she answered, all she could hear was chanting. The female voices were haunting, and she couldn't find the strength to pull the phone away; she was entranced. When silence filled the line, she looked at the call duration on her screen and was shocked to find that it had lasted three hours. She remembered mere minutes of it.

Callie changed her number the next day, yet the calls continued. In a single week, she lost over thirteen hours, according to her call logs. She couldn't remember answering the phone half the time. The message from Olivia had been the last time her phone rang. Callie recognized the number and let it go to voice mail. When she woke up the next morning, her feet were sore. Upon inspection, she noticed that two of her nails had turned black. When she touched the nail on her big toe, it stuck to her finger and, with a sticky rip, had come away from the foot. She pushed this to the back of her mind. She had a presentation at work that day.

The following day, the rest of her nails were the same shade of black. They popped off when she put her feet on the floor. She screamed as she walked into the bathroom. Her shoulders were covered in white nubs. They looked like engorged spots and were painful to the touch. With shaking hands, she had called into the office and explained that she had a bug and wouldn't be in for a few days. She didn't need to put on a sickly voice, as the sound that escaped her throat was convincing enough. In a state of panic, she ran her hand through her hair. That simple action would ground her.

Panic exploded in her stomach when a handful of blonde locks came away from her head. Fear froze her. Not her hair! Anything but that! Every time she touched her scalp, more strands came loose. Vomit erupted out of her throat in a hot stream. She didn't reach the toilet as her back arched and more of the burning liquid escaped her. It dripped down the walls; it coated the floor. Retching and crying, she backed out of the ensuite. Her reflection in a full-length mirror in the bedroom showed a balding monster. Screaming in disgust, Callie threw her phone at the creature. Her phone began ringing, but she didn't want to answer. Her gut told her not to. Trembling, she ignored her instincts.

"Hello?" she whispered with a voice that didn't sound like hers.

"I warned you," Olivia stated calmly on the other end.

"Please," Callie cried, "help me." She felt her skin vibrate.

"It's too late for you." Olivia's voice whispered almost sadly. "You brought this upon yourself."

"I didn't know," Callie wailed.

"But you didn't stop. I warned you. I've been saying it since the start: Women should support women."

"P-p-please." Callie struggled to form her words. Her tongue suddenly felt too big for her mouth. Coughing slightly to try and dislodge a blockage from her throat, she was horrified when three teeth clattered to the floor.

"You don't have long left now, Queen Callie," Olivia whispered.

"Y-y-you. W-w-what did you..." Callie's stomach lurched as another stream of vomit erupted from her. Hunched over, she let the phone fall from her hands as a spasm ripped through her body. Crawling on her hands and knees, she reached a shaking hand to the phone.

"You're a beautiful woman, Callie." Olivia laughed coldly. "Sorry. You *were* a beautiful woman. I noticed that very quickly. Men were drawn to you."

Callie's skin burned as the white spots on her shoulder started to pulsate. "You might want to put me on loudspeaker, you know. This next part isn't going to be pretty."

Callie did as instructed.

Olivia's voice filled the room: "I begged you, Callie. I begged you to tell the truth."

Callie screamed as her skin ripped, and bloodied brown tips pushed through around her shoulders.

"But you wouldn't listen. You used your beauty against me."

Watching in horror, she observed the tips continue to grow. Her mind couldn't comprehend at first that they were feathers.

"Of course, Owen was going to believe you. You lured them into a truth you created. He couldn't see past your beauty. None of them could. Not only did you go out of your way to destroy another woman, but you also enjoyed it." Olivia whispered, "There's always a cosmic punishment for those who betray their own, Callie."

Callie's body slammed to the floor as her toes stretched. There was a wet shredding sound as a rough talon pushed through the taut skin.

"All those people you lied to … They all listened to your song. That's always been your gift. That beauty lures people to the wrong choices."

Callie choked when one of her teeth fell into her tightening throat.

"So, now that will be your punishment. Anyone who listens to the lies you sing,"

Callie heard her bones breaking before she felt them. A deep snapping filled her mind as her arms twisted at an angle that defied their design. The flesh tore as the bones forced themselves into the air.

"Well, they will be as doomed as you are." Olivia's laugh bounced off the walls.

Callie's screams filled the space soon after.

The day had darkened and passed as she ate. Her stomach was bulging, and she felt lazy from gorging. Ruffling her feathers, she used her right talon to push the bones off the rocks and into the water. The boat had long since drifted away with the gentle current. She would have to move on soon. There would be too many questions about missing teens after this meal. It felt like a problem for tomorrow. In the gentle white moonlight, her soft face knotted in worry. How long could this continue? She couldn't think of an answer. Opening her mouth, she allowed her voice to fill the night air. Her sadness rose to the sky, giving her wings. Soaring through the night air, she allowed her sorry to fall on the land below. Flapping her great wings, she rose higher. Unable to escape the body she was trapped in, she knew that peace was her only option. She had accepted three truths about herself:

She was different.

She was a predator.

She was death.

This was just the start of her journey. Her song would be the destruction of all those she encountered.

Endless, He Said

Anton Cancre

Images began to form behind his eyes. Not in flashes or floods, but a sludge-slow trickle. Chemicals leaking from dendrite to dendrite, swimming lazily through the gaps between neurons. Disparate pieces of a jumbled puzzle linking in random locations.

Red. Bright. Too much. Over everything. Drowning the room. The world. Filling him. Leeching his life.

Then black. Seeping in.

Eyelids heavy, he forced them open. The room was a blur of colors and shapes. Angry, painful light burst through open curtains.

Someone didn't like those curtains. Too bright. Too busy. Too grandma. Who? Couldn't remember.

Something gray. Pale. Limp and crumpled in on itself. Laying under the window. In the shadow. Too close to that misshaped black lump. Too close to the puddle of pink. He didn't like that lump, so he looked away from it.

The lump was bad. He didn't like looking at it. His neck popped and groaned as he turned toward anything else.

The soft, round, brown, and oblong shape had to be the couch. It wrapped around him. Cradled him. He wanted to feel comforted, but something jabbed at his mind like a thorn. Something was wrong.

It was supposed to be white. There had been arguments. Something about stains and cleaning. Someone was a sloppy little pig.

He knew he should get up. He wanted to. He needed to do something. Maybe hunger? His stomach wasn't growling, but he felt empty. There was food somewhere in the house. There had to be. All he had to do was get up.

A simple request. Stand up. Walk. Defy gravity. Coordinate hundreds of strands of muscles and ligaments. Put one foot in front of the other without falling over somehow.

The thought exhausted him.

His neck ached. Not screaming agony but insistent. A steady moaning buzz of angry nerves. He could lift his arm to check on it. That much was possible. It had to be.

The muscles were stiff and sore, but they complied. His hand rose slowly. Eventually, it reached the source of the ache. He expected pain. The bright jolt of a poked bruise. Instead, there was nothing. Not just a lack of pain. Nothing at all. An absence where the skin of his neck should have been. Raw, cold meat on deeper probing. Still, no real pain. Certainly not the agony he expected from an open wound.

There were teeth. And dull green eyes that should have shone like emeralds, staring from beneath black felt. Gray hands grabbing him like steel claws. His pain rested on the edges of those teeth and in the emptiness of that gaze.

He remembered weight, too. Cold, blunt steel in his hand. The momentum and the crunch of a cracked skull, making his stomach lurch. Over and over until the hands let go and the teeth and the eyes fell away. Then the red came.

"You know what they said," Hunter said.

"Yeah," Jade replied. Short and stern with those deep green eyes boring holes through him. "Buncha face-flapping toadies paid to keep us all terrified. Locked in our homes and under control. You damn well know better than to fall for that bullshit."

His pale, rail-thin arms flailed as he spoke, building momentum for the soapbox, a pastor psyching himself up for the choir. He hadn't hit his stride yet, but Hunter knew he was saving that for the pulpit. He couldn't help wondering if the ashes from the end of Jade's cigarette might catch on the carpet. Then they'd both have no choice but to break curfew.

To be out there.

In the street.

"I know it sounds crazy." Hunter tried to keep his voice even. Concentrating on the rhythm of the words and pushing to keep it measured. "There's no reason to believe a word of it. I get it."

He took a breath, looking Jade directly in the eyes. "But you weren't there when it happened. You didn't see them all together. YOU didn't feel how still the air got. Didn't watch what they… I…" Hunter trailed off, his tongue frozen in his mouth. Words lost form in the images, and his mind stopped dead.

"You saw people acting up and acting out."

There it was. The cherry of that damn cigarette pointed right at him. There might be no congregation, but it was still time to preach.

"You saw people who finally had enough of this bullshit. You saw people who realized there was no way out. You saw people with no other options left. YOU saw them stand up and lash out for a change."

That silly goddam night-black bowler with the sillier pink ribbons hanging from the brim bounced around on his head. It would have been funny without sound. So much fury and such a flurry of motion. Jade always

188

tended toward the dramatic, and he became a tornado when he was passionate.

"It's what we've always dreamed of...happening right in front of us. All around us. How many times did you scream at the TV that we needed to burn the whole thing down? The match has finally been lit.

"It's happening on our own doorstep. You were there when the flame hit the floor. You were there, and YOU could have doused the place with gasoline. Instead, you cowered with your tail between your legs."

Jade's hand was on the doorknob. His cigarette trailed smoke. Hunter knew he should say something. Grab his shoulder. Kiss him deeply. Or punch him in the jaw. He knew he should scream at Jade about the all too real blood in the streets. His lungs froze in his chest, and his lips turned to stone.

Time passed. The shadows were longer or deeper. Maybe there were just more filling the room.

Had he slept? He didn't remember losing consciousness. He didn't remember much of anything. Maybe the shadows were always this dark. He wanted them to back off and give him space. Maybe he dreamt they were shorter before, back when he was...

The thought slipped through his fingers. He waved them in front of his head, trying to grab it   before it disappeared. They were too stiff, too clumsy, and too slow, and it passed away into nothing. Maybe it would have stayed put if it really mattered at all.

Food.

That's what he needed. Something solid that would sit in his stomach like a rock. He wasn't supposed to eat red meat. Reasons and attendant arguments hid in the muck of his memories, but they didn't matter. A steak would do the trick. Rare and bleeding. Then he could think straight.

But the floor was so…comfortable? No, that didn't seem like the right word. His back was sore and stiff. His ass felt flat and swollen. It felt like something was moving underneath his thighs.

Maybe comforting. It was solid. Stable. So much better than the couch he had slid off of. It didn't reach out to smother him like the damnable black fingers reaching out from the corners. It didn't ooze out from under him like every thought while he tried to make sense of himself. The floor was there. It had always been there. The floor would always be there.

Endlessly unchanging.

It was the same on both of their shirts. Stark red on white cotton in gorgeous, delicate script. The back told a different story. Simple block lettering, bold and invasive. The alternating colors of the rainbow blending smoothly: SSDD. Resting atop a single coil of deep brown, piled pyramid-like to give the impression of concentric circles. An inwardly spiraling cone spotted with yellow.

Hunter caught those green eyes fluttering over to his several times throughout the night. Quick, like squirrels jetting after a stray nut, but noticeable. Hunter couldn't bring himself to go over, though. His mouth turned into a wadded mass of cotton whenever he considered it. The room was too small. The stark white walls, with those garish thick pink stripes slashing across them, closed in around him. There were too few people to hide among. And everywhere he went, those eyes were there, peeking out from behind a swoop of black hair.

There wasn't enough liquor to loosen his tongue or pry

his feet from their spot cemented into the floorboards. He could drown his liver in vodka and gin and still never have enough to move. What would he say if he did? Some fool pickup line?

Come here often?

Was your father a thief?

Those pants are fabulous, but they'd look better on my floor.

How quickly would those full, round lips turn sharp if he did? What fire would spill from between them and leave him a smoldering pile of ash? Any amount of self-hatred he was guaranteed to feel in the morning had to be better than that.

In the end, the decision was made for him.

Shouting. A thin, black cigarette punctuated each bellow with a thrust. The cherry getting closer and closer to the other man's face. The words, and any sense they may have held, were lost in the thunder. The other one looked like a friend of Nixon's, who had a thing for muscle-bound giants. A sense of righteousness, no matter how well earned, and a tiny bit of flame wouldn't stand a chance where this was headed.

Hunter didn't think about what he was doing. His feet moved on their own, striding with purpose. His left hand reached out, snatched the cigarette mid-thrust, and dunked it into his drink. It was a waste of good vodka, but the insistent hiss silenced the room.

"These kids today." The words flowed smoothly off his tongue as if coming from someone else. "All hopped up on the cloves and starting shit with houseplants."

His right hand pressed firmly on the back. Bone jutted sharply beneath trembling skin. There was pressure. Turning. A slight nod to the host.

"It was a lovely evening," Hunter said to no one in

particular, "but I think we'd better get to rehab before he burns the whole house to cinders."

The door opened.

"Nice shirt," Jade said as they stepped into the night together.

The sun was in his eyes. It definitely moved. He had to think to blink and concentrate on making the muscles move to make it a reality. The sound they made, a soft rasp, as they scraped across his eyes worried him. The sunlight, harsh as it was, failed to bother him as much as the nagging thought that something wasn't right.

Something was supposed to be there, blocking the light. Blocking THEM. Something important.

Something to keep him. No, not him; them. Something to keep them both safe.

Something that didn't work.

He wanted to do something about it. The boards were right there, next to the gray lump on the floor beneath the window. The hammer had to be nearby. There must be nails somewhere, too. His legs didn't feel so stiff anymore. A quick, easy task…

It would still be there later, though. The damage was done. No point in worrying about it now. Besides, he might come home soon.

Another day done, Hunter was on his way home. Usually, there wasn't much traffic this late. One of the few perks of working retail—selling the same fucking print of the same fucking flowers to the same fucking idiots to hang over the same fucking table in their dining rooms. But the later shifts meant sleeping in later and that he didn't have to deal with the traffic jams everyone else complained about. It was usually smooth sailing coming in and going home.

Tonight was different. Likely, some asshole jumped the gun on a light, and everyone was gawking. The radio was off. An old bastard with a tape deck and an older Erasure tape stuck in it. The choice was Ship of Fools or nothing, so he chose nothing. His half-blown-out speakers wouldn't have been able to cover the cacophony of blaring horns and curses being hurled around anyway.

At least the air conditioner worked, so he could keep the windows up. There was too much exhaust built up from all the cars sitting stagnant, and the buildings crammed on top of each other over the street kept the wind from blowing it away. He coughed enough from the clove smoke in the house; he didn't need to do any further damage to his lungs.

A woman walked along the sidewalk toward his car, slouching wearily as if toward Bethlehem. From the matted brown dirt in her hair and torn, stained clothes, he assumed she was homeless.

"Just walk on by," he mumbled to himself, hoping the words would work. "Think I'd drive a piece of shit like this if I had any money?"

They didn't. She didn't. She approached the passenger side window and pawed at the glass like a cat begging to come in. Her hand left thick streaks of crimson down the glass. He worried that it might not be mud all over her, but there was nothing he could do to help.

I'm not a damn doctor, he thought.

She wasn't taking the hint, so he gave up pretending he didn't notice her. Her jaw worked in slow, steady circles. She looked him dead in the eye. Then her left fist began pounding on the glass while the right continued sliding, scraping. It was too much for him to handle.

"Look," Hunter screamed, "I don't ha—"

There was a sharp crack, like thunder. An explosion of red, gray, and white burst across the window. He thought he heard a faint thump on the ground outside the door. More thunder rolled down the street and out from the alleys.

He looked out the windshield but couldn't make sense of what he saw. It was all too far removed from prior experience and context. Olive-green and khaki figures swarmed across the road. Rifles held ready in their hands, muzzles flashing noon-sun white. People. Just regular people in severe black and white business suits and bright green housedresses were everywhere now. Just walking through it all. Every once and a while, one would jerk once or twice and fall to the ground.

One of the soldiers was in the middle of a group. Close enough that Hunter could hear the curses he yelled between shots fired. Most of the people around him dropped, but not all. They were moving in closer. Hunter didn't see any weapons. They didn't seem to be yelling or showing any usual signs of anger. Just walking toward him slowly, methodically. Two reached him from behind and grabbed him by the shoulders, pulling him to the ground. Shouts turned to screams, screams to undefined vowels. Vowels that drew out until they finally disappeared.

Someone stepped out of the car in front of him. A woman in a slinky blue dress and three-inch heels. Hunter couldn't make out what she said, but she shouted whatever it was. Her head flew back and forth as she strode over to a teenager with bright blue hair and shredded jeans. His back was to Hunter, but he must have said something, done something. The bright red rage drained from her face, and her hands dropped to her sides. She started to back away from him. Her foot must've caught on a rock or something because she tumbled down backward. With the racket of the air conditioner blocking out the sound from outside, it was almost funny. All that self-possessed, entitled anger turning to fear and a well-deserved slip on the pavement. The terror on her face was too clear, though, even from a distance. Eyes wide as she frantically pulled herself up, she was nearly standing when the teenager reached her.

Hunter expected blows to fall. Punches. Kicks. Maybe some spitting. The usual street fight stuff. He didn't expect the teen to lunge in, face-first and mouth agape. Didn't expect to see teeth clamp down on the flesh of the forearm she threw up in defense and continue forcing their way through skin and muscle. He'd been bitten before, once by a pissed-off dog and again by an even more pissed-off eight-year-old. The dog left some punctures in the skin, and both bruised his muscles all to hell. The pain was terrible. But neither of them tore anything loose. He flinched in sympathetic agony and watched her scream into the sky, slapping and pushing at the teen with her other hand. The teen finally released her with a backward yank that tore free the last strings of skin, muscle, and tendon. Blood ran down from the wound. She tried to turn, probably to run back to the relative safety of her car, but he lunged at her again, throwing both of them to the ground.

Hunter couldn't handle any more. The confusion, the fear, and the impotent anger overwhelmed him. His lizard brain took over. Conscious thought was shut down. He crawled into the back seat and pulled the emergency thermal blanket over him. Curled up in a ball, he whimpered softly to block out the sound of the screams and the gunfire.

Something small, gray, and furry pulled on his little toe. Somehow, he didn't notice it chewing through his shoe. Now, it was gnawing on HIM. A dim memory expected pain or shock or anger. There was nothing. He should be swatting at it. Screaming and kicking and stomping. He couldn't bring himself to stand up. Just stared.

He thought about how warm it must be. Pulsing with blood and meat. Wriggling. Squealing.

His arm acted independently, grabbing the rat before he knew what it was doing. The expected squeals came. It fought back against his grip. Tiny claws shredded the skin of his fingers. Teeth sank into his knuckle. Warm, yellow liquid spilled down over his hand. His grip didn't loosen. When he pulled it to his mouth, his teeth and jaws did their work. Clamping down. Crushing small, brittle bones and tearing through both fur and skin.

The squeals stopped. So did the wriggling. His tongue pushed warm, wet meat down his throat to fill the empty pit inside.

The rest of the bites were easier. Less fight meant less work. The skin was tough, the meat stringy. Fur didn't catch in his throat quite as he expected it would. He pounded its head against the floor to free its brain from the cage of its skull. Ultimately, he chewed the remaining fragments of bone anyway.

His clothes were a mess. The volume of blood in something that small surprised him. It was everywhere. Flies were already settling on his shirt. The yawning gulf in him didn't feel any fuller.

"They consider it a delicacy there," Jade said, a smile stretching his lips into thin crescents. "Starch said so."

He was seated across the small, plastic kitchen table, picking at the remains of a chicken leg on his plate. Those thin, dexterous fingers snatched little meat morsels from the crooks of gristle and bone. They were greasy, shining orange and yellow in the light of the single candle. With each bite, he slid them part of the way into his mouth, sucking at their tips. The seduction wasn't subtle. Nothing Jade did was subtle. At the same time, Hunter was mesmerized.

"I think it's a given," Hunter said, trying to keep his focus, "that anything people cook on the street isn't a delicacy. Sounds more like a quick way to contract every foodborne illness on the face of the planet. That's the type of thing people only eat when they have no choice…or if they're tourists."

He forced a laugh. Half-heartedly tossed a kernel of corn at Jade, who ducked aside with a dramatic flourish. Every moment was a show for him.

"But that's why I'll have to eat it," he said. "It's part of the experience, both good and bad. You're just scared I'll like it. That I'll come back demanding rat kebab every night, and you'll have to find some dark stall at the farmer's market where they're willing to admit what the pale, shaved meat actually is. Or that I won't be able to leave the convenience of charred rodent, grilled to order right on every corner."

The last bit hit a little too hard. The façade slipped a little. Hunter's eyes dropped to his plate, to his own trembling hands. His breath caught in his chest. The laughter choked off.

"Shit," Jade said, taking hold of Hunter's hands. The grease smeared tracks along them. "You know I don't mean that. Six months is a damn long time. It'll be hard on me, too. But I don't have a choice about it."

Jade lifted Hunter's hands and placed them against his cheeks. He stroked them down along the soft fuzz. At twenty-three, he still couldn't grow a proper beard. It was a bit of a joke between them that he was trapped at prepubescence. An eternal teenager who would never get to be an adult, like Peter Pan. The sensation soothed Hunter, even as his heart beat faster. Hunter's breathing calmed, and the trembling stopped.

"I have a plane to catch in the morning, but we still have tonight. Let's not ruin it by getting all weepy." Jade stood up and walked around the table without releasing his grip on Hunter's hands, even when they passed over the candle's flame. "Besides, I know you'll wait for me. 'Until the world burns and the roads go silent. Until the last of us shuffles off into oblivion. Endlessly.' Isn't that how you put it?"

The sun was in his eyes again. Not as strong this time. Filtered and gray with smoke that wafted lazily through the remains of the window. The last of the screams died out last night. Or last week. The memories were fading again. Getting tougher to hold onto. Everything was blurring.

He knew he had eaten something at some point from the feather stuck in his teeth. Something black and loud had pecked at his tongue. He had bitten its head off when it thought it was getting an easy meal. There was no point in going out to hunt, not when food brought itself to him.

He was comfortable here. At least, as comfortable as he could be with tendons drying out and tightening. In his spot against the wall, he could see the door, the window, and that crumpled form beneath it. Flesh too far gone to be any good to him. If someone were to come in, he'd know. He'd be ready.

He had to wait. Some part of him knew, somehow, that it was important to stay here. Stay vigilant. A name danced on the tip of remembrance. It wouldn't stay still. Wouldn't let him grasp it. But it mattered. More than the smoke or the gaping empty inside, it mattered. And he had all the time in the world.

Trauma

Jason Lavelle

It's not exactly haunted, Raena told herself, closing the closet door in the bedroom for the third time in the last half hour. *It's just an old house. It has quirks.*

Her mother used to talk about houses settling and pipes popping all the time when she was growing up, and they had always lived in older homes. And though this was Raena's first home that was truly hers, it definitely wasn't new. Constructed in 1960, the house was thirty years older than she was.

"So, a few people are coming over tonight," she said into the air of her bedroom, thankful no one was there to hear her. "I'd really appreciate it if you could maybe tone down the strangeness a little, ok?"

"Sorry, I'm just nervous. This is my first dinner party." Raena shook her head at herself and walked out of the bedroom. As she reached the threshold to the hallway, she heard the squeaky click of the closet door popping open. She sighed and continued to the kitchen to scrub the grout on her tiled countertop.

She rinsed out the stiff yellow scrubbing pad and tossed it in the sink.

"You know you *could* put less effort into banging cupboards around and try helping me with the cleaning," Raena said.

"Who are you talking to?"

"Jesus fuck!" Raena screamed as her knees went out from under her.

"Door was unlocked," her best friend said. Audrey squatted beside her, a goofy grin on her face.

"You bitch." She felt her crotch with one hand. "I pissed my pants, Audrey!"

The short redhead snorted a burst of laughter.

Raena held out her hand. "Help me up, loser."

"Fine, but I'm not taking the piss hand. Give me the other one." Audrey pulled her up off the ground.

Raena gave her a quick peck on the lips. "You're early."

"Thought I'd help you clean up, but it sounds like you've got an imaginary friend helping you already."

"Yeah, yeah. It's just the house. I'm always cleaning; figured it could give me a hand." Raena brushed long dark hair away from her face.

"Shit, I wish." Audrey grabbed a few dishes off the counter. "You ought to go shower. I'll finish picking up."

"You're the best, queen."

"I know."

Raena stood in front of her bathroom sink, head down, drying her hair gently to avoid damaging the extensions.

Audrey knocked twice.

"Enter, my child," Raena said in a dramatic voice.

Audrey came in, unsurprised to find her friend still topless. Years ago, they had actually dated, so there wasn't a whole lot they hadn't seen of each other. The brief relationship was the last Raena had been in while still in 'boy mode,' as she called it. Thankfully, the failed romance had turned into a fierce friendship.

"So, I know, woo woo woo and all that, but I just wanted to remind you that you're a badass twenty-nine-year-old woman, and you have nothing to worry about tonight. It's just a few people, and you already know you love Marcy and Regina."

"What about Chad?" Raena leaned against the sink, pulling her fingers through her hair.

"Don't be a shit. You know how picky I am about boyfriends. Aside from being named Chad, he's pretty awesome."

"But you've only known him like two months, right?"

"Yes, and I like him, and he's nice. So please don't worry."

"Anxiety all over my face?" Raena asked with a frown.

"It's not so bad, honey. I just know how you think. You can't get so wound up that you don't enjoy yourself."

Raena stuck her tongue out. "$300 a week for therapy, and I could just talk to you."

"Oh, hell no. This is special occasion therapy, so the rate's double."

Raena rubbed conditioner between her palms and ran her fingers through her hair again. "You know it's been tough for me to get out there and be social again. I don't do it on purpose, the anxiety and all."

"I know it, especially with people you knew before you came out. I don't know what it feels like, but I know you have to take the time you need."

Raena sniffed a little and nodded. Her dark brown hair bounced around her shoulders, softly curling like a model's, like she'd always dreamed. "Ok, that's enough of that. I don't need a cry headache."

Audrey grinned. "Fine, I need to go pick up Chad anyway. Cover up those tits. I don't need you stealing my new man."

Raena laughed. "I'd never date a Chad, honey."

Her best friend flipped her off and left.

She looked at herself in the slowly clearing mirror, but as she watched, an invisible finger traced the details of her face. She closed her eyes and let out a long breath. The bathroom was still warm, but that couldn't stop the chill that rippled over her body. She knew the marks on the mirror would still be there when she opened her eyes, so she turned, eyes still closed until sure she couldn't even catch a peripheral glance, and walked out of the bathroom.

In her closet, by the light of a single bulb hanging above her clothes, she breathed deeply, concentrating on steady breaths and the feeling of air inflating her lungs. She selected a black cami with silver accents around the neck and a built-in bra. She pulled the garment over her head and left the bedroom to stand in the hall at the perfect spot. From there, she could see into both bedrooms, the bathroom, and the dining room.

Slow, calm breaths. *Feel the air in my lungs. Feel the floor beneath my feet. Smell the plaster and paneling and the bite of lemon-scented cleaner.*

"Ok, so I've never freaked out about sharing this house," she said loudly. "I know you've been here longer than me. I'm asking you nicely; please go easy on me tonight. I'm stressed out and need a break, ok? Please."

She listened to the sounds of the house, those that every residence should have, and those extra, special sounds that hers had. She'd only been living there for two weeks when the first strange shadows appeared, doors started moving on their own, and sensations that shouldn't be there existed. But it never felt bad in the house, only warm, dusty, and welcoming.

She heard no response and saw no shadow in the second bedroom. "Thank you. It's just for tonight."

Marcy and Regina, two friends in their forties, were from the other side of the state.

Regina was a boisterous black woman who taught Yoga and Zumba at several studios. She had a body to die for, and the biggest smile Raena had ever seen. She was one of those people who made everyone around them feel good.

Marcy had been a kindergarten teacher for ten years before an anxiety disorder made the classroom impossible. She rallied, though, and now coached softball for a community college. She was a bigger girl who wouldn't be caught without a baseball cap and high-waisted jeans. Regina liked to say that Marcy was the most lesbian a person could possibly be. They also claimed that the two of them had been gay since before gay was cool.

Food covered the table and counters. Spicy lil' smokies filled a small crock pot. She served bruschetta with tomato and feta cheese relish with an assortment of crackers and cheese dip. And Raena's homemade Parmesan garlic wings. Raena had always firmly believed that the best kind of dinner was a bunch of appetizers.

Her dining room table was a thrift store find, round with a parquet wood pattern, sealed with what she assumed was a toxic '70s varnish. They had to squish a little, but the five of them fit. Audrey sat to the left of Raena, eating a meal of mostly cheese dip and crackers, with her new boyfriend Chad to her left.

The house and whatever unseen forces occupied the space with her had remained quiet just as she requested, but she felt something in the air, an odd tension that made her nervous. It had begun around the time everyone arrived, so it was difficult to tell if there was something paranormal happening or just her superhuman anxiety. She picked at her food but focused more on her wine, drinking too much too fast. When it was time to clear off the table, Raena was already tipsy.

Audrey stood next to Raena and pulled on her arm. "I need to pee. Come with me."

Raena raised an eyebrow, so Audrey jerked her a little harder.

"Chad, can you help clear off the table?" Audrey asked.

"Happy to," he said, standing.

He was a handsome man, Raena thought—tall, six foot or so, with the trim athletic build of former military. His hair was a dirty blond, short up the sides and slightly shaggy on top. He carried himself with confidence but not what she'd call swagger. It was obvious why he appealed to Audrey; thus far, he'd been polite and attentive. Raena knew men sometimes just behaved well in front of company, like children, so she reserved judgment. But for now, there were no bright red flags.

Audrey pulled her. The bathroom was fewer than a dozen paces from the table, but Raena could feel the dizzying pull of alcohol on her equilibrium. *I'm in trouble. I've done something wrong.* Otherwise, why would Audrey be dragging her off?

Her bestie pulled her into the bathroom and shut the door. Then she hiked up her cotton dress and sat on the toilet. She sighed when she began to pee.

"Tell me what's wrong, honey," Audrey said. "And don't say nothing. I can see it in your face and the amount of wine you've been guzzling."

Raena leaned against the sink. "I'm a big girl; I can drink if I want." She pressed a hand into her lower belly. "God, I have to pee too."

Audrey wiped herself and flushed the toilet but didn't stand. "I'm not getting up 'til you talk to me. Don't be a pansy. Just tell me what's on your mind."

"Pansies are actually quite ni—"

"Raena!" She snapped.

"Fine, I'm just kind of mildly having a freakout."

"Ok, nothing I haven't seen before. Any triggers? Any particular thing that's setting you off? If you tell me, I might be able to help." She stood and motioned for Raena to switch places with her.

"Thank god. It's like, suddenly, I was gonna pee my pants."

"That would be twice today," Audrey said with a smirk.

"I don't know if it's any one thing. I mean, having people over is an obvious stressor, then meeting your guy. Like, I'm really happy for you, but it's kind of weird. He seems nice and all, but I don't really know anything about him."

Her mind, still fuzzy around the edges, began to clear. The more she talked, the more coherent she felt. "And, like, you and I are done, and I'm not jealous or anything. But still, we were together once, and it's just weird. I'm just a mess, honey."

Audrey nodded. "You know, Raena, I don't think any of this is irrational, and that's a good thing. Your stressors are legit, nothing crazy at all, so you don't need to feel like you're being extra or losing it. All of this is ok. Is there anything I can do to help?"

Raena blew out a long breath. "Why am I always nervous to tell you stuff? I'm an idiot."

Audrey shrugged. "We're moving on now. How can I help?"

"We were gonna play some games," she said, flushing the toilet. "Can you kinda take charge of that?"

"Definitely, and I want you to do something for me."

Raena raised an eyebrow as she stood and got herself tucked away in her leggings.

"I want you to remember that your best friends are here with you. We love you, and we'll support you. You're safe with us."

Raena nodded and hugged Audrey. "Thanks, babe." She opened the door and returned to the kitchen to find Chad, Regina, and Marcy gathered at the counter.

"On three," Chad said. "One, two, three!" The three knocked back what looked like a double shot of... oh Christ, tequila.

"Whew!" Marcy cried. "Get over here, you two."

"Oh, my god," Audrey said.

"Shit's getting real now, I guess," Raena said. "Fuck it. I'm easy, breezy, relaxed."

Tequila is a bad idea every time, and this time was no different, but damn if they hadn't been having fun. Raena put the finishing touches on her drawing of a penis held down by chains just as Regina called time. She set her dry-erase marker down, and they all exchanged pads to guess what the others had drawn.

"*What* is going on?" Chad said, looking up at the light fixture above them.

Raena groaned inwardly. This was the third time the lights had pulsed since they sat back down. She'd really hoped no one had noticed.

"Nothing to see here, folks, nothing to see," Raena said, "just my friendly household ghosts making an appearance." She waved to the light fixture. "Thanks for stopping by, ghosts." Then she flopped back in her seat.

Audrey chuckled, her face flushed from alcohol. Her cheeks and eyebrows always held the rosiness longest, whether she was drunk, happy, embarrassed, or, well, excited.

"You have the coolest voice," Chad said, his words a little slurred. "It sounds really, like, smokey."

Raena stared at Chad for a moment, eyes swimming. Her gaze flicked to Audrey, whose eyes had grown wide.

"That's because I'm a tranny, honey. Didn't you know?" Raena said with a dramatic flourish, her stomach's contents sloshing angrily as she did so.

The smile faded from Chad's face as he tried to make sense of her words. "A… tranny? Like a drag queen?"

The light overhead pulsed sharply, and Raena felt a hum in the air like some great piece of machinery was laboring in the room with them. The hairs of her arms stood erect, tickling her skin, an unseen static charge building around her. She opened her mouth, not knowing what she would say but feeling a spark of truculent excitement.

Audrey wasn't about to let it happen. "Oh shit!" she said, pouring her glass of wine down her dress. She stood quickly to show off the deep stain. "Chad, help me out." She grabbed her phone from the table and pulled Chad to the bathroom with her. "Sorry, girls."

Once the door shut, Regina scolded Raena. "Why did you say that? You could have just said, 'Yeah, thanks,' or told him you're trans. But to use that word? Ugh."

"I can't say what I want about myself? Don't I have that right?" Raena said, her face flushed with a mixture of frustration and embarrassment.

Marcy shook her head. "Of course, but remember you own what you say about yourself. I hate to think that dude thinks he can call you a tranny now. I'd fucking beat his ass."

Regina pointed a dramatic finger at Marcy and nodded her head.

Raena blew out a breath. She was hot—her face, her body, and now she felt like hot tears might be coming. "I'm drunk. I'm an idiot. Sorry, girls."

Regina leaned over and squeezed her arm. "We love you, honey. You're not an idiot."

Raena squeezed her eyes shut, then leaned her head back. *Ugh, not a good idea.* The air still hummed, but no one else seemed to hear it. She gently leveled her head and opened her eyes, glancing toward the hallway. A shadow waited there, where the light of the dining room bled out into the darkness of the hall. It was not a well-formed shadow, nothing she could have pointed to and said, 'There, see that?' But it was out of place just enough so she would notice. She hissed out a sigh through her teeth.

"I asked you nicely," she whispered. "I asked you for one night of peace." She spoke to the shadow in the hall, the flickering lights, and the hum in the air.

The bathroom door opened, and the shadow dissipated. Chad emerged with Audrey on his arm. Audrey waved drunkenly.

"Hey, girls, sorry to be the party pooper. We're gonna head home," Audrey said. She looked at Raena and smiled. "I had a lot of fun, darling."

"How are you getting home?" Marcy asked.

"Our Uber should be here any second," Chad answered.

Raena gave Audrey a hug and a kiss on the cheek. "Call me tomorrow, love."

"What, no kiss for me?" Chad said with a wink.

Raena's stomach twisted, and she let out a sharp-smelling belch.

"Get out of here, Chad!" Regina said with a laugh. "Bring more tequila next time."

Chad waved to the room, and Raena quietly stood while they turned and left. Once the door closed, she turned back to the table.

Marcy, watching her, raised an eyebrow when she approached. "Everything peachy, my dear?" she asked Raena.

She smiled weakly. "Just coming off the drunk. You two heading out?"

"Gonna crash in your living room if that's all right," Marcy said.

"It's all yours, ladies. Close the blinds if you're gonna get weird. The neighbors already think I'm suspicious."

Regina blew her a kiss.

"I'm gonna crash. Just leave everything, and I'll get it in the morning."

"Goodnight, honey," Marcy said.

She walked down the hall toward her bedroom. *The wood floor under my feet, the smell of warm dust blowing up from the furnace, the sound of Marcy and Regina chatting behind me.* Once she closed herself in her room, she stripped off her clothes and her undies, feeling relief as she let her muscles relax. She sat on the edge of her bed. Her comforter was still cool and pleasant against her skin. She told her smart speaker to play 'fan noise.'

Raena hunched over herself in the dark, letting her body relax, when the closet door snicked open. She shook her head and got up, opening the closet and pulling on the light. She grabbed a t-shirt off a hanger and a pair of loose-fitting boxers from a shelf. She gave the closet door a good shove to close it before heading back to bed.

She checked her smartwatch before tucking herself in. Just before one in the morning. "Ok, world, I'll see you in about ten hours."

She woke with gooseflesh crawling up, moving over her groin and across her belly. Tiny pricks of ice sank into her skin and burrowed into her chest. Her eyes opened, and she saw only the shadowed plaster ceiling above her with a darkened ceiling light, the frosted dome yellow with age and displaying the carcasses of all the houseflies it had lured to their deaths with its luminance. She looked at her watch. It was 3 am, and her heart rate was 92. There was a silent alert about changing weather conditions. *Why the fuck am I awake?*

At 3:01, she heard the sound. A delicate thing, soft like a butterfly's wing but not like a wisp of cloud. A long scraping sound… no, rubbing, like the tip of a finger dragged along aluminum siding just outside her window. She was up on her elbows. The electric venom of adrenaline shot so hard through her body that she momentarily saw white, and the sharp smell of ammonia rushed down her throat.

The sound stopped.

Her watch tapped her wrist lightly, startling her. Heart rate: 132. She swung her legs off the side of the bed. When they touched the cold wood floor, her closet door clicked open and then shut again rapidly. Heat crept through her groin, into her bladder and bowels, signaling their willingness to betray her at the next provocation. She stood, shaky but willing strength into her legs.

211

I feel the floor under my feet. I smell the...ammonia. I hear—

The sound was back, just outside, less than six feet from where she stood. She tried with everything in her heart to be brave. Someone or something dragged their finger over her siding. The thrum of pressure on the aluminum was dull but with the higher pitch whine of metal.

She took two staggering steps toward the window. *It's just a tree; it's just the wind.* She was almost close enough to reach the curtains; she could almost feel the ancient cotton fabric between her fingers.

The soft thrum stopped, and a loud grating sound peeled down the siding, nails scraping across an aluminum chalkboard. Heat charged through her body, and she tasted tequila. Tequila, chips, summer sausage, thick creamy cheese dip, and— "Oh no!"

She fell to her knees as a wave of thick, choking vomit poured from her mouth. Her body jerked to expel it, and her bladder let go. She couldn't breathe, the vomit wouldn't stop, and the smell of partially digested food and alcohol clogged her nose.

Then the light in the bedroom flicked on, and Marcy rushed in. "Oh, dammit! Regina!" she yelled. "Come on, honey. You're gonna be ok. Come on, let's get you in the tub."

The morning after is never nice. By the time Raena dragged herself from her room, the sun was high. She heard voices and the clatter of dishes as she made her way down the hall, squinting against the light.

"Well, look at that sexy beast," Regina called from the kitchen. She was drying dishes and popping them up into the cupboard.

Raena groaned.

"Don't you get crabby," Marcy said. "We were up all night, too, babysitting you."

Raena waved one hand in the air. She slumped against the kitchen counter, watching as Marcy drained soapy water from the sink. "You girls ok?"

"We're good, honey," Regina said. "Glad you didn't die last night."

Raena squinted at Regina. "Are you wearing my t-shirt?"

"My t-shirt now. You puked on mine last night."

Raena hung her head with another long groan.

"Yeah, you puked on me too, but unlike little miss fitness, I brought a change of clothes."

"I'm so sorry," Raena said. "I really appreciate you two."

Regina closed the glass cupboard. "Hey, you remember anything you were telling us last night?"

Raena looked at her closely. "I-I don't think so."

"What about anything that happened after the party but before, you know, the puke fest?"

Regina and Marcy stared at Raena while she thought, dredging up murky memories of frightening sounds in the late hours of the night. Finally, she nodded. "I do. I-I told you about it?"

"Mm-hmm," Regina said. "Pretty scary, actually." She filled up the coffee maker and started a pot that looked strong enough to jump-start a tractor.

"Is any of it real?" Marcy asked.

"Jesus, girls. I mean, you're already mopping up my pukey mess, and I don't really want you to think I'm insane."

Regina laughed and started to say something, but Marcy waved her off. "Be nice, Reggie." She looked at Raena with sincerity. "We don't think you're crazy. We, uh, we just want to know more."

"And we have some ideas," Regina said, eyes full of mischief.

"Oh my god, you two are ghost lovers, aren't you?"

"Paranormal enthusiasts," Marcy corrected, "and it sounds like we're here for a reason."

"Argh!" Raena cried. But then Regina set a cup of coffee in front of her, and the ugly hangover demon started to quiet.

After an hour of explanation into her experiences in the house, the gentle tapping, lights going on and off, the closet door opening on its own, and—the one they *oohed* and *ahhed* over—the finger that liked to draw on the bathroom mirror, Marcy and Regina were practically drooling.

"Ok, I've got a plan," Marcy said, slapping one meaty thigh. "It's pretty much stage one, right from Ghosthunters. We're gonna do an EVP session."

Regina was just about trembling on the couch. A forty-year-old woman, almost bouncing in her seat like a child.

Raena sighed. "Ok, so, I love you two, but remember what I said about last night? I mean, I was drunk, yeah, but that scared the shit out of me. I do not want to do anything to provoke whatever's in this house."

"No no no, honey, that's not what this is about," Regina said. "We aren't trying to provoke anything. We're going to reach out, make some contact, and give these spirits a chance to communicate with us if they want."

Raena blinked several times. "Ok, that seems like a good thing. Sounds like you know a lot about it."

"Oh my god, I know so much!" Regina said. And we have everything we need—a phone with a voice recorder."

"Let's get the house ready," Marcy said.

"How?

"We're gonna close all the blinds and drapes; make it as dark as possible."

Raena let out another groan, but the girls were already off the couch.

She regretted it. Oh hell, how she regretted it. They walked through the house, through every room, into every closet, any dark corners they could find. The whole time, Marcy and Regina called out questions into the still air.

Raena stayed quiet. She tried to be amused, to think it was silly or stupid, but, in truth, she became more unsettled in the hour they were at it.

"Who are you?"

"Why are you here?"

"Do you mean Raena any harm?"

"Why were you at the window last night?"

"What are you trying to tell us?"

The questions continued: in the bathroom, the musty basement, the two bedrooms. They even ventured into the tiny, one-car garage. It was eerie and unsettling, exploring the house she knew but in a way she never had before. And when they returned to the dining room table, Raena was cold down in her bones.

"I need another coffee," Raena said. "You two want any?"

Regina motioned to both her and Marcy and nodded.

215

"This makes me nervous, Marcy," she said as she started the coffee pot.

"I'm excited," Regina said.

Marcy just nodded, doing something on her phone, her fingers stabbing at the screen.

Raena was quiet as she watched the coffee pot fill. "I think when you're the one living the experience, you react differently." She poured coffee into mugs and walked them over to the table.

The chair squeaked beneath her as she sat. She wasn't especially heavy, 150 pounds, but the table and chairs were likely older than her. She hoped to have quality furniture someday, but that would take a long time on a disability check and a part-time internet gig.

"You ready?" Marcy asked Regina.

Regina nodded vigorously.

Raena chimed in: "Yeah, I'm ready, too…you know, the one whose house is haunted."

Marcy set her phone down on the table. "Ok, this is the EVP app. It cuts out all dead silence and boosts quieter signals, so all we should hear are our questions and any potential responses."

"Reggie, don't drool on the phone," Raena joked.

"Regina flipped her off."

"Quiet children. Here we go," Marcy said, tapping the play button.

Raena kissed the girls goodbye and shut the door before they made their way to Marcy's blue Toyota pickup. It was midafternoon, and the sun was still high enough to warm the chilly air. Once the door was shut, Raena walked to the kitchen, opened her junk drawer, and pulled out her THC vape pen. She took a long hit and returned to the couch in the living room. She lay on her side, phone in one hand, vape pen in the other.

What. The. Fuck.

She took another long drag from the pen, enough to soften the blow of what she had heard, but she couldn't keep it from coming back to her.

"What do you want?"

"*Danger.*"

The voice was a stream, soft and gentle but filled with gravel, bubbles, and tiny eddies. It was only just audible above the amplified static yet there. Undeniably there.

"Why are you here?"

"*Leave.*"

"What are you trying to tell us?"

"*He is coming.*"

She lay on her side, tears soaking into her ancient couch. Raena was not weak; she'd survived horrors and endured traumas that most people never have to consider. Her body had been broken and remade after years of abuse as a child, then years of self-harm as an adult. Though her mind had come a long way in healing from her traumas, it still had far to go. But she was alive, and there were no fresh lines on her wrists, no empty pill bottles at her bedside. If nothing else, Raena was a survivor.

"And now," she said to the room. "I'm being haunted."

The shower was a little less than scalding, not so hot that her skin sloughed off, but hot enough to draw blood to the surface until she had pinked all over. The last eighteen hours had been pretty much shit, and Raena was ready to let herself melt away, to be washed down the drain with all the hot water.

She grabbed the green bar of Irish Spring off the shower rack and lathered her body. The soap's thick scent and shower steam made it hard to breathe. She turned her face into the shower spray and opened her mouth, holding the hot spray on her tongue until it started overflowing her lips. Then she spat it against the shower wall.

I taste the water. I smell that godawful soap. I feel the tiny bumps on the tub beneath my feet. I hear the tapping.

The tapping? Why was there tapping? She closed her eyes and stepped out of the spray, listening.

Tap tap tap. Tap tap. Tap tap tap.

That's not the pipes. She shuddered.

Tap tap tap...

It was in the house. Christ, it could almost be in the room with her. She leaned her head against the shower wall.

Tap tap tap. Tap tap.

Right there, clear and hard enough that she could feel the vibrations. It seemed to emanate from the other side of the wall, in the second bedroom. It was definitely in the house.

Raena wrapped her arms around her chest. Her whole body hunched forward, shaking. Her nails dug into her sides, just below her breasts. *It isn't real. It's the ghosts or spirits or whatever they are. They don't want me here anymore. But they can't hurt me; they can't do anything.*

Then she felt a slight change in air pressure as the bathroom door opened from the hallway. The shower curtain rippled with the cool air that rushed in. She couldn't control her breathing; she sucked and gulped hot air and shower spray, inching her way to the very back of the tub. Her eyes remained glued to the curtain as the steam drifted away, leaving her completely bare, totally exposed.

For a long moment, she thought there was nothing. Then one loud footfall thumped. And a tall, man-shaped silhouette stood on the other side of her curtain. She screamed like she never had before. Her voice strained, cracked, and finally disappeared into a pained, hoarse gasp. Her feet went out from under her, and she crashed onto the tub's floor, somehow hitting every bone in her body along the way. She curled instinctively into a tight fetal ball and watched as a single silhouetted hand brushed down the outside of the shower curtain.

Then the dark figure walked from the room, and it was gone. Raena even heard the bathroom door close behind him. *What the hell kind of ghost opens and closes doors to walk through them?*

She may have laid there for twenty minutes or two hours—she couldn't tell—but the water falling on her felt like shards of ice biting into her skin. When she finally crawled over the tub's edge, she brought a tide of water with her, sloshing over the ancient tile. She dragged herself to the counter, pulled herself up, and grabbed her phone from beneath her bra. Her hands shook violently; her fingers pruned so deeply that she couldn't operate the screen.

"Siri, call Audrey," she said in a whisper.

The call connected. "What's up, ho-bag?" Audrey said.

"I need you," Raena said, her voice so frail she worried it wouldn't reach the other end of the line. "Please come."

"Are you hurt? Do you need an ambulance?"

"I don't know," her voice trembled. "I can't get out of the bathroom."

"I'm on my way, honey. Ten minutes."

The call disconnected, and Raena slid down into the pool of water on the floor. It was ice cold but for the puddle of tears beneath her face.

By the time Audrey arrived, Raena was in a wrestling match with hypothermia, and she was losing.

"Fuck," Audrey cursed. She bent over her friend. Raena's skin was pale as a vampire's complexion, but she still breathed. Audrey pulled Raena's cold bottom lip down to reveal near-white gums. "Shit." She scanned the countertop and trash can for pill bottles and razors, seeing nothing but a well-worn bra and undies.

"Here we go, baby," she whispered, pulling Raena up into a half-sitting position and leaning against her body. She was immediately soaked with cold water. Audrey dragged two towels out of the wicker stand at her left and bundled Raena up.

"Raena—listen to me, honey—did you take anything? Did you hurt yourself?" Audrey scrubbed at Raena's chest with a towel, creating as much friction as she could to heat the skin. At the same time, she dragged her friend backward out of the bathroom. It was no small feat since Raena was taller and forty pounds heavier.

But Audrey was very strong, one hundred and ten pounds of rock-solid muscle, her small breasts the only bit of fat on her. Years of competitive gymnastics had given her strength that surpassed most men she knew. When she had Raena in the hall, she rubbed her whole body down, sopping the water off her legs and abdomen.

"Raena, I'm so sorry, but your lips are still blue. You're going to the hospital."

Audrey opened her phone and dialed 911.

Raena regained consciousness in the ambulance, though she was hardly coherent. Not until she was properly hooked up and covered with heated air blankets in the emergency room did she look over at Audrey, who sat beside her. "My hero," she said.

Audrey rolled her eyes. "You better hope I don't die before you, or you're completely screwed."

"So, tell me the news."

Audrey nodded. "First of all, I'm your sister if anyone asks. I had to tell them about your history of self-harm. I'm sorry."

"It's fine. You did right."

"They did the standard bloodwork and checked every inch of you to make sure you hadn't hurt yourself. Didn't find anything, though."

"I'm not surprised. Because I didn't do anything."

"Bottom line is that you were hypothermic, and you've got a few bruises from hitting the floor."

Raena grimaced. "Yeah, I can feel them."

"So, now that you're making me late for date night, you better tell me what the hell happened."

Raena took a deep breath. "Hold on to your socks, honey."

A very cute nurse finished checking Raena's stats, and when he left, Audrey leaned forward, resting her chin on her hands. "Ok, so you've mentioned the house 'ghosts' before. Just silly stuff, weird enough that it could be paranormal or just a quirky old house."

"Right. Then I started seeing the weird shadowy blobs or whatever. Nothing threatening, though, not at all."

"But the night of the party—last night—things went sideways," Audrey said, tucking some stray hair back from her face. "So, I think you need to ask what changed. What was different last night?"

"I had a group of people over. We were loud. We listened to music. We had fun. Maybe I pissed off the spirits."

Audrey sighed. "Or maybe it's not spirits at all; maybe something else is happening."

"Like what?"

"I don't know, but what you experienced today…" She shook her head. "Look, I don't want to scare you more than you already are, but this bathroom shit that happened today seems like a real flesh and blood person fucking with you."

Raena pressed her head back into her pillow. "Well, I guess this is just one more thing to add to my CPTSD. My therapist will be thrilled."

Audrey cleared her throat. "Feel like you're making any progress with the therapy?"

"It's good to talk, you know. But she's told me, more than once, that this isn't something that can be cured."

"Only managed, right?"

"It's a delicate balance. She says she wants me to get to the point where I can be more functional in society, but that may take years."

The nurse came back to let Raena know she was being discharged. Raena 'discreetly' pointed at him and waggled her eyebrows at Audrey.

"Shut up, Raena," Audrey laughed.

The nurse turned to go but looked back at Raena. "All right, I don't want to see you back here. But, you know, I wouldn't mind seeing you back here." He winked, then left.

Audrey busted out laughing, pointing at Raena's reddening face.

Raena cleared her throat. "If I were into dudes, I would ride that hottie all the way home."

"Mmhm," Audrey agreed. "And then some."

Only after Raena insisted it was safe did Audrey drop her off at home and leave for her night out with Chad. She promised to keep her phone next to her in case she was needed.

Raena hated being in the hospital. She'd spent months of her life in various hospitals and treatment centers. Which made stepping into her small, aged home feel all the better. It felt like hers, the slightly uneven wood flooring beneath her feet, all the surfaces badly in need of dusting, the Black Friday special flatscreen TV. All hers, all safe, nothing dangerous at all, except maybe the furnace, which would have to go in the next five years.

"I'm not leaving," she said out loud. "This is the first place I've ever felt safe."

She walked through the house, touching the walls. "We can be safe together. I will respect you and our home."

She tried to sound confident; she tried to feel confident. Perhaps if she didn't show her fear, didn't show the house and its otherworldly occupants the panic swirling inside her like a tornado, they would give her peace. But the panic was there, like bile rising in her throat, and she could not hold it back much longer.

The sun was long gone, and night descended, bringing all its promised terror. Her false confidence had evaporated. Fear and panic ran raw and unchecked through her veins. She couldn't sleep in her bed anymore; it was too close to the window where her phantom antagonist waited to drag unseen fingers across her siding and window. She couldn't sleep on her couch, not so close to the hall where the shadow waited, roaming from the kitchen to the bathroom.

The bathroom. An hour ago, unable to hold it anymore, Raena rushed in, dropped trou, and squeezed out the quickest shit of her life, a painful, humiliating affair. She'd sobbed as she wiped, staring at the door to the hallway, waiting for someone or something to burst in.

There was little in Raena's house left to her, little space where she didn't feel afraid. So she dragged two pillows and her comforter into her bedroom closet.

She stared at the ceiling and its single bare lightbulb with nowhere else to go. She couldn't afford a hotel every night and didn't want to couch surf at Audrey's apartment, especially on date night. She felt lost, adrift in this darkly surreal nightmare, not trusting her senses. She doubted everything.

For months she'd thought the house was a little haunted, with strange, benign disturbances that cropped up and amused her, sometimes frustrated her, but that had all changed. This was harassment; these phantoms were stalking her. She was terrified in her own home. But the very worst of it was that she no longer knew if any of it was real. She'd been willing to believe there may be playful spirits in the house, and she'd been willing to share her space, but things had gone too far. In fact, things had gone from possibly paranormal to Hollywood horror. And what did that say about her? If these things were impossible, then she must be losing her mind.

An hour went by in the tight closet. It took two Benadryl and a Xanax, washed down with a blackberry Whiteclaw, before the panic started to subside. The closet was cold, a deep chill from the basement rising up through the polished wood floors to creep into her bones. The tang of mildew also came up through the floor, pinching her sinuses. She lay with the comforter half beneath her and half folded over the top like a taco. It wasn't enough, but she couldn't bring herself to leave her refuge until morning. She reached up and pulled sweaters off their hangers, cringing at the loud noise of the metal and plastic implements popping off the rod.

"Jesus," she whispered, draping the sweaters over herself. "House, whoever's in the house, I just want you to know that I am genuinely sorry for whatever I did to offend you. And I really mean that. It's not like when a man tells you that, and it's bullshit—I really mean it. I just want to live here and be happy, and I'll do anything you need me to do. Just please stop scaring me. I think I'm going over the edge here."

Above her head, with a quiet *snick*, the closet light turned off.

The refrigerator door opened sometime in the dark of night. Raena rose quickly from sleep when she heard the *clink* of the Worcestershire and cocktail sauce bottles, which were too small for the door's top shelf. She lay in absolute silence, with only the gentle sound of her breathing disturbing the stale closet air. More muted clinks from the kitchen, one glass bottle hitting several others. *Beer bottles*. The refrigerator door slammed shut, and a moment later, a loud hiss reached down the hall, and then the *tink tink tink* of the bottle cap hitting the floor.

The dusty closet air mixed with the sharp tang of fear and jabbed at her sinuses. She swallowed very carefully, terrified any tiny irritation in her throat might trigger a coughing fit. She pulled her phone out—1:43 am, and her heart rate was 118. Her fingers flew over the glass screen as she listened. It was toying with her. Whatever it was, it was actually fucking with her.

When the first loud footsteps echoed through the hall, a new wave of cold air seeped through her mound of sweaters. The steps were unhurried, a large shoe or boot with a heavy occupant, calmly violating her home. The thin, wispy hairs on the back of her neck tickled as goose flesh rose from her scalp all the way down to her butt. After the third footstep, she heard a *thunk* and then a loud scraping sound in the hallway. More footsteps, closer now. Raena wriggled her way around so her head was right near the door. The scraping—it sounded like something dragged along the wall: a screwdriver, a knife, some type of weapon.

Raena pushed her hand against her chest as if to keep her galloping heart from bursting out. She squeezed her eyes closed, but the tears were already there waiting for her. This didn't feel like an apparition, paranormal activity, or whatever the hell the crazies called it. This was real, and Raena knew this might be her last night on Earth.

It was almost to the bedroom. She could feel that deep scraping in her teeth, right down to the roots. Then, suddenly, the next step was in the bedroom, less than ten feet from her hiding spot. Her own warm breath brushed her face as she exhaled against the backside of the closet door. She clenched her fists as shivers rocked through her. The steps stopped. She heard the wooded *thunk* as the beer was set on her dresser. *Oh my god! Oh my god! Oh my god!*

Then came a strange sound, something heavy but crinkly landing on the bed. More crinkles, like plastic. It was loud, similar to something being opened. *Something plastic is being laid out on my bed.* Her watch alerted her that her heart rate was very high. She squeezed her phone with one hand; it couldn't save her. In fact, even the vibration of a text message arriving could give her away in the quiet bedroom. She held down the power button until the device went totally dark.

The crinkling finally stopped. A blessing, as it had become like fingernails on the chalkboard of her mind. Then more footsteps, but not toward her. They left the bedroom, then trod down the hall. Once the heavy steps faded, she heard her front door open and then close.

"What the actual fuck?" she whispered. "Must be going out to his car to get something." She waited thirty more seconds. *This is probably my only chance to get out of the house.* She felt frozen on all fours in the closet, her knees burning, fingers like claws. *Just do it!*

"Ok, I'm doing it." She reached for the doorknob and released the latch. The door began to swing open, then quickly closed again. Not hard, not as if someone slammed it from the outside, but like a gentle unseen force had influenced its motion. She grumbled, pushed the door open, and crawled forward on her hands and knees.

She didn't feel the presence until her head and shoulders were exposed. A huge hand clamped down on her head, digging into her hair and pulling her, screaming, into a back-bent standing position.

Her hair, the pain—oh god, the pain!—it was tearing out. There were only six inches of natural hair under the extensions, but she felt as though he had every bit of it. Then the hand thrust her forward, smashing her face into the wall. In an instant, her vision went white as a lightning strike, and pain just as hot soaked into her skull. Blood

227

flowed from her mangled nose down her throat. She gagged, trying to vomit the thick metallic liquid, but the hand in her hair would not let her wretch. She screamed and choked on the blood. Her fingers, attempting to pry the hand away, clawed uselessly at the tight leather glove.

Then it stopped, and the pressure—oh, that bastard pressure on her scalp—just released. She stood facing the wall, blood pouring down her face and throat, piss dribbling down her legs. She shook, every nerve in her body dancing to its own funeral dirge. Then she picked up the smell. Such a strange smell, like that of a high school boy, sweat and musk and Coolwater cologne.

"Turn around," he commanded, with a voice both deep and young and something else. Amused.

She didn't hurry to follow the voice's order. She was terrified, after all, so she took small steps like a child as she moved to face her attacker. *Motherfucker!*

"Hello again, Raena. I'm so glad we could do this." He smiled at her. He actually fucking smiled at her.

"Chad! You piece of shit!" Raena raged and lunged at him without thought, swinging at his face.

Chad was more than ready for her, and as her right hand arced clumsily toward him, he buried his fist deep in her gut. She couldn't hear the rib break over the sound of her scream, a grotesque animalistic cry, and then her air was gone. She heaved over and over, but the air would not come, her lungs either unable or unwilling to draw another breath. She hit the floor on her knees.

"Hurts like a bitch, I know. Just give it a minute."

She stared up at him through gasping, ineffective breaths. Her eyes shot through with blood, and her face erupted with pain. Chad shuffled back and forth, looking bored and impatient. He allowed her to wheeze and gasp for another thirty seconds.

"Up," he ordered, motioning with one hand. "Come on now."

Still unable to completely fill her lungs, Raena pulled herself to her feet.

"This has all been you? Why the fuck are you stalking me?" she asked. Her tongue felt odd in her mouth, and the blood that had leaked down her throat was now bubbling with a fresh batch of bile, ready to make an appearance at any time.

He grinned widely. "I wanted to really get your blood moving. I thought it might be more fun for us this way. What do you think?"

She swallowed, uncertain how long she could keep her stomach down. She glanced around the room. He had her pinned quite well between the closet and the bed. *Oh my god, the bed.* The bed was covered with clear plastic sheeting. *Oh christ.* Tears rolled down her face. She cleared her throat. "Yes, I was terrified. But I don't know why you're doing this."

"Of course, Raena. See, I've fucked just about everything under the sun, had a good old time of it, but I've never fucked something like you." As he spoke, he unsheathed a knife from his belt. "So there's your explanation. Nothing fancy."

"You didn't think of maybe hiring a sex worker?" she asked, not giving a good goddamn but trying to buy a little more time before the raping and murdering began.

He snorted. "Hey, I don't need to pay for it, ok? Almost all my conquests have been perfectly willing. I'm not some loser."

"'Course not. Look—"

"It's getting late, and I'm getting bored. Let's get on with it. Clothes off. Now," he demanded, motioning to her shirt with his knife.

Her hands trembled, and her arms locked into place.

"Raena, I will put this knife up under your ribs. I'll puncture your lungs and still have my way with you, but you'll be in fucking agony." He didn't sound angry but remained perfectly flat, just laying out the facts.

Her head shook, but she pulled her t-shirt off and let it drop. The chill of the room immediately bit into her skin, and her shoulders hunched forward. She tried to cover her breasts with her arms, but he shook his head.

"Arms down now. Now!"

She dropped her arms. His eyes were illuminated with desire, hot and unstoppable.

"Now the boxers," he demanded.

The growl of his voice jabbed into her mind. A mind already weak with fear. His stink—sweat, beer, testosterone, and the oozing lust in his pants—filled and burned her sinuses.

The drift started in her mind. She tried to hold on. *I feel the cold air. I see—*

But she was far from grounded, and the flashback took her.

Red lockers with chrome latches scratched raw from years of use and vandalism.

Cinderblock walls, painted an off-white that always looked dirty, stacked so much taller than her.

Stone tile, cold beneath her feet, gritty, moist, slimy, like mud at a pond's edge.

Bodies moved around her. She could not see them, but she felt them. Felt their heat, too, close to her body. And she smelled the nauseating tang of pubescent male sweat.

Water sprayed elsewhere in the room, and steam filled the air. She tasted the cheap soap in the back of her throat.

She knew the place, the smells—special torments among so many others—and she could do nothing to help her younger self, standing topless in the room, trying to keep her body covered. Laughing and jeering from all around her as the eighth-grade boys watched her misery.

A fat, red face atop a giant body that stank of sweat and, yes, beer, shouted down at her. "Everyone must shower!"

The words boomed through her like a fire engine horn next to her head. His big hand jabbed at her face over and over.

"I can't," she screamed for what felt like the fiftieth time because her voice was hoarse.

Pain dug into her shoulder, his giant hand squeezing into her thin body. A finger the size of a bratwurst jabbed her forehead. "Take your shorts off now, or I will do it for you!"

She saw only the bright silver whistle bouncing at his chest and could hear only blood in her ears.

"Why can't you, dammit?"

"Because I'm a girl!"

Those words. Once they were out, they could never be caught. Those words would cause so much misery for many years before finally freeing her.

His face blurred, the room quieted, and for the millionth time in this horrible memory, she thought it was over. Then large hands grabbed the waistband of her shorts and yanked them to the floor. Exposed, overflowing with hot shame for all to see. The silence broke, and the laughter poured in.

She barely felt him drag her into the shower, shoving her under the hot spray. She only felt the shame, the terrible humiliation, and the loss she could not possibly understand.

Raena was back in the moment she'd left, just as horrified and helpless as that day in the locker room.

The overhead light flicked on and off like an ancient strobe on a sick dance floor.

Chad waved his knife through the air as if he were suddenly attacked by invisible insects. He growled in anger and confusion.

Raena tried to dart past him. But Chad whipped back around at that moment and lashed out at her, cutting a long line across her chest. It was lava, bright and hot and deep, burning across her breasts.

"Please, Chad, no!"

"Take your fucking boxers off now!" He made to jab at her with the knife again.

"Ok!" she cried. Pushing the boxers down over her hips, she stepped out of them. She stood bare before him, trembling in horror, anger, and a fear that only the world's prey ever knew. To her absolute disgust, his lips parted, and a rivulet of saliva escaped his maw.

"Yeah, we're gonna have some fun now," he said breathlessly.

"I don't think so," said a hard voice behind him.

Raena hadn't even heard her come through the door, but now she was there, six feet behind him.

Chad spun around.

Audrey didn't cock the gun dramatically or rack the top slide. She was a practical woman and had done that in the car.

There was only the unbelievably loud gunshot in Raena's small bedroom. It smelled like fireworks and tasted like burnt ash in her throat. Chad's head whipped sideways as the bullet gouged out his cheek and ripped one ear from the side of his head. He screamed like a monstrous creature. And before Audrey could pull the trigger again, he darted forward and swung his blade, burying it in her side, under her arm, right up to the hilt.

Audrey screamed.

Chad was still roaring.

Raena cried out for her friend.

Audrey collapsed onto the floor, jerking and crying, with the blade sunk deep into her side.

Chad stalked over to Raena's best friend, hands outstretched to choke the life from her.

Drums pounded in Raena's head, panicked and terrified. *Fuck!* She had no weapons, nothing with which to save Audrey. She didn't even have her fucking clothes on. She scanned the floor. Nothing but discarded clothes.

The closet light clicked on, and what sounded like half the hangers in her closet suddenly landed on the floor, clacking and skittering, until a single metal hanger spun out to rest at her feet.

Holy shit.

Raena bent down and scooped the wire hanger off the floor. She yanked the triangle's hypotenuse until she had formed a diamond, then rushed at Chad. She didn't have time to think, didn't have time for a plan. Chad was hunched over Audrey, hands on her throat. Raena slipped the hanger over his head like she was catching a stray dog. Then she yanked back with all her might.

Chad cried out, a strangled sound that was aborted before it reached its full potential. He tried to turn on her, but Raena twisted the hanger in her grip, turning the elongated diamond into an impossible noose. He thrashed and kicked back at her, but she danced away from him, pulling and twisting, tighter and tighter, the thick wire constricting against his throat with terrifying finality. The wire bit into her hand, grinding her fingers together until it felt like it was chewing her bones. She cried through the pain, letting the tears rush down her face as they danced the dance of death.

I taste the blood in my mouth. I feel the searing pain in my hands. I smell fear and urine. I see his desperation.

But not only his desperation. Raena needed to get to Audrey. Her friend needed help. Chad stumbled drunkenly, the oxygen he needed no longer reaching his brain. At last, Raena had her chance. She kicked him in the back of his knees, and he went down. In a final act of desperate savagery, she dropped herself onto his back. Kneeling on his writhing body, she pulled up on the wire with every bit of the strength she had left. A grinding crunch traveled up the hanger wire. She felt it in her hands: the bones, the cartilage, life itself. There was no grand finale, no cinematic spasms; his body just stopped. She stayed on his back, holding the wire tight, unable to pry her fingers open.

"Rae," Audrey said softly, "he's dead."

Audrey lay curled on one side, blood pooling beneath her, the knife still lodged under her arm.

"Rae, call 911. Hurry, honey."

Raena screamed as she pried her fingers open, sure she had ruptured tendons or ligaments or whatever the hell made fingers work. She army crawled into the closet and retrieved her phone, thanking god she could just click the power button a few times because she didn't think she could use the touchscreen with her mangled fingers.

She dialed emergency and returned to Audrey on the bedroom floor.

As she held Audrey's head in her arms, the closet light clicked off. Raena barely had the strength to roll her eyes.

"Your ghosts," Audrey whispered.

"Yeah," she said quietly, petting Audrey's head. "Probably saying, 'I told you so.' Cheeky bastards."

"I saved you again," Audrey said.

"Took you long enough to get here. Were you sleeping when my text came through?"

"Fuck off," Audrey said and winced. "I think I'm done with this hero shit."

As Raena listened to the distant sound of sirens approaching, she was overwhelmed with gratitude. It wasn't only Audrey who had saved her, and while she still didn't understand it all, she looked up into the air around her and whispered, "Thank you."

"Hospital chairs are shit for comfort," Raena said. She leaned to crack her back, winced at the fractured rib, then settled again. She set her crocheting down in her lap. Currently, she was hooking a teal scarf she'd likely never wear.

Audrey chuckled softly. Even with her auburn hair a mess, with no makeup, and wearing naught but a thin hospital gown, she still looked beautiful. "The bed isn't so bad. At least you can go home. I've been trapped here four days now."

"I'd stay up here if they let me, honey, you know that." Raena sighed. "I haven't been getting any sleep anyway. It's hard to be in that room, you know, where it happened."

"Anything new from the police?"

"Yeah. I was kinda hoping you wouldn't ask, though. Pretty dark stuff. You sure you want to hear?"

Audrey hesitated, then nodded. "Yeah, I want to know."

"Broad strokes," Raena said. "They found a lot of pics on his phone, tons of different women. They're trying to find all the girls and get their stories. They found some stuff in his apartment, mostly jewelry. Though they didn't use the actual word, they sounded like trophies. So there may be other assaults, maybe worse."

"Jesus," Audrey whispered.

"He didn't have friends outside the lumber mill. The guys there said he didn't talk to anyone, so they don't have a lot of insights into his personality."

"They were up here after I came out of surgery," Audrey said, "asking me a million questions about what he was like, where he'd been, and all that." She shook her head, "Surprising how little I actually knew about him. I mean, I'd been seeing him for a few months."

"They found a lot of porn on his computer too, and not good porn either, a lot of non-consensual stuff, real nasty. He started looking for trans stuff as soon as he got home from the party."

"So, it was all about you being trans?"

"Looks like it. My therapist said guys like him get something in their head, like what's in my pants, and just start obsessing."

"I never cared about what was under your clothes," Audrey said, smiling at Raena from her hospital bed, with soft green eyes that had only ever been honest with her.

Raena knew that Audrey carried some guilt over bringing Chad into their lives, but that was all bullshit. The guy was just trash. "Yeah, well, this stuff happens, you know. Guy starts to fetishize trans women or any other kind of person, and he's just a couple of steps removed from assaulting them. Until he's not."

"Fuck them," Audrey said. "Fuck those men. I'll move in with you. We can be spinsters together."

Raena snorted with laughter. "You? You never clean up your dishes, you pig." She smiled at Audrey, seeing that the sparkle was beginning to return to her friend's eyes. The dark circles beneath them had lightened. And her lips were flushed with pink instead of that ghastly white they had been on that night when Audrey had saved her life and almost given her own.

Audrey raised an eyebrow. "What are you thinking about?"

Raena smiled back at her as her eyes began to water. "I'd absolutely love to have you."

THE END

A note from the author:

This is a work of fiction. However, there is a dark and terrible theme in this story that is absolutely true—the victimization of trans women around the world. Of all people, trans women, and especially trans women of color are the most vulnerable in our society, suffering more assaults, more rapes, and more murders than any other group of people. Their lives are not fiction, and some live through real horrors. Trans people are people, deserving of love, peace, and respect, and they desperately need our support to end the violence against them. Even if love is all you have to give, please give your love to all of our trans friends who want only the chance to live their lives in peace and happiness.

About the Authors

JUDITH SONNET

Judith Sonnet is a prolific and active horror writer, reader, and fan. Her books include *No One Rides for Free*, *The Clown Hunt*, and *Magick*. She's also known for creating the "Ten Day Challenge," where she and other selected indie authors write, edit, and publish novellas in ten days or less. She currently lives in Utah, where she collects old books and Italian splatter movies.

HAILEY PIPER

Hailey Piper is the Bram Stoker Award-winning author of *Queen of Teeth*, *The Worm and His Kings* series, *Cruel Angels Past Sundown*, and *No Gods for Drowning*, which shares its world with her *We're Here* story. Her short fiction appears in Pseudopod, Vastarien, Cosmic Horror Monthly, and other publications. She lives with her wife in Maryland, where their occult rituals are secret. Find Hailey at https://t.co/tiWoS6bp8X or on Twitter as @HaileyPiperSays.

ANGELIQUE JORDONNA

Angelique Jordonna is an author of darkly intense horror, thrillers, and paranormal romance. Her books take you into the depths of depravity while still having elements of the strong love bonds between characters. The rich descriptions pull you right into the story, whether she's detailing a gruesome murder or dropping subtle hints at a burgeoning romance. Angelique has a love for all things creative, and she devours books and music like they were the finest cuisine, sustaining her better than the finest wines, better than a five-star meal, better than ... sex? Well, maybe not that good. angeliquejordonnaauthor.com

SUMIKO SAULSON

Sumiko Saulson is a Bram Stoker nominated poet and award-winning author of Afrosurrealist and multicultural sci-fi and horror. Author of the Bram Stoker nominated *The Rat King: A Book of Dark Poetry* (Dooky Zines, 2022), *Happiness and Other Diseases* (Mocha Memoirs Press, 2022), and the LOHR Reader's Choice Award-winning collection *Within Me Without Me* (Dooky Zines, 2022), and the novel. Winner of the HWA Scholarship from Hell (2016) BCC Voice "Reframing the Other" contest (2017), Mixy Award (2017), Afrosurrealist Writer Award (2018), HWA Diversity Grant (2020), LOHR Fiction Grant (2021), and the HWA Richard Laymon President's Award (2021). They have an AA in English from Berkeley City College, write a column called "Writing While Black" for a national Black Newspaper, the San Francisco BayView is the host of the SOMA Leather & LGBT Cultural District's "Erotic Storytelling Hour," and teach courses at the Speculative Fiction Academy.

MICHAEL R. COLLINS

Michael R Collins was born at a very young age in the wilds of southern Idaho. After a few decades, he finally got his fill of all the sagebrush and rattlesnakes he could eat, so he struck out into the world. After slinging some bass guitar, and general shenanigans in Austin, Texas, he currently lives in Pennsylvania with his partner Mel. He is a Bi author who has most recently published Miracles For Masochists (with James G. Carlson) and Verum Malum. He has a plethora of short stories, and a few alibis. (Just in case) He is also a co-host of the Bi+ Podcast.

PIPPA BAILEY

Pippa Bailey is a foul-mouthed queer horror author, voice actor, reviewer & all-round good person. She lives in a tiny cottage in the Scottish Highlands with her husband, Myk Pilgrim, and her hairy babies, Bodkin and Poppet. When Pippa isn't writing, she spends her time collecting tasteless memes, drinking too much tea, making terrible puns, and generally bothering the local wildlife. You can sneak up on her if you are very, very quiet, but it is not advisable. Pippa's work has appeared alongside Clive Barker, Ramsey Campbell, Jack Ketchum, Joe R Lansdale, and the marvellous Myk Pilgrim in *Dark Faces Evil Place 2*. Also in *13 Wicked Tales: A Wicked Library Anthology*, featured on the Wicked Library podcast, Frisson Comics, Sirens Call Magazine, & Holiday-themed horror collections *Poisoned Candy: Bite-sized Horror for Halloween*, *Bloody Stockings: Bite-sized Horror for Christmas*, *Rancid Eggs: Bite-sized Horror for Easter,* & *Devil's Night: Bite-sized Horror for Halloween.* Her story "Achromatica" appeared in *Chromophobia: A Strangehouse Anthology* by Women in Horror, edited by the brilliant Bram Stoker award-winning Sara Tantlinger and published by Rooster Republic Press in 2022.

RUTH ANNA EVANS

Ruth Anna Evans is a writer, anthologizer, and cover designer who lives in the heart of all that is sinister: the American Midwest. She has been composing prose of all types since childhood but finds something truly delightful in putting her nightmares on the page. She has published the horror collection *No One Can Help You: Tales of Lost Children and Other Nightmares*, along with novellas, novelettes, and several short stories. She is the editor of *Ooze: Little Bursts of Body Horror.* Follow Ruth Anna on Twitter @ruthannaevans, on Facebook at Ruth Anna Evans, on Instagram at ruthannaevanshorror, or at her website www.ruthannaevans.com for updates on her work.

EVAN J. PETERSON

Evan J. Peterson is an author, game writer, and Clarion West alum. His latest book is *METAFLESH: Poems in the Voices of the Monster* (ARUS Entertainment), and recent work includes *Drag Star!* (Choice of Games), the world's first drag performance RPG, and *Arkham Horror: The Road to Innsmouth* (Asmodee/Fantasy Flight). Evan edited the Lambda Literary Award finalist anthology, *Ghosts in Gaslight, Monsters in Steam: Gay City 5*, and his writing appears in *Weird Tales, PseudoPod, Tales to Terrify, Queers Destroy Horror, Boing Boing,* and *Best Gay Stories 2015.* Evan's novel, *Better Living Through Alchemy*, will be published in 2024 by Broken Eye Books. Evanjpeterson.com can tell you more.

DAN B. FIERCE

Dan B. Fierce loves humor and horror alike, and many things in between. A long-time fan of authors like Stephen King, Dean Koontz, and Edgar Alan Poe, he lets his darker side come out in the macabre "Revenge," demonstrates the tension caused by the corona virus with "Mistaken," and gives the reader a taste of dark humor with "Warning Shot," all contained between the covers of the *2020 Indie Authors' Short Story Anthology*. His suspense-filled story "Abandoned Bikes," published in *Crimes and Culprits: An Anthology by the Indie Author Group*, won second place in the Missouri Writer's Guild's 2022 President's Award Contest. Both books were put out by Heathory Press. In 2022, he made his first solo short story publication, *Roadkill King* and had his story "The Nothing" included in Woodneath Press's *Community Voices III* anthology. He has also recently had a poem published in the Horror Writers Association's *Poetry Showcase IX*. 2023 kicked off with his story "El Cangrejo" finding a home in the first volume of the *HorrorScope* anthology series.

He has over twenty years of experience writing stand-up and sketch comedy, and over 10 years of competitive creative writing in online forums. He has also had some opinion pieces published in *KC Lifestyles Magazine.*

Dan resides in the Kansas City, Missouri, area with his long-time husband of twenty-plus years.

Social media links:
Facebook: https://www.facebook.com/DanBFierce/
Instagram: https://www.instagram.com/danbfierce/
Twitter: @DanBFierce1
Tumblr: https://www.tumblr.com/danbfierce
WordPress: https://www.firecefantoms.com

JAMES LEFEBURE

James Lefebure is a Scottish-born, Liverpool-living horror author. Splitting his time between watching horror, reading horror and writing horror, he can often be found arguing with people that Jason would whoop Michael. His two novels *The Books of Sarah* and *God in the Livingroom* have proven to his long-suffering, fantasy-reading husband that James will probably never write a story about dragons or an orphan with a destiny. He can be found on Tiktok, (jameseylefebure) Instagram (Jameseylefebure), and facebook (JamesLefebureWriter). He does have a Twitter but doesn't understand how it works enough to use it.

ANTON CANCRE

Anton Cancre's mother wasn't really pregnant with them when she went to see The Exorcist, but they tell people that anyways because it sounds cool. Their poetry collections, *Meaningless Cycles in a Vicious Glass Prison* and *This Story Doesn't End the Way We Want All the Time* as well as their nonfiction book about Silent Hill, *Nightmares of Blood and Flesh*, are available from Dragon's Roost Press. They're also a luddite who still has a blogspot website (antoncancre.blogspot.com).

JASON LAVELLE

Jason LaVelle is a father, photographer, and animal wrangler from West Michigan. They're one of those restless souls who has tried out just about every job there is, which at one time earned them the moniker, 'Most interesting person in Holland.' ADD folks, that's all it is. That and they can't stomach the thought of being a real adult with a real job. Throughout all the years and the many changes, a desire to create has been one of the few constants in their life. Though an award-winning habit of procrastination did everything in its power to stop them, LaVelle has authored five novels and one large collection of short stories. Drawing from a lifelong love of horror, thrillers, and mystery, all of LaVelle's works aim to give readers a dark ride on a rickety coaster. LaVelle is one of those people who would definitely 'like' their own posts, were it acceptable to do so. More than anything, as they enter their twilight years (early forties), LaVelle wants to do whatever they can to help those who are oppressed in this world.

Acknowledgments

First, a huge thanks to the individuals who proved instrumental in planning and carrying out this project: Angelique Jordonna, Mick Collins, and Ruth Anna Evans. Also, much appreciation to all the talented authors involved. Without their contributions, this book wouldn't have been possible. And lastly, thank you, dear reader, for purchasing a copy of *We're Here: An Anthology of LGBTQ+ Horror* and supporting not just indie horror but a good cause.

Printed in Great Britain
by Amazon